FATHERS AND SONS

MODERN LIBRARY COLLEGE EDITIONS

Fathers and Sons

By IVAN S. TURGENEV

Newly Translated from Russian by
Bernard Guilbert Guerney

With the Author's Comments on His Book
and a Foreword by the Translator

The Modern Library · New York

Salient Data

Ivan Sergheievich Turgenev was born in Orel on November 9, 1818 (New Style). He entered the University of Moscow in 1832, and in 1833 changed to St. Petersburg, forming his first literary contacts; he also went to Berlin to round out his studies, and there made further contacts. Life abroad led to his becoming a Westernizer. In 1840, after a brief stay in Russia and a trip to Italy, he returned to Berlin, where he shared quarters with Bakunin. In 1842, he entered the chancellery of the Minister of the Interior, where his chief was V. I. Dahl, well known as a writer, lexicographer and proverbiologist. In 1843 he resigned his post; first appeared in print (anonymously) with "Parasha," a rather long poem; and in the same year made the acquaintance of Belinsky. By 1846 Turgenev was thinking of abandoning literature but, in 1847, he scored with the publication (by Nekrassov) of "Hor and Kalinich," the first of his *Hunting Sketches,* the appearance of which *Sketches* as a collection in book form, as well as the publication of an essay on the death of Gogol (all three events occurring in 1852), won for Turgenev the infallible recognition of the government: in his case a month in jail and two years of house-arrest on his country estate. In 1856 *Rudin* was published; in 1858: *Nest of Gentlefolk;* 1860: *On the Eve;* 1862: *Fathers and Sons;* 1867: *Smoke;* 1877: *Virgin Soil,* his last novel. The last work to be published during his lifetime was *Senilia: Poems in Prose,* which appeared in the December, 1882, issue of the *Messenger in Europe* (the first cycle, to be precise, consisting of fifty of these exquisite pieces; a second cycle was first published in Russian—with a facing French translation—in Paris, 1930, but, although discovered as far back as 1927, these thirty-one pieces, together with a considerable number of other miscellanea by Turgenev, still await the honor of publication as a book in English). Turgenev died on September 3, 1883 (New Style), at Bougival, a country place near Paris.

Translator's Foreword

Justice demands the admission that *Fathers and Children,** the work of the well-known writer Ivan Turgenev, has exerted a salutary influence on minds. Standing at the head of the contemporary Russian men of talent and enjoying the sympathy of cultured society, Turgenev, unexpectedly to the younger generation, which had been recently applauding him, has by means of this work branded our hobbledehoy revolutionaries with the mordant name of *nihilists,* and has shaken both the doctrine of materialism and its proponents.

> *Special comment in the* Report for 1862 *of the nefarious* Section III (*the unspeakable secret police*).

Turgenev did not know how to define his problem: instead of depicting the relations between "fathers" and "children" he wrote a panegyric to the "fathers" and an exposé of the "children" and, besides, has actually failed to understand the latter; instead of an exposé the result in his hands turned out to be a calumny . . . the novel is nothing else but a merciless and . . . destructive criticism of the younger generation.

> *M. Antonovich: "An Asmodeus of Our Time," a review in the* Contemporary, *an organ of the younger radicals (1862).*

Turgenev has pondered deeply on Bazarov as a type and has such an understanding of it as not a single one of our young realists is capable of. . . . Bazarov is a representative of our younger generation; grouped in his person are those characteristics which, in minute quantities, are scattered as dust among the masses, and the image of this man emerges vividly and distinctly before the imagination of the readers.

> *D. Pisarev, radical critic and a leader of the young generation (1862)*

* *Fathers and Children* is the literal title.

Were the question put: Which work of Turgenev's created the greatest sensation—it seems inconceivable that any other title could be named in answer save *Fathers and Sons*. To put it baldly: even the *succès de fou* of *Doctor Zhivago* did not come within an ocean's breadth of the *succès de scandale* of *Fathers and Sons*, which not only awakened more interest than any previous or subsequent work of Turgenev's but aroused more controversies than any other Russian novel of the nineteenth century, controversies the heat of which persisted literally for decades and which has not died out in certain quarters to this day. *Fathers and Sons*, we are assured by a contemporary witness, was read (and even bought) by those who had never opened a book since their school days and whose souls were taken up only with the price fluctuations of axle-grease in Astrakhan. What sort of book was it—progressive or retrograde? Whom was the author glorifying, both critics and readers wanted to know, and whom was he denigrating?

Indubitably, the author is by no means tongue-tied about his book, but, after all, we do have the advantage of a century's wisdom-after-the-event. I am under the persistent impression that no archaeological dredging up of pictographs, hieroglyphs, cuneiform inscriptions, scrolls has ever failed (or ever will fail) in restating (or antedating) all previous puttings-forth of the proposition that Crabbed Age and Youth cannot live together, and at first glance *Fathers and Sons* may seem to have congealed into a classic on that theme.

Yet the book was very much more than that in its beginnings; the conflict it dealt with was more than merely intratribal, merely regional. All of Russia (literate Russia, that is) was split into two camps: Slavophiles and Westernizers. The Slavophiles may be described, not too uncharitably, as 100 percent Russians, professed and professional, as patriots who made both heads of the Imperial Eagle scream—"for such Saviors of the Fatherland had at that time cropped up even in our Russia"; they put up villas that were grandiose take-offs on the log huts of the peasants; got themselves up in long shirts of Irish linen, worn outside balloon-pantaloons of British broadcloth tucked into high boots of French kid, and, by way of coats, sleeveless garments of Italian velour reaching to below the knees (which outfits had, of course, to be sent to London or Paris to be properly laundered and cleaned); they ate their truffles and *pâté de foie gras* off peasantish earthenware and drank champagne out of mouzhikian wooden cups—the Slavophiles were, in short, all those who were perfectly willing to do anything on earth for the dear little mouzhik except get off his back. The Westernizers, on the other hand, were fighting to spread enlightenment; believing that the future and progress of Russia lay toward the West, they wanted to emulate Peter the Great by breaching a few more windows into Europe and letting the light and fresh air of civilization into benighted and stifling Russia.

Despite Hertzen's witticism to the effect that Ivan Sergheievich never went in for politics, "except for a fortnight on the Isle of Wight, when he discussed the alphabet with Robinson Crusoe," Turgenev had always (and justly) prided himself on his awareness of current history and political trends, and on his sensitiveness to the possible reaction of his readers. Among the very numerous and conflicting counsels he had received from sundry friends had been the advice of one well-wisher that he should waste no time in burning the new novel while it was still only a manuscript; Turgenev himself had wanted to postpone publication, owing to a number of unfavorable circumstances, mostly political: the book was decidedly topical, filled with references and details that were fraught with the utmost significance to the public of that day. Even when the reader was informed that certain actions were *not* performed, such information was not pointless. Why was he told, for instance, in the opening sentence of Chapter 4, that "no throng of domestics trooped out onto the front steps to welcome the masters"? Because not the least of the shadows cast by coming events was that of 'mancipation, as that flunky-soul Feerss shapes the word in *The Cherry Orchard*.*

"The only good trait about a Russian," to quote none other than Bazarov, "is that he has a most atrocious opinion of himself." And, coupled with this pejorative pride (or mania) there is, not altogether illogically, something very like xenophily, a naïve admiration for non-Slavs: "There, see how clever them Germans are—they even invented monkeys!"

Could anybody but a Russian, then, be the laziest man in the world? And whom else could Goncharov choose as a foil to Oblomov except an impossibly energetic and enterprising German? Could anybody but a Russian hit upon so droll a swindle as trading in so whimsical a commodity as dead souls? And whom did Gogol pick to be a guide and a shining light unto his Chichikov? Why, an incredibly upright and knowledgeable businessman but, of all things, a Turk!

* The White Negroes of Russia were freed (and that without an internecine war) almost two years before the black ones in the U.S.A. However, the Americans were almost ten times faster in assassinating their Emancipator than the Oblomovian Russians were about polishing off theirs.

No such all-Russian monoliths of vice as Oblomov, Chichikov, old Karamazov, Little Judas are to be found in Turgenev's magnificent gallery of characterizations; but, somehow, he did not escape the pitfall of xenophily: when he needed a positive, strong revolutionary as a hero for *On the Eve* he produced Insarov, who decidedly filled the bill but who was a Bulgarian. Wasn't an all-Russian *hero* possible (the critics sniggered)—just for a change?

The master obliged by creating Bazarov, whose all-Russian status was as indisputable as his positive nature. Early in 1861 he had written P. V. Annenkov concerning *Fathers and Sons:* "I have worked long, assiduously, conscientiously. . . . The goal I had set myself was a true one, but whether I have attained it, God knows." Every seasoned artist takes both brickbats and bouquets in his stride; the hurtful, the shocking thing is to have the bouqets tendered by life-long enemies and the brickbats flung by old friends. Turgenev had held a true mirror up to Russia and was bewildered to hear so many voices berating both him and the mirror for what they saw therein. Only two men, according to Turgenev himself, grasped his intentions, and one of them was Dostoevsky—but Dostoevsky was the leading cantor of the congregation of Slavophiles. And one of the very few who perceived the true image of Bazarov was Pisarev, whose authoritative tone in due time persuaded the younger generation actually to accept Bazarov proudly as their authentic prototype.

Not the least important effect of the harsh reception of *Fathers and Sons* was that which it had upon the author himself. Not being as tough-skinned as Leskov, he left Russia and did not revisit it except for stays of short duration, and died in his self-imposed exile. That he could not forget the hurt inflicted by the misunderstanding on the part of the youth of Russia of his motives in writing this book is attested to by the embitterment evident in " 'Thou Shalt Hear the Judgment of the Fool' " —a poem in prose written sixteen years after the publication of *Fathers and Sons* and brought out in print twenty years after that publication: in 1882, less than a year before his death.

One indisputable contribution of *Fathers and Sons* was the currency it gave to *nihilist* and *nihilism,* at first in Russia and subsequently throughout the world. The *Encyclopaedia Britannica* (© 1956) devotes exactly five lines to NIHILISM, of which no more than three are misinformative: *nihilism* was *not* "first used by Ivan Turgenev"; neither was *nihilist:* both words, as political terms, were first launched in print as far back as 1829 by N. E. Nadezhdin, who in his turn had borrowed them from the muzzy terminologies of philosophy and theology, and who, according to a contemporary, defined nihilists as "people who know nothing, who do not base themselves upon anything in art or life." As used by Turgenev *nihilist* meant *materialist, realist, extreme skeptic, atheist,* and he suggested, specifically, that whenever it was used as a term of abuse it ought to be read, properly, as *revolutionary*. It was not long before *nihilist* was bandied about by the penny-a-liners as loosely as *anarchist* was at the turn of the twentieth century and as *communist* is today, while Leskov, Goncharov and Pisemsky in their novels shortly reduced the honest image of Bazarov the Nihilist to the stock-caricature of the popeyed, bushy-haired bomb-thrower, until in the popular so-called mind *nihilist* became synonymous with *terrorist,* and was used in that sense even by such skilled wordsmen as Wilde (*circa* 1880) and by France, who lumped *nihilists* and *anarchists* together as late as the eve of World War I. In current Russian-English dictionarese *nihilist* is equated with *negationist, negativist* and even *negator,* but not *terrorist.*

Turgenev's fears have proven groundless: his name, free of any shadow, has not been forgotten nor is likely to be—at least until such time as the ultimate model in atomic bombs s unleashed, while his Bazarov has not only stepped over the threshold of the future but will, *strontium volens,* go on striding through the further future as one of the major heroic and tragic figures of all literature. For *Fathers and Sons,* even in our fissionable day, is still something more than a present-ment of the ever-recurring conflict between the Wise Old Ones of the Cave and the Young Hotheads of the Tribe. After all, imprudent as it may be to point it out at this febrile moment of a shift in literary fashions, with fiction headed for the scrap-heap, this masterwork remains, and will indefinitely remain, an engrossing tale, superbly told by one of whom George Moore, himself no mean teller of tales, has said: "The best storytellers are the Russians, and the best among them was Turgenev."

I have been assured, upon percipient authority, that a few remarks, not too shrilly pitched, concerning the intent and possible merits of this translation will not necessarily be taken amiss. Let me state then, at the very outset, that it is new, from first to last, and that, whatever other virtues it may have, it can definitely claim four points of advantage by comparison with other renderings, even though all four points happen to be negative: it is not abridged, it is not Victorian, it is not prissy and, *slava te gospodi,* it is not a feminine version of a male writer's work.

Any literary classic (meaning thereby a work which persists in being irrepressibly alive, rather than some sorry monster kept perversely on exhibition in a pickle of pedantic formaldehyde: Rabelais, as against Racine) —any classic, in its original language, is certain of its tenure of decades, centuries, or even millennia. Any *translation* of any classic is in an altogether different case: the number of translations into English which no longer abide our judgment as secondary classics will not exhaust the count of fingers of one hand, since the presentation of any classic in a new dress inevitably calls for a comparison of times and languages.

In the case of the *Odyssey,* for instance, the original time and language are set for the translator; in the case of a classic of the nature of *Fathers and Sons,* however, the original time and language are still fluid and demand the utmost wariness on the part of the translator. For this work is, assuredly, no costume piece and should not be treated as such; still less should it be presented in modern dress, even if such presentation were possible in translation, which I exceedingly doubt. Modern dress has been put over on the stage, of course, but according to my observation neither too often nor for very long. And, naturally, there would be no insuperable difficulty in turning Turgenev's polemical masterpiece into a Novel of Our Day: after all, *Madame Bovary* was transmogrified successfully enough into *Main Street.* Yet such cobbling, too, calls for a much shallower, though showier, skill than that of honest translation.

Obviously, *Fathers and Sons* could be tagged as a period piece, but it is that only insofar as its periodicity is recurrent in almost every generation—at the present writing it is recurring in our own nefandous South, in a conflict between the none-too-strenuous New Southrons and the die-hard professional Whites, over emancipating the colored serfs into Desegregation. The translator is therefore faced with a task as difficult as it is delicate: he must have his reader feel, subconsciously, that he is reading a classic of another day and land, yet at the same time make him aware, through indirection, that the theme, the story line, the characters of that classic all could be of his own land and day. And that would seem to demand modernization—although, as I have already tried to point out, that turnpike is *verboten* (and rightly so!) to any such literary camp-followers as translators.

Yet the problem is merely difficult, not insoluble. I am, not unnaturally, rather reluctant to divulge any secrets of a hard-bitten trade, but a hint as to how a Russian circle can be squared in English may be harmless enough, I think. There are at the disposal of any fairly competent translator certain time-tested sleights which will enable him not to modernize, exactly, but to create the *impression,* or *effect,* or even *illusion* of modernity. The trick is honest enough, since it involves no betrayal of the author, nor any deception of the reader greater than that which has always been the basis of all dealings between the readers and the writers of fiction.

If I have succeeded in this *escamotage* (and I can merely express the hope, perhaps not unjustified, that I have), such success would constitute the main point in favor of this new translation. Should its immediate reception encourage the belief that it may be found viable through its first term of copyright I will, assuredly, be content; should it be still readable for another term of twenty-eight years, so much the better, all around; and if it should survive for any length of time thereafter—well, even my poltergeist, I suppose, will be gratified.

The preparation of the entertainment offered herewith has required practically two years instead of the six months which a more accommodating conscientiousness would have taken; it also involved a dozenth rereading of the original—and at no point did I find it anything but fresh and challenging. Reader, I can see no reason, then, why you should find this new version unrewarding, even if you have already gone through some previous rendering (or renderings).

Nu vot, droozya moee—chitaite da oomeelyaitess!

BERNARD GUILBERT GUERNEY

At the Sign of the Blue Faun
New York
Winter of 1960-61

The Author on His Book*

I was taking sea baths at Ventnor, that smallest of little towns on the Isle of Wight (this was in the month of August, in the year 1860), when I first conceived the idea of *Fathers and Children,* that tale thanks to which the predisposition toward me of the younger generation in Russia has ceased—and, apparently, has ceased for all time. More than once I have heard, and read in critical articles, that in my productions I "set out with an idea" or that I "bring out an idea"; some have bestowed praise upon me for this, others, on the contrary, have reproved me. For my part I must confess that I never essayed to "create an image" unless I took as my point of departure not an idea but some living person to whom suitable elements were gradually added and applied. Since I am not possessed of a great deal of untrammeled inventiveness I have always had need of some specific ground that would be firm underfoot. This was also the case with *Fathers and Children:* the personality of a certain young provincial physician who had made a striking impression upon me was used freely as the basis of the book's leading figure, Bazarov. (This young physician died shortly before 1860.)

In this remarkable man there was incarnated, before my eyes, the barely nascent, still fermenting beginning of that which subsequently acquired the name of nihilism. The impression this personality had made upon me was very powerful and, at the same time, not altogether clear; I myself, at the very outset, could not arrive at any thoroughgoing estimate of him and I kept intently

* From *Reminiscences of Literature and Life.*

listening to and observing everything around me, desirous of checking, as it were, the veracity of my own perceptions. I was made uneasy by the following fact: in not a single production of our literature did I encounter as much as a hint at that which I imagined I saw everywhere; willy-nilly the doubt sprang up: Was I not, after all, pursuing a will-o'-the-wisp?

There was, I remember, a certain Russian living on the Isle of Wight at the time I was there, a man endowed with quite refined taste and a remarkable sensitivity toward what the late Appolon Grigoriev used to call the "influential ideas" of the epoch. I imparted to him the thoughts which were engrossing me—and was dumbfounded to hear him remark: "Why, you've already presented such a type in . . . Rudin, I believe?" I let this pass in silence. Rudin and Bazarov—one and the same type?

These words had such an effect upon me that during the course of several weeks I avoided devoting any thought at all to the work I had undertaken; however, upon my return to Paris I buckled down to it anew; the *fabula* little by little took shape in my head; during that winter I wrote the opening chapters, but I finished the tale only in July [1861], when I was back in Russia, living in the country. That autumn I read it to some friends, corrected a thing or two and made some additions, and in March, 1862, *Fathers and Children* appeared in the *Russian Herald*.

I shall not dilate on the impact made by this novel; I will content myself with saying that upon my return to St. Petersburg, on the very day of the notorious fires in the Apraxin Palace, the term *nihilist* had already been caught up by thousands of voices, and the first exclamation that burst from the lips of the first acquaintance I encountered on Nevsky Prospect was "Just see what *your* nihilists are doing—they're burning down Petersburg!"

The impressions I received at that time, although they differed in kind, were uniformly depressing. I noted an iciness, bordering on indignation, on the part of many friends whom I had found sympathetic and who had been close to me; I was the recipient of congratulations, of something very like kisses, from persons belonging to the camp that opposed me, from enemies. This confused me, it caused me chagrin; my conscience, however, did not reproach me; I was well aware that my attitude toward the character I had brought out* was an honest one, and that it was not only devoid of prejudice but was fraught with sympathy; my respect for the calling of an artist, of a litterateur, was too great for me to be a casuist at heart in such a matter.

"Respect" is actually not altogether appropriate here: I simply could not and did not know how to do my work differently and, finally, there was no motive for me to act otherwise. My critics pinned the label of "pamphlet" on my narrative; they did not forget to mention my "exasperated," my "wounded" vanity—yet why should I have embarked on writing a pamphlet against Dobroliubov, whom I hardly ever saw but whom I valued highly as a man and as a talented writer? No matter how

* I will take the liberty of citing the following extract from my diary: "Sunday, July 30th. An hour and a half ago I at last finished my novel. . . . I don't know what success it will have —the *Contemporary* will probably shower me with disdain because of Bazarov, while ———— will never believe that throughout the writing of the book I felt involuntarily drawn to him. . . ."

modest an opinion I may have of my gifts, I nevertheless considered—and still consider—the composition of a pamphlet, of a pasquinade, as being beneath them, as unworthy of them. And as far as my "wounded" vanity is concerned, I will merely remark that Dobroliubov's review of *On the Eve*—the *immediate predecessor* of *Fathers and Children* among my works (and he was rightfully considered the spokesman of public opinion) —I will merely remark that this review, which appeared in 1861, is filled with the warmest and (I say this in all sincerity) most undeserved praises.

Yet Messieurs the critics found it necessary to represent me as an offended pamphleteer—*"leur siège était fait"*—while no further back than this year it was possible for me to read the following lines in Supplement No. 1 to the *Cosmos* (p. 96): "Finally, *everybody knows* that the pedestal upon which M. Turgenev stood has been demolished, chiefly by Dobroliubov . . ." While further on (p. 98) there is mention of my "rancor," which, however, the critical gentleman "can understand and, if you like, even excuse."

———————

In general, Messieurs the critics do not have an altogether correct conception of those things which take place in the soul of an author, of those precise things which constitute his joys and woes, his aspirations, his successes and failures. The critics do not, for instance, as much as suspect that delight which Gogol mentions and which consists of castigating one's own self, one's own shortcomings, in the depiction of characters which one has invented; the critics are fully convinced that the only thing the author inevitably does is "bring out his ideas"; they do not want to believe that the exact and powerful representation of truth, of the reality of life, constitutes the highest happiness for the man of letters, even if such truth does not coincide with his own predilections. I will take the liberty of giving a brief example. I am an ingrained, incorrigible Westernizer and have never made, nor am I now making, the least secret of the fact. However, despite this, I took particular pleasure in bringing out, in the character of Panshin (in *A Nest of Gentlefolk*), all the comic and vulgar aspects of Westernizing; I made the Slavophile Lavretsky "demolish him at every point." Why did I do so—I, who consider the Slavophile doctrine false and sterile? Because *in the given instance, according to my notions, that was precisely how life had formed itself* and I wanted, above all, to be sincere and truthful.

In drawing the character of Bazarov I excluded from the range of his sympathies everything of an artistic nature; I endowed him with a brusqueness and unceremoniousness of tone—not out of any incongruous desire to insult the younger generation* but simply as the result of my observations of my acquaintance Dr. D., and individuals like him. *"That is how* this life has formed itself," experience again told me—experience that was in error, perhaps, but (I repeat) conscientious. There was no reason for me to indulge in finesse—and *that was precisely how* I was in duty bound to depict this doctor as a figure in my story. My personal inclina-

* Among a host of proofs of my "rancor" against the youthful element I was confronted even with the fact that I had forced Bazarov to lose at cards to Father Alexei. "The author, you see, is up against it when it comes to needling and humiliating this fellow! There, he doesn't know even how to play cards!" There isn't the least doubt that if I had forced Bazarov to win, the same critic would have cried out in triumph: "Isn't it an open-and-shut case? The author wanted to make us understand that Bazarov is a card-sharp!"

tions meant nothing in this case, yet probably many of my readers would be surprised were I to tell them that, with the exception of this character's views on the arts, I share almost all his convictions. Yet I am being assured that I am on the side of the Fathers—I, who in the figure of Pavel Kirsanov have actually transgressed somewhat against artistic verity and have overdone the thing, reducing his shortcomings to the point of caricature, making him mirth-provoking!*

All the fault in the misunderstanding, all the "trouble," so to speak, lay in that the Bazarov type I had

* People abroad simply cannot understand the merciless accusations brought against me because of Bazarov. There were several translations of *Fathers and Children* into German; here is what one critic writes in discussing the latest one, which appeared in Riga ("Vossiche Zeitung," *Donnerstag, d.* 10 *Juni, zweite Beilage, Seite* 3):*"Es bleibt für den unbefangenen . . . Leser schlechthin unbegreiflich, wie sich gerade die radicale Jugend Russlands über diesen geistigen Vertreter ihrer Richtung (Bazaroff), ihrer Ueberzeugungen und Bestrebungen, wie ihn T. zeichnete, in eine Wuth hinein erhitzen konnte, die sie den Dichter gleichsam in die Acht erklären und mit jeder Schmähung überhäufen liess. Man sollte denken, jeder moderne Radicale könne nur mit froher Genugthuung in einer so stolzen Gestalt, von solcher Wucht des Charakters, solcher gründlichen Freiheit von allem Kleichlichen, Trivialen, Faulen, Schlaffen und Lügenhaften, sein und seiner Parteigenossen typisches Portrait dargestellt sehn."*

I.e.: "To an unprejudiced . . . reader it remains utterly incomprehensible: How could the radical youth of Russia, because of such a representative of its convictions and aspirations as Turgenev has drawn in Bazarov, have flown into such a rage that it has subjected the author to formal disgrace and showered him with every sort of abuse? One would rather suppose that every modern radical, in a mood of elation and satisfaction, recognizes his own portrait, his own sympathizers in such a proud image, endowed with such force of character, such complete freedom from all that is trivial, vulgar and false."

brought to the fore had not had time to go through the gradual phases which literary types usually undergo. No epoch of idealization, of sympathetic exaltation, such as had fallen to the lot of Oneghin and Pechorin, had fallen to his. At the very moment of the appearance of Bazarov—the New Man—the author assumed a critical, an objective, attitude toward him. This it was which led many people astray and—who knows?—there was in this something which, while it may not have been an error, may yet have been an injustice. The type of Bazarov had at least as much right to idealization as the types that had preceded him. I said just now that the author's attitude toward the personage he had brought to the fore had led the reader astray: the reader is always discomfited, he falls an easy prey to perplexity, even to vexation, if the author treats the character portrayed as a living being—that is, if the author perceives and exhibits both the bad and the good sides of that character but, most important of all, if he evinces no patent sympathy or antipathy for his own brain child. The reader is on the verge of getting angry: he is faced with the necessity of breaking his own trail instead of following a way already laid out for him. "No great need to work so hard!" the thought is involuntarily engendered within him. "Books exist for diversion—not for racking one's brains; there, what would it have cost the author to tell me what I'm supposed to think of such and such a personage—or what he himself thinks of him!"

But if the author's attitude toward this personage is of a still more uncertain nature, if the author himself does not know whether he loves or does not love the character he has brought forth (as was the case with me in respect to Bazarov, inasmuch as that "involuntary attraction" which I mentioned in my diary is not love)—why, matters are in an altogether bad way! The reader is prepared to saddle the author with extravagant sympathies or extravagant antipathies—anything to get out of disagreeable "uncertainty."

"Neither Fathers Nor Children," a certain witty lady told me after having read my book, "there's the real title of your novel—and you yourself are a nihilist." A similar opinion found a still more forceful utterance upon the appearance of *Smoke*. I will not take it upon myself to offer objections; it may well be that the lady has spoken nothing but the truth. In this business of creative writing every man (I am judging by myself) does not do that which he wants to do but that which he is able to do—and as much as he can succeed in doing. I suppose that works of fiction ought to be judged *en gros,* and, while conscientiousness on the part of the author should be strictly demanded, the remaining aspects of his activity should be regarded—well, I would not say with apathy, but with equanimity. Still, with all my eagerness to pleasure my critics, I cannot plead guilty to any absence of conscientiousness.

I have accumulated a quite curious collection of letters and other documents having to do with *Fathers and Children*. Comparing them is not devoid of a certain interest. At the same time that some of the writers are accusing me of affronting the younger generation, of being behind the times, of obscurantism, informing me that they are burning photographs of me "with contemptuous laughter," others, on the contrary, indignantly reproach me with groveling in the dust before that very same younger generation. "You are crawling at the feet of Bazarov!" one correspondent proclaims. "You are merely pretending to condemn him; in reality you are fawning upon him and are hoping for a single condescending smile of his as if it were alms!"

One critic, I recall, in strong and eloquent terms addressed directly to me, presented Mr. Katkov* and myself in the guise of two conspirators, hatching out in the quiet of a secluded study our cabal, our calumny against the young forces of Russia. The resultant picture was an effective one! In reality this is how our "conspiracy" occurred. When Mr. Katkov received from me the manuscript of *Fathers and Children,* as to the contents of which he hadn't had even an approximate notion, he felt perplexed.† The type of Bazarov struck him as "all but an apotheosis of the *Contemporary*," ‡

---

* Michael N. Katkov (1818-87) was the editor of the decidedly reactionary *Russian Herald.—Trans.*

† I hope that Mr. Katkov will not resent my citing a few passages from the letter he wrote me at the time: "Even if M'sieu' Bazarov has not been exalted into an apotheosis," he wrote, "still, one cannot help confessing that he has, somehow, found himself on a very high pedestal. He actually does overwhelm everything about him. Everything he confronts is either ol' clo's or weak and unripe. Was that the desired impression? In this novel one feels that the author wanted to characterize the beginning of something he had little sympathy for, but he apparently was wavering in his choice of tone and unconsciously submitted thereto. One feels a certain constraint in the author's attitude toward the hero of the novel, a certain awkwardness and stiffness. It seems as if the author were at a loss before him and had no liking for him—and yet feared him all the more!" Further on Mr. Katkov regrets that I had not made Odintsova treat Bazarov ironically, and so on—everything still in the same tone! It is clear that one of the "conspirators" was not quite satisfied with the efforts of the other.

‡ The *Contemporary* was definitely on the radical side.— *Trans.*

and I would not have been surprised had he refused to run my novel in his periodical. *"Et voila comme on écrit l'histoire!"* one might exclaim at this point—but then, is it permissible to bestow such a high-sounding name on such small matters?

On the other hand, I understand the reasons for the wrath aroused by my book in a certain clique. These reasons are not groundless and I—without any false modesty—accept, in part, the reproaches aimed against me. The word "nihilist," which I had given currency to, was taken advantage of at that time by many people who had been simply waiting for an opportunity, for a pretext, to halt the movement which had taken possession of Russian society. It was not as a form of reproach, not for the purpose of giving offense, that I used this word, but as an exact and appropriate expression of a fact—an historic fact—which had manifested itself; the word was transformed into a weapon of denunciation, of irrevocable condemnation—well-nigh a brand of infamy. Several unfortunate events which had taken place during that epoch supplied additional fuel to the suspicions that were being engendered and, apparently confirming the widely diffused apprehensions, justified the efforts and concern of our Saviors of the Fatherland—for such Saviors of the Fatherland had cropped up even in our Russia. Public opinion, still so indeterminate among us, came rushing in a returning wave. Nevertheless a shadow was cast upon my name. I am not deceiving myself: I know that shadow will not depart.

But, just the same, there were others—others before whom I am far too deeply conscious of my own insignificance—who could, after all, have uttered the great words: *"Périssent nos noms: pourvu que la chose publique soit sauvée*—let our names perish, as long as the common cause is saved!" And so, in emulation, I too can console myself by reflecting on the resultant benefit. This reflection outweighs the unpleasantness of undeserved reproaches. And, truly, of what importance are they? Who will remember, twenty or thirty years from now, all these tempests in a teacup? Or my name— with a shadow or without a shadow?

However, enough of talking about myself—it is high time to terminate these desultory recollections which, I fear, will afford little satisfaction to readers. I would merely like to say a few words to my young contemporaries, my confrères who are entering the slippery arena of literature. I have already declared on one occasion, and am ready to repeat the declaration, that I am not blinding myself as to my position. My "service to the muses," of twenty-five years' duration, has come to an end amid the gradual cooling-off of the public—and I do not see any reasonable prospect of a renewal of its warmth. New times are upon us, new men are needed; literary veterans are like military ones: they are almost always invalids—and blessed are those who are able to hand in their resignations voluntarily and in good time!

It is not in the tone of a preceptor (to which, incidentally, I have no claim whatsoever) that I intend to deliver my farewell words, but in the tone of an old friend, who is heard to the end with half-condescending, half-impatient attention—provided he does not overindulge in orating. That is something I shall try to avoid.

And so, my young confrères, it is you whom I address.

Greift nur hinein in's volle Menschenleben!

I would say to you, quoting the words of our mutual master, Goethe:

Ein jeder lebt's—nicht vielen ist's bekannt,
Und wo ihr's packt—da ist's interessant!

"Plunge your hand into the very depth of human life! Each one lives thereby—not many are familiar therewith; and wherever you may seize hold of it, that will prove of interest!"

It is only talent which bestows the power of "seizing hold," of this "capturing" of life, and talent is beyond self-bestowal; yet even talent, by itself, does not suffice. What is needed is constant communion with the milieu which you undertake to reproduce; what is needed is truthfulness, a truthfulness that is implacable as far as your own reactions are concerned; what is needed is liberty, complete liberty of views and conceptions. And, finally, what is needed is culture, what is needed is knowledge!

"Ah, we're catching on! We can see where you're heading!" many are likely to exclaim at this point. "Potughin's bright ideas, Ci-vi-li-za-tion, *prenez mon ours*—all old stuff!" Exclamations of that sort would be no novelty to me, but neither would they make me fall back a hair's breadth. Learning is not only light (as the folk-saying has it), it is also liberty. Nothing liberates man like knowledge—and nowhere is liberty as necessary as it is in the functioning of art, of poetry. It is not in vain that even in bureaucratese the arts are styled as "liberal." Can man "seize hold of" or "capture" that which is all around him if he is all in knots within? Pushkin felt this profoundly; not in vain did he say in his immortal sonnet, that sonnet which every beginning writer ought to get by heart and to remember as a testament:

> . . . along a *free* road
> Go thou where'er thy *free* mind may draw thee . . .

It is the absence of such liberty, among other things, which explains why not a single one of the Slavophiles, despite their undoubted gifts,* has ever created anything with life in it: not a one of them has managed to remove—if for but a moment—his tinted spectacles. The saddest example, however, of the absence of true liberty, which has its source in the absence of true knowledge, is provided for us by the latest work of Count L. N. Tolstoi (*War and Peace*), which at the same time, owing to the power of a creative, poetic gift, stands well-nigh at the head of everything that has appeared in our literature since 1840. No, without education, without freedom in the widest sense of that word—freedom in relation to one's own self, to one's own preconceived ideas and systems, even to one's own people, one's own history—the true artist is not to be thought of. Without that air one cannot breathe.

———

As for the ultimate result, the ultimate appraisal of

* One cannot, of course, reproach the Slavophiles either with boorish ignorance or lack of culture, but what the bringing about of an artistic result requires is (to use the latest phraseology) an interaction of many "factors." The factor lacking in the Slavophiles is liberty; there are others who are in need of culture, others still, of talent, and so on.

a so-called literary career—well, even here one must perforce recall the words of Goethe:

> *Sind's Rosen—nun sie werden blüh'n.*
> (If these be roses, they will bloom.)

There are no unacknowledged geniuses, even as there are no merits which live beyond their appointed time. "Every man sooner or later lands on his own little wall bracket," the late Belinsky used to say. If, at the proper time and the proper hour, you have offered up your utmost mite—even that is cause enough to be thankful. Only the chosen few are able to transmit to posterity not only the content but also the *form* of their thoughts and views, their personality, which, generally speaking, is of no concern to the masses. Ordinary individuals are condemned to evanishment in the continuum, to being engulfed in its torrent; nevertheless they have increased its force, have widened and intensified its swirling— what more could be desired?

I am putting down my pen. . . . One more last counsel to the young literati, and one more last request. My friends, never seek to justify yourselves, no matter what slander may be brought up against you; don't exert yourselves to clear up any misunderstanding; avoid the wish either to say *the last word* yourselves or to hear it said. Keep on doing your work—as for the rest, it will all straighten out eventually. In any event, let a decent interval of time elapse first and then take a look, from an historical point of view, at all the past bickerings, as I have tried to do here.

Let the following instance serve for your edification. Throughout the course of my literary career I made only one attempt to "set the facts straight." To be specific, I made this attempt only when the editorial department of the *Contemporary* took to assuring its subscribers, through advertisements, that I had been turned down on account of the unsuitability of my convictions —whereas it had been *I* who had turned the editors down, despite their solicitations: something concerning which I have documentary proof—I did not have sufficient strength of character and made a public statement of just what was what—and, of course, met with an utter fiasco. The younger generation's indignation against me became still greater. How dared I to raise a hand against their idol! What difference did it make that I happened to be right? I should have kept quiet!

That lesson proved of benefit to me; I wish you, too, may derive benefit from it.

———————

As for my request, it consists of the following: Guard our language, our splendidly beautiful Russian language, this treasure trove, this hoard transmitted to us by our predecessors, and it is Pushkin, once more, who stands at their head, refulgent in his glory! Treat this mighty weapon with respect; in skilled hands it can work miracles. Even to those who find "philosophical abstractions" and "poetical cooings" not to their taste, practical people in whose eyes language is nothing else but a means for the expression of thought, nothing else than a simple lever—even to them I would say: Respect, at least, the laws of mechanics; extract all the possible good from every object! For otherwise, really, as the reader runs through certain wishy-washy, vague, impotently long-winded perorations in the periodicals, he will not be able to help thinking that it is precisely the *lever* which you are replacing by primitive props—that you are reverting to the very infancy of mechanics. . . .

Enough, however—or else I myself will succumb to loquaciousness.

BADEN-BADEN
1868-69

Letter to Sluchevsky*

Paris, April 14, 1862.

I hasten to answer your letter, for which I am very grateful to you, my dear Sluchevsky. One cannot help but treasure the opinion of young men; in any event, I very much wish that there should be no misunderstandings concerning my intentions. I answer point by point.

1. The first recrimination is reminiscent of the accusation made against Gogol and others: Why aren't any good people shown among the evil ones? After all, Bazarov does overwhelm all the other *personae* in the novel (Katkov found that I had presented him as an apotheosis of the *Contemporary*). The traits assigned to him are not casual ones. I wanted to make him a tragic figure—there was no room here for sentimentalities. He is honest, truthful and a democrat to his very fingertips. And

* In answer to K. K. Sluchevsky, a poet, who had written of the unfavorable impression which *Fathers and Sons* had created among the young Russians studying at the University of Heidelberg.—*Trans.*

yet you fail to find any good aspects in him. He recommends *Stoff und Kraft* precisely as a popular—*i. e.,* a trifling—book; his duel with Pavel Petrovich (Kirsanov) is introduced precisely as graphic proof of the inanity of exquisitely aristocratic chivalry, presented with well-nigh exaggerated comicality—and how could Bazarov have declined to fight: why, Pavel Petrovich would have thrashed him. Bazarov, as I see it, is constantly demolishing Pavel Petrovich and not the other way around; and if he is called "nihilist"—why, the name should be read as "revolutionary."

2. What you say about Arcadii, about the rehabilitation of the *Fathers* and so on, merely indicates—I beg your pardon!—that you have not understood me. *My entire novel is directed against the gentry as a leading class.* Look closely at the faces of Nicholai Petrovich Kirsanov, Pavel Kirsanov, Arcadii: weakness and flabbiness, or narrow-mindedness. Aesthetic sensitiveness compelled me to take precisely the *good* representatives of the gentry, so as to prove my theme all the more truthfully thereby: if the cream is poor, what must the milk be like? To take quill-drivers, bureaucratic generals, rapacious officials and so on would have been crude—*le pont aux ânes* [hackneyed, trite, commonplace]—and bogus. All the true negators whom I have known (Belinsky, Bakunin, Hertzen, Dobroliubov, Speshnev *et al.*) were, without an exception, the offspring of comparatively kindhearted and honest parents, and this fact is fraught with great significance since it removes the least tinge of *personal* indignation, of *personal* irritation from the *men of action,* the negators. They follow their path only because they are more sensitive to the demands of the life of the people. That little Count, Salias, is incorrect in saying that persons

such as Nicholai and Pavel Kirsanov are our grandsires: Nicholai Kirsanov is I, Ogarev, and thousands of others; Pavel Kirsanov is Stolypin, Yessakov, Bosset—they, too, are our contemporaries. Nicholai and Pavel are the best of the gentry and that is precisely why they were chosen by me—to prove the bankruptcy of that class. To present, on the one hand, the bribetakers and, on the other, an ideal young man—that is a pretty little picture which I would rather let others paint. I was after bigness: in one passage (I discarded it, because of censorship) I had Bazarov saying to Arcadii—that same Arcadii in whom our Heidelberg friends see a "more successfully done type"—"Your father is an honest fellow; but even if he were a super-bribetaker you still wouldn't go beyond genteel resignation or getting genteelly steamed up, since you are one of the gentry."

3. Good Lord! Kukshina, that caricature, is, according to you, the *most successfully done* character of all! One actually can make no answer to that. Odintsova *falls in love* with Bazarov to the same extent as with Arcadii—which is not much; how is it you do not perceive this! She, too, is a representative of our idle, dreaming, inquisitive and frigid nobly-born she-Epicureans, our she-aristocrats. Countess Salias* had a clear understanding of *this* character. Odintsova wanted, at first, to stroke the shaggy coat of the wolf (Bazarov) —anything to keep him from biting—then to stroke the curls of the little boy (Arcadii), and yet at the same time go right on lying on velvet, all fresh from her bath.

4. The death of Bazarov (which Count Salias calls *heroic* and consequently criticizes) was supposed, as I

* E. A. Salias (Evgenia Tur), an authoress who hung out with the younger liberals.—*Trans.*

saw it, to put the final stroke to his tragic figure. And yet your young people find it incidental!

I conclude with the following comment: If the reader will come to *dislike* Bazarov with all his coarseness, heartlessness, pitiless harshness and brusqueness—if the reader should come to dislike him, I repeat, it is I who am at fault, and I have failed to attain my goal. But to turn syrupy (to use Bazarov's words) is something I did not want to do, even though, by doing thus, I probably would have had the young people on my side right off. I did not want to buy my way into popularity through concessions of that sort. It is better to lose a battle (and it does look as if I have lost it) than to win it through a ruse. I had visions of a somber, savage, great figure, grown half its height out of the soil, mighty, rancorous, honest, yet still doomed to perdition, since it was still standing at the threshold of the future—I had visions of a certain strange pendant to Pugachev, and so on; yet my young contemporaries tell me, shaking their heads: "You have come a cropper, little brother, and have even wronged us; there, your Arcadii turned out to be a somewhat neater job—it's a pity you didn't put in more work on him." All that remains for me to do (to echo a Gypsy song) is to "doff my hat and bow real low." I will try to send you a copy of my novel, but for the present, enough of this. I am not traveling by way of Heidelberg, yet I would like to take a look at the young Russians there. Give them my regards, even though they consider me behind the times. Tell them that I ask them to bide a little longer before they pronounce the final sentence. You may show this letter to whomever you will. I clasp your hand hard and send you my best wishes. Work, work, and do not be in a hurry to tot up the score.

Fathers and Sons

1

*Dedicated to the Memory of
Vissarion Grigorievich Belinsky*

"Well, Peter? Nothing in sight yet?" a hatless gentleman of forty and a bit over, in dusty overcoat and checked trousers, asked as he emerged on the small low porch of the inn on the road to S——; he was questioning his servant, a young round-cheeked fellow with whitish down on his chin, and eyes that were tiny and lackluster. It was the twentieth of May, 1859.

The servant, everything about whom—his turquoise earring, and his hair (mottled and slicked down with pomatum), and the deferential wrigglings of his body—betrayed a man of the new, perfected generation, glanced condescendingly along the road and replied: "No, nothing yet, sir."

"Nothing?" repeated his master.

"Nothing, sir," the man replied a second time.

His master sighed and perched on a small bench. We will make the reader acquainted with him as he sits there with his feet tucked in and looking about him in a reverie.

They call him Nicholai Petrovich Kirsanov. He owns, twelve miles or so from this small inn, a good estate of two hundred souls or (as he puts it after having come to an agreement with the peasants concerning the boundaries between his land and theirs and starting a *farm*) one of almost five and a half thousand acres. His father, a general who had fought against Napoleon in 1812, a semiliterate, coarse, yet not an ill-natured man and thoroughly Russian, had been a shaft-horse all his life, first as the commander of a brigade and then of a division, and had lived all the time in the province where, because of his rank, he had played quite an important rôle. Nicholai Petrovich had been born in the south of Russia, just like his elder brother Pavel, of whom more will be said later, and up to the age of fourteen had received his education at home, surrounded by none too well-paid tutors, his father's free-and-easy yet fawning aides and other regimental and staff personnel. His mother, née Kolyazin, who had borne the name of Agathe when she was a girl but as a general's wife was known as Agathocleia Kuzminishna Kirsanova, was one of those matriarchal officers' ladies who are styled commanders-in-skirts; she wore exuberant caps and dresses of swishing silk; in church she was the first to walk up to the cross; she had a great deal to say and said it loudly; allowed her children to kiss her hand in the morning and blessed them at night. In short, she lived for her own pleasure.

Nicholai Petrovich, as a general's son—although he not only was not outstanding for bravery but actually deserved to be called a bit of a coward—had been slated for the army, just as his brother Pavel was, but he had broken his leg on the very day when word of his enrollment in a military school arrived and, after spending two months in bed, was left with something of a limp for the rest of his life. His father washed his hands of him and let him try for a career in the civil service. Right after his son's eighteenth birthday he took him to Petersburg and entered him at the University. Just about this time his brother graduated as an officer and entered a regiment of the Guards; the young men took rooms together and began living there under the remote supervision of Ilya Koliazin, an important official and a first cousin, once removed, of their mother's. Their father returned to his division and his spouse and communicated with his sons only rarely, sending them quarto sheets of gray paper covered with line upon line of a sweeping clerkly hand; these quarto sheets were adorned with the signature of *Petrus Kirsanof, Major-General,* painstakingly encircled by sundry curlicues and flourishes.

In 1835 Nicholai Petrovich graduated from the University, and that same year General Kirsanov, forced into retirement after a review that had gone wrong, came to Petersburg with his wife to live there. He took a house near Tavrichesky Park and joined the English Club, but then died suddenly of a stroke. It was not long before Agathocleia Kuzminishna followed him; she could not get used to the dull life in the capital; the tedium of an existence in retirement finished her off.

At the same time, even while his parents were still

alive and to their by no means small disappointment, Nicholai had contrived to fall in love with the daughter of Prepolovensky, a government clerk who was his landlord. She was a darling to look at and, as the phrase goes, a progressive girl—she read the serious articles in the *Science* sections of periodicals. He married her right after the termination of his period of mourning and, resigning his position in one of the ministries where he had been placed through his father's influence, lived in clover with his Masha, at first in a country house in the neighborhood of the Institute of Forestry, then in town, in a small and darling apartment with a well-kept staircase and a rather chill drawing room, and finally in the country, where he settled for good and where, shortly thereafter, his son Arcadii was born. Husband and wife led a very pleasant and quiet life; they were practically never away from each other; they read together, played pieces for four hands on their grand piano and sang duets; she went in for raising flowers and kept an eye on the poultry-run; he busied himself with his estate and occasionally went hunting. As for Arcadii, he kept on growing and growing, also very pleasantly and quietly.

Ten years went by, like a dream. In 1847 Kirsanov's wife passed away. He barely survived this blow, his hair turning gray in a few weeks; he was all set to go abroad, in quest of some distraction, no matter how slight—but then the revolutionary year of 1848 arrived. Willy-nilly he went back to the country and after quite prolonged inactivity busied himself with the reorganization of his estate. In 1855 he took his son to the University of St. Petersburg, spent three winters with him in the capital, hardly ever going anywhere and trying to get on a friendly footing with Arcadii's young comrades. Last winter he had been unable to go to Petersburg, and so we see him here in the month of May, 1859, altogether gray by now, rather on the plump side and a trifle stooped, as he waits for his son who has gained a degree, even as he himself had once done.

The servant, out of a sense of propriety and, perhaps, also because he did not wish to stay under his master's eye, had stepped into the gateway and lit his pipe. Kirsanov let his head sink and took to staring at the timeworn porch steps; an overgrown speckled chick was staidly pacing over them, tapping hard with its big yellow feet; a bedraggled cat, demurely curled up on the railing, eyed it from time to time, not at all amiably.

The sun was scorching; the odor of freshly baked rye bread was wafted from the half-dark entry of the little wayside inn. And our Nicholai Petrovich was plunged in daydreams. *My son . . . Arcasha . . . a graduate*—the words kept going around in his head with never a stop; he attempted to think of something else but the very same thoughts persisted in coming back. He recalled his late wife. "She did not live to see it!" he whispered despondently. A plump bluish-gray pigeon alit on the road and hastily set out for a drink from the puddle near the well. Kirsanov began watching it, yet his ears had already caught the rattle of approaching wheels.

"They're coming, by the sound of it, sir," the servant reported, darting out of the gateway.

Kirsanov sprang up and his eyes followed the road. A tarantass came into view, drawn by a troika of post horses; in the tarantass the father glimpsed the band of a student's cap, the familiar outline of a face dear to him.

7

"Arcasha, Arcasha!" Kirsanov shouted, starting to run and wave his arms. A few moments later his lips were clinging to the beardless, dusty, and tanned cheek of the young graduate.

2

"Do give me a chance to shake some of the dust off, Dad," Arcadii was saying in a voice hoarse from travel yet ringing and youthful, in gay response to his father's caresses. "I'll get you all dirty."

"It's nothing, nothing!" the father kept saying with a beatific smile, and he slapped a couple of times at the collar of his son's uniform cloak and his own overcoat. "Let's have a look at you, now—let's have a look at you," he added, backing away a little, and immediately started off with hurried steps toward the inn, to the refrain of "This way, this way—and let's hurry about the horses!"

The father seemed considerably more moved than his son; he was apparently a little at a loss, apparently abashed. Arcadii stopped him: "Dad," said he, "allow me to introduce you to my good friend Bazarov, about whom I've written to you so many times. He has been kind enough to accept an invitation to stay with us."

Nicholai Petrovich quickly turned back and, walking up to a tall man in a long dust coat trimmed with tassels who had just clambered out of the tarantass, clasped hard the gloveless reddened hand which the other had been a little slow in extending.

"I am heartily glad," Kirsanov began, "and grateful for your intention of staying with us; I trust . . . may I have your name and patronymic?"

"Evgenii Vassiliev'," Bazarov answered in an indolent but manly voice and, having turned down the collar of his dust coat, let the other see him full-face. Long and gaunt, broad of forehead, with the nose flattened at the bridge but pointed at the tip, the eyes big and greenish, and the drooping side-whiskers of a sandy hue, this face was animated by a calm smile and expressed self-assurance and intelligence.

"I trust, my most amiable Evgenii Vassil'ich, that you won't find it dull at our place," Nicholai Petrovich went on.

Bazarov's lips stirred the least trifle but he said nothing in answer, merely tipping his cap a little. His hair, blond but of not too light a shade, did not, although it was long and thick, conceal the big bulges of his capacious cranium.

"Well, what do you say, Arcadii?" Nicholai Petrovich spoke up again, turning to his son. "Should we harness the horses right now, perhaps? Or would you like to rest up a bit?"

"We'll rest at home, Dad; tell them to harness the horses."

"Right away, right away," the father concurred. "Hey there, Peter—you hear? See to it, brother—and be lively about it."

Peter, who in his status of a perfect servant had refrained from walking up to the young master and kissing his hand but had merely made him a distant bow, disappeared again through the gateway.

"I came here with a carriage, but there's a troika for your tarantass as well," the father fussed as Arcadii drank water from a metal dipper which the hostess of the inn had brought out to him; as for Bazarov, he had lit his pipe and walked over to the driver of the tarantass, who was unharnessing the team. "The thing is, though, that the carriage seats only two, and so I don't know what to do about your friend—"

"He'll ride in the tarantass," Arcadii broke in in a low voice. "Don't you stand on ceremony with him, please. He's a wonderful fellow and so unassuming—you'll see."

Nicholai Petrovich's coachman led out the horses.

"Come on, get moving, you with the thick beard!" Bazarov turned to the driver of the tarantass.

"Did you hear what the gentleman called you, Mitiukha?" chimed in another driver who was standing near, with his hands thrust through the slits in the back of his sheepskin jacket. "You do have a thick beard, sure enough—"

But Mitiukha merely tossed his head so that his cap wiggled, and dragged the reins off the sweated shaft-horse.

"Lively, lively, lads—lend a hand!" Nicholai Petrovich called out. "There'll be something for vodka!"

The horses were harnessed in a few minutes; father and son got into the carriage; Peter clambered up on the box; Bazarov hopped into the tarantass, letting his head rest against a leather cushion, and both vehicles rolled away.

3

"So that's how it is—you're a graduate at last and have come home," Nicholai Petrovich was saying as he patted Arcadii now on the shoulder, now on the knee. "At last!"

"And what about Uncle? Is he well?" asked Arcadii, who, although he was filled with a sincere, almost childlike delight, wanted to shift the conversation from an emotional mood to an everyday one as quickly as possible.

"He's well. He wanted to come along with me to meet you but for some reason changed his mind."

"And were you waiting for me long?" asked Arcadii.

"Why, five hours or thereabouts."

"Good old Dad!"

Arcadii quickly turned to his father and kissed him resoundingly on the cheek. Kirsanov indulged in the quietest of chuckles. "What a glorious horse I have readied for you!" he began. "You'll see. And your room has been papered."

"But what about Bazarov—is there a room for him?"

"We'll find a room for him as well."

"Please, Dad, be good to him. I can't begin to tell you how greatly I value his friendship."

"Did you make his acquaintance recently?"

"Yes, recently."

"No wonder I didn't see him last winter. What is he taking up?"

"He's majoring in the natural sciences. But then he knows everything. He wants to get his M.D. next year."

"Ah, he's going in for medicine," the father remarked and lapsed into a short silence. "Peter," he resumed, and pointed, "aren't those our mouzhiks, by any chance, driving along over there?"

Peter threw a glance in the direction indicated by his master. Several carts drawn by unbridled horses were rolling at a spanking pace along a narrow side-road. Each cart held a mouzhik (or two mouzhiks, at the most); their sheepskin jackets were all unbuttoned.

"Exactly so, sir," Peter spoke up.

"Where are they heading—for town, or what?"

"For town, one would suppose. To the pothouse," he added disdainfully and leaned a little toward the coachman, as if for corroboration. But the other did not as much as budge: he was one of the old school, hard as nails, and did not share the latest views.

"I'm having a lot of difficulties with the mouzhiks this year," Kirsanov went on, turning to his son. "They're not paying their rent. What can one do?"

"What about your hired hands—are you satisfied with them?"

"Yes," Nicholai Petrovich got out through clenched teeth. "They're being stirred up against me, that's the trouble, and—well, there's still no real effort on their part. They damage harnesses. They haven't done so badly in tilling the land, however. You can't grind meal without some dust rising. Why, are you finding agronomy engrossing now?"

"You have no shade—that's where the mischief lies," Arcadii remarked, evading the last question.

"I've put up a big marquee over the balcony on the north side of the house," Kirsanov commented. "We can now dine out of doors, actually."

"That'll make it look too much like a summer residence, somehow. However, all that doesn't amount to much. But what air you have here, to make up for that! What glorious fragrance! Really, it seems to me that there's no such fragrance in all the world as one finds in these regions! And this sky, too—" Arcadii stopped abruptly, casting a cautious look over his shoulder, and fell silent.

"Of course," Kirsanov commented, "You were born here—everything here can't fail but impress you as something extraordinary—"

"Come, Dad, it's all the same where a man happens to be born."

"However—"

"No, it's all the same—absolutely."

Kirsanov gave his son a look, and the carriage had covered almost half a mile before they resumed their conversation.

"I don't recall whether I wrote you about it," Nicholai Petrovich began, "but your old nurse Egorovna has passed away."

"Really? Poor old woman! But what about Procophich—is he still living?"

"He is, and not changed in the least. Grouses in the same old way. On the whole, you won't find any great changes in Maryino."

"Have you still got the same clerk?"

"Now that's one change, if you like; I have replaced the clerk. I have resolved not to keep any freed houseserfs about me, or at least not to give them any positions involving responsibility." Arcadii looked significantly in Peter's direction. *"Il est libre, en effet,"* * Kirsanov commented, lowering his voice. "But then, he's a valet. My present clerk is a burgher—seems to

* "He is free, practically."

13

be a businesslike fellow. I've given him a salary of two hundred and fifty roubles a year. However," he added, running his hand over his forehead and eyebrows, which in his case was an invariable sign of inward perturbation, "I told you a little while ago that you wouldn't find any changes at Maryino—that's not altogether so. I consider it my duty to forewarn you, even though—" He brought himself up short for an instant and then continued in French: "A strict moralist would find my frankness inappropriate; but, in the first place, there is no concealing this thing and, in the second, as you know, I've always adhered to exceptional principles as to the relations between father and son. Still, you would be right in condemning me, of course. At my time of life. . . . In a word, this—this girl, whom you've probably already heard about—"

"Phenechka?" Arcadii asked, perfectly at his ease.

"Please, don't mention her name aloud." Nicholai Petrovich turned all red. "Why, yes—she's living at my place now. I have put her up at the house—there were a couple of small rooms available. However, everything can be changed."

"Please, Dad—whatever for?"

"Your friend is going to stop with us—it'll be embarrassing—"

"Don't you worry about Bazarov, please. He's above all that sort of thing."

"Well, there's yourself, after all. The trouble is, that small wing of the house is so bad—"

"Please, Dad," Arcadii broke in, "it looks as if you were making apologies—aren't you ashamed of yourself?"

"I should be ashamed, certainly," the other answered, his face turning an ever deeper red.

14

"That'll do, Dad, that'll do, if you please!" Arcadii smiled with affection. The things he's apologizing for! he thought, and a feeling of condescending tenderness toward his kindhearted, gentle father, mingled with a sensation of a certain secret superiority, filled his soul. "Stop it, please," he reiterated, involuntarily taking delight in an awareness of his own progressiveness and freedom.

His father gave him a look from under the fingers of the hand he was still running over his forehead and he felt a twinge in his heart—but immediately turned it into self-accusation.

"Now this is where our fields begin," he let drop after a long silence.

"And that forest ahead—that's ours, I think?" Arcadii asked.

"Yes, it's ours. Only I've sold it. They'll be cutting down the timber this year."

"What made you sell it?"

"I needed the money; besides that, the land is going to the mouzhiks."

"The same ones who aren't paying you their rent?"

"That's up to them, now; still, they're going to pay it some time."

"It's a pity about the forest," Arcadii remarked, and began looking about him.

One could not call the places they were driving through picturesque. Fields, nothing but fields stretching to the very horizon, now rising gently, now dipping anew; here and there one caught glimpses of groves, while ravines filled with low, scanty brushwood wound along, visually recalling similar ravines as they are figured on the antique plans going back to the times of Catherine the Great. They also happened upon small

15

rivers with eroded banks, and diminutive ponds with ill-kept dams, and hamlets with little squat huts under darkened roofs, their thatching half gone, as likely as not; and small threshing barns, tilting over, their walls woven out of deadwood and their clumsy gates gaping close to the deserted threshing-floors; and churches, either of brick, with the stucco fallen off in this spot or that, or built of wood, with tilted crosses and grave-yards fallen into utter decay.

Little by little Arcadii's heart contracted. As if intentionally, the humble mouzhiks they came across were all raggedy, driving the wretchedest of little nags; willows, with their bark stripped and their branches broken, stood by the wayside like beggars in tatters; cows, shaggy and as gaunt as if they had been gnawn clean, were hungrily nibbling the grass along the ditches. It seemed as if the sorry creatures had just struggled free from the death-dealing claws of some dread being and, evoked by the pitiful appearance of the worn-out beasts, there sprang up in the midst of the splendid spring day the white specter of dismal, never-ending winter with its blizzards, frosts, and snows. No, it occurred to Arcadii, this is not so rich a region; it doesn't overwhelm one either by its prosperity or its industriousness; it can't remain like this—it simply can't; radical changes are imperative—but how is one to put them through, what approach can one make?

Thus did Arcadii ponder the matter—but, even while he was pondering, spring was having its way. All things around and about him—all the trees, bushes and grasses—were greening with an aureate tinge, all things were stirring in broad and gentle waves and giving off a sheen under the soft breath of a warm breeze; everywhere the larks were trilling in endless ringing rivulets

16

of song; the lapwings alternated between screaming in erratic flight over the low-lying meadows and running silently over the hillocky clods; the rooks were strolling about, handsomely black against the tender green of the still-low summer corn or disappearing in the rye which had already whitened a little, their heads bobbing up only at infrequent intervals out of the hazy waves of the grain. Arcadii gazed and gazed and his reflections, weakening little by little, were vanishing. He threw off his student's cloak and looked at Kirsanov so gaily and in a way which made him seem so much like a very young boy, that the father hugged him once again.

"It isn't much further," Nicholai Petrovich remarked. "All we've got to do is go up that small hill and you can see the house. You and I will be living in clover, Arcasha; you'll lend me a hand in running the estate —if you don't get fed up with it, that is. We've got to get close to each other now, get to know each other rather well—isn't that so?"

"Of course," Arcadii assured him. "But what a wonderful day this is!"

"In honor of your homecoming, my soul. Yes, spring is in all its glory. Still, I go along with Pushkin—there is a passage in *Evgenii Oneghin* you will recall:

'How your arrival saddens me
Springtime—springtime, love's own season!
What—' "

"Arcadii!" Bazarov's voice came loudly from the tarantass. "Send me a match; I haven't a light for my pipe."

Kirsanov fell silent while Arcadii, who at first had listened to him not without a certain surprise, but also not without sympathy, hastened to get a silver match-box out of his pocket and sent Peter with it to Bazarov.

"Care for a cheroot?" Bazarov called out again.

"Let's have it," Arcadii answered.

Peter came back to the carriage and, together with the matchbox, handed him a thick black cigar which Arcadii immediately lit, spreading all around him such a strong and acrid odor of fermented tobacco that his father, who was a life-long non-smoker, could not help constantly turning his nose away, although he did it unobtrusively so as not to offend his son.

A quarter of an hour later both vehicles stopped before a new house built of wood, painted gray, and with a red metal roof. This, then, was Maryino, likewise known as New Borough or, to use the designation the peasants gave it, Lackland Croft.

4

No throng of domestics trooped out onto the front steps to welcome the masters; the only one to appear was a girl of twelve, while right after her there emerged from the house a young fellow who very much resembled Peter, garbed in a livery jacket of gray trimmed with white armorial buttons—servant to Pavel Petrovich Kirsanov. Without saying a word he opened the door of the carriage and unfastened the apron of the tarantass. Nicholai Petrovich with his son and Bazarov started to cross a dim and almost empty hall, where they caught a glimpse of a young woman's face peering from behind its door, and headed for the drawing room, the furnishings of which were indisputably in the latest taste.

"Well, we're home," remarked Nicholai Petrovich, removing his cap and tossing back his hair. "First and foremost, we must sup and then rest up a bit."

"A bite wouldn't be at all a bad idea," Bazarov put in, stretching, and lowered himself upon a divan.

"Yes, let's have supper—let's have supper without delay." For no apparent reason Kirsanov stamped his feet. "And, apropos, here comes Procophich."

A man of sixty or thereabouts entered, white-haired, gaunt and swarthy, in a brown frock coat with copper buttons, and with a pink kerchief swathed about his neck. He smirked, walked up to Arcadii to kiss his hand, then, after making a bow to the guest, backed toward the door and put his hands behind his back.

"There he is, Procophich," Kirsanov began. "He's come home at last. Well? How does he strike you?"

"He's looking his best, sir," declared the old man and indulged in another smirk, but the next moment knit his thick eyebrows. "Will you order the table set?" he asked impressively.

"Yes, yes—please. But wouldn't you rather go to your room first, Evgenii Vassil'ich?"

"No, thank you; there's really no need. But you might give orders to have them lug my wretched traveling bag there—and this bit of a garment," he added, taking off his dust coat.

"Very good. There, Procophich, take the gentleman's cloak." Procophich, acting as if he were in perplexity, picked up Bazarov's "bit of a garment" with both hands and, raising it high above his head, withdrew on tiptoes. "And you, Arcadii—are you going to your room for a minute?"

"Yes, I must clean up a little," Arcadii answered and was just about to start for the door, but at that moment a man of medium height, clad in a dark *suit* of English cut, with a modishly slim cravat and shod in kidskin low-shoes, stepped into the drawing room: Pavel Petrovich Kirsanov. He appeared to be forty-five or so; his closely clipped gray hair gave off a dark sheen, like minted silver; his face, jaundiced but unwrinkled, unusually regular in features and clean-cut, just as if it had been outlined by a fine and delicate graver, showed traces of remarkable good looks; particularly fine were his radiant eyes, dark and elongated. The entire bearing of Arcadii's uncle, elegant and thoroughbred, preserved the gracefulness of a youth and that earth-spurning striving for the upper regions which for the most part vanishes after a man's twenties.

Pavel Petrovich took his beautiful hand with long pink nails out of his trouser pocket, a hand which appeared still more beautiful because of the snowy whiteness of the cuff, linked with a large opal solitaire, and offered it to his nephew. After consummating a preliminary European *shake hands* he kissed him three times, in the Russian way—that is, he allowed his fragrant mustache to touch the other's cheeks three times—and bade him "Welcome."

Kirsanov introduced him to Bazarov; Pavel Petrovich bent slightly from his supple waist and slightly smiled but did not offer his hand and even went to the extent of thrusting it back in his pocket.

"I was already thinking that you would not arrive today," he began in an agreeable voice, rocking genially, shrugging, and showing his teeth in all their resplendent beauty. "Why, did anything happen on the road?"

"Nothing happened," Arcadii answered. "We were just delayed a bit. That's why we're ravenous as wolves right now. Make Procophich hurry, Dad—I'll be right back."

"Hold on, I'll go with you!" Bazarov called out, rising impetuously from the divan. Both young men left the room.

"Who is this individual?" asked Pavel Petrovich.

"A friend of Arcadii's—a very intelligent fellow, he tells me."

"Is he going to be our guest?"

"Yes."

"That hairy fellow?"

"Well, yes."

Pavel Petrovich drummed a little on the tabletop with his nails.

"I opine that Arcadii *s'est dégourdi*," * he commented. "I'm glad he has come home."

There was little talk during supper. Bazarov in particular said hardly a word, but he ate a lot. Nicholai Petrovich told various incidents of his life as a farmer, as he put it, gave his opinions on the forthcoming government measures, on committees, on deputies, on the need for the introduction of agricultural machinery, and so forth. Pavel Petrovich was leisurely pacing up and down the dining room (he never indulged in supper), taking a sip from a small glass of red wine at rare intervals and, still more rarely, letting drop some comment—or rather interjection, on the order of "Ah! Aha! Hm!" Arcadii imparted several items of news from Petersburg, but he felt a slight awkwardness, that awk-

* Is more at his ease.

21

wardness which takes possession of a young man when he has just done with being a child and has returned to a locale where others had become accustomed to regarding and treating him as a child. What he had to say was unnecessarily protracted, he shunned using the term "Dad" and once actually substituted the term of "Father" for it—getting it out through his teeth, it is true; with excessive nonchalance he poured into his glass much more wine than he really wanted and downed all of it. Procophich never took his eyes off him and could do nothing but champ his lips.

They all dispersed immediately after supper.

"You have a rather pernickety uncle, I must say," Bazarov told Arcadii as he sat by his bedside in a bathrobe and puffed hard at a stubby pipe. "Just imagine, such dandyism in the country! Those nails of his, those nails, now—you could send them to an exhibition!"

"Well, you don't happen to know it," Arcadii answered, "but he was a lion in his time. I'll tell you all about him some day. Why, he was an Adonis—turned the heads of all the women."

"So that's it! That means he's keeping it up for old times' sake. There's nobody to captivate here, though —the more's the pity. I couldn't stop looking at him: what amazing collars he wears—they look as if they were carved out of stone—and his chin is so painstakingly shaved. Isn't it absurd, Arcadii Nichola'ich?"

"If you like. But really, he is a fine person."

"An archaic phenomenon. Your father, though, is a splendid fellow. Reading poetry won't do him any good, it's hardly likely that he understands farming, but he is a good-natured man."

"My father has a heart of gold."

"Have you noticed how timid he is?"

Arcadii shook his head, as if he himself never felt timid.

"They're amazing, these little elderly romantics!" Bazarov continued. "They develop the nervous system to the breaking point and, naturally, all equilibrium is upset. Oh, well—good night! I have an English washbasin in my room—but the lock on the door won't work. Still, English washbasins are something to be encouraged—they represent progress!"

Bazarov left the room. A happy feeling came over Arcadii; it was delightful to fall asleep in one's own home, in a familiar bed, under a quilt that had been sewn by beloved hands, the hands of his nurse, perhaps, those caressing, kindly, tireless hands. Arcadii called Egorovna to mind, and sighed, and prayed that the Kingdom of Heaven might be hers. But he offered up no prayer for himself.

Both he and Bazarov fell asleep shortly, but there were others in the house who still remained awake for a long while. His son's homecoming made Kirsanov feel keyed up. He went to bed but, instead of extinguishing the candles, propped his head on his hand and plunged into deep, deep thoughts. His brother sat on in his study until far beyond midnight in a capacious armchair of Hambs workmanship, before the fireplace with its feebly smoldering coals. He was still fully clothed, except that he had changed his kidskin low-shoes for Chinese slippers, red and without heels. He was holding the latest issue of Galignani's *Messenger* but he was not reading; his eyes were fixed on the fireplace where a bluish flame quivered, now dying down, now flaring up. God knows where his thoughts were wandering, but they did not wander only in the past—his expression was absorbed and morose, something which does not hold true of a man who is taken up with memories alone. And, in a small room toward the back of the house a young woman by the name of Phenechka, in a warm sleeveless jacket of blue and with a white kerchief over her dark hair, was seated on a large trunk and, between naps, she kept listening intently or looking at the open door of an adjoining room through which one could glimpse a child's crib and hear the even breathing of a sleeping baby.

5

Next morning Bazarov was up before all others and stepped out of the house. Well! he reflected after glancing about him. This spot isn't much by the looks of it!

After Kirsanov had reached an agreement as to the boundaries between his land and that of his peasants, the area he had to assign for his new manor consisted of eleven acres in an utterly flat and denuded field. He had built a house and outbuildings, laid out a farm, planted a garden and dug a pond and two wells; but the young trees did not take kindly to the soil, the pond had little water in it and the well water proved to have a brackish taste. Only one arbor of lilac bushes and acacias had attained a decent growth; occasionally they had tea or dined there. It did not take Bazarov more than a few minutes to explore all the garden paths, to look in at the barnyard and the stable, to find a couple of urchins, with whom he immediately struck up a friendship, and to go off with them on a frog hunt in a small bog a mile or so from the manor house.

"What do you need frogs for?" asked one of the boys.

"Well, I'll tell you what for," answered Bazarov, who had a special ability of inspiring confidence in the humbler folk, although he never humored them and treated them offhandedly. "I'll take a frog and slit it open and see how its insides work, and since you and I are no different than frogs, except that we walk upright, I'll get to know how our insides work too."

"But what do you need to know that for?"

"Well, so's to avoid mistakes if you should happen to fall sick and it were up to me to treat you."

"Why, are you a doctor?"

"Yes."

"You hear that, Vasska? Master says you and I are no different than frogs. Sounds funny to me!"

"I'm scared of them frogs, now," remarked the seven-year-old Vasska, whose hair was as white as flax; he was wearing a gray cossackeen with a standing collar and was barefooted.

"What are you scared of? Do they ever bite?"

"There, get into the water, you philosophers," Bazarov told them.

In the meantime Nicholai Petrovich also had awakened and gone to Arcadii's room, where he found him fully dressed. Father and son stepped out onto the balcony under the marquee; on a table near the railing, a samovar, set between big bouquets of lilac, was already steaming. A little girl appeared, the same one who had been the first to meet them on the front steps when they had driven up yesterday, and informed them in a piping voice: "Theodosia Nicholaievna isn't feeling too well; she said for me to ask you if you were wishing to pour the tea yourself or if she should send Dunyasha to you?"

"I'll pour myself— I'll pour," Nicholai Petrovich quickly broke in. "What do you take with your tea, Arcadii, cream or lemon?"

"Cream," Arcadii answered and, after a short silence, called him questioningly: "Dad?"

"Yes?" the other responded.

Arcadii lowered his eyes. "Excuse me, Dad, if my question strikes you as inappropriate," he began, "but your own frankness yesterday encourages me to be frank—you won't be angry?"

"You can speak."

"You make me bold enough to ask—isn't it because Phen . . . Isn't it because I am here that she won't come here to pour the tea?"

Kirsanov averted his face a little. "It's possible," he spoke at last, "that she supposes . . . She feels ashamed—"

Arcadii quickly looked up at his father. "There's no reason for her to feel ashamed. First of all, you are familiar with my way of thinking"—Arcadii found the utterance of this phrase most gratifying—"and secondly, would I want to interfere, even in the slightest way, with your life, with your habits? Then, too, I feel certain you could not have made a poor choice; since you've permitted her to live under the same roof with you it follows that she has earned the right. At any rate, a son cannot sit in judgment on his father—especially such a son as I, and especially such a father as yourself, who has never in any respect interfered with my freedom."

26

At first Arcadii's voice had been unsteady; he had felt in a magnanimous mood, yet at the same time he was aware that he was delivering something very like a preachment to his father; the sound of one's own speechifying, however, acts strongly upon a man, and Arcadii pronounced his concluding words firmly, even effectively.

"Thank you, Arcasha," Nicholai Petrovich began in a stifled voice, and his fingers again began fidgeting over his eyebrows and forehead. "Your suppositions are actually just. Of course, if this girl wasn't worthy . . . This is no frivolous whim. It's embarrassing for me to be talking about this with you, but you understand that it was not easy for her to come while you were here, particularly on the first day of your arrival."

"If that is the case I'll go to her myself!" he exclaimed, as a new wave of magnanimous emotions swept over him, and he sprang up from his seat. "I'll make it clear to her that she has no cause to be embarrassed before me."

The father also stood up. "Arcadii," he began. "Do oblige me—how could you possibly when . . . when there's a . . . I haven't informed you that—"

However, Arcadii had stopped listening by now and dashed away. Nicholai Petrovich followed him with his eyes and, confused, sank back in his chair. His heart pounded. Had he a prevision at that moment of the ineluctable peculiarity of the future relations between him and his son? Was he realizing that Arcadii would have evinced probably still greater respect for him by not concerning himself with this matter at all? Was the father reproaching himself for being so weak? It is difficult to say. All these emotions affected him, but only as sensations, and even these were none too clear; nevertheless a flush would not leave his face and his heart was pounding.

He caught the sound of hurrying footsteps and Arcadii came out onto the balcony. "We know each other, Father!" he called out, his face expressing affection and kindliness. "Theodosia Nicholaievna is really not feeling well today and will come later on. But how is it you never told me I had a brother? I would have kissed him every bit as hard yesterday as I did just now."

Nicholai Petrovich wanted to say something, wanted to stand up and open his arms for an embrace. Arcadii threw his arms about his father's neck.

"What is this? Embracing again?" Pavel Petrovich's voice came from behind them.

Father and son were equally pleased about his entrance at that point. There are situations from which, despite their touching nature, one wants to extricate oneself as quickly as possible.

"Come, what do you find so surprising about it?" Nicholai Petrovich said gaily. "I've been waiting for ages and ages for Arcasha to come. I actually haven't had a chance to have a good look at him since yesterday."

"I don't find it in the least surprising," Pavel Petrovich remarked. "I myself would not object to embracing him."

Arcadii approached his uncle and his cheeks once more felt the light touch of the other's perfumed mustache.

Pavel Petrovich took a seat at the table. He was wearing a fine morning suit, quite British; a small fez graced his head. This fez and a neat, negligently knotted cravat suggested the relaxation of life in the country, but the close-fitting collar of his shirt (not a white shirt, true enough, but with a small colorful design, as befitted morning wear) propped up his meticulously shaved chin as inexorably as always.

"Where is your new friend?" he asked Arcadii.

"He's not in; he gets up early as a rule and goes off somewhere. It's best not to pay him any attention—he isn't fond of ceremony."

"Yes, that's noticeable." Pavel Petrovich began buttering a piece of bread leisurely. "Will he be staying with us long?"

"That depends on circumstances. He's stopping awhile on his way to his father."

"And where is his father's place?"

"In this very province, sixty miles or so from here. He has an estate there, quite small. He was a regimental doctor at one time."

"That's it, that's it! No wonder I was asking myself all the time—where did I happen to hear that name Bazarov? If my memory serves me right, Nicholai, there was a sawbones by the name of Bazarov in father's division, wasn't there?"

"There was, I think."

"Exactly, exactly. So his father is a sawbones. Hm!" His mustache twitched. "Well, what about M'sieu' Bazarov himself—just what is he?" he asked with a drawl.

"What is Bazarov?" Arcadii smiled. "I'll tell you just what Bazarov is—would you like me to, Uncle?"

"Do oblige me, Nephew."

"He is a nihilist."

"How?" Nicholai Petrovich asked, while his brother lifted up his knife with a pat of butter at its tip and arrested his hand in midair.

"He's a nihilist," Arcadii repeated.

"A nihilist," his father uttered. "That comes from the Latin, *nihil,* meaning *nothing,* if I am any judge; the word, then, designates a man who . . . who recognizes nothing?"

"Say: one who respects nothing," Pavel Petrovich interjected and went back to buttering his bread.

"One who regards everything from a critical point of view," Arcadii commented.

"But isn't that all one?" his uncle queried.

"No, it's not. A nihilist is a man who does not accede to any authority, who does not accept a single principle on faith, no matter how great the aura of respect which surrounds that principle.

"Well, and is that a good thing?" Pavel Petrovich cut him short.

"That all depends on the person, Uncle. One man may find it a very good thing for him, while another may find it very bad."

"So that's how things are. Well, now, I can see that's outside our province. We who belong to an older age, we go upon the assumption that without principles"—he gave the word a soft pronunciation, after the French manner, while Arcadii, on the contrary, gave it a harsh sound, placing the accent on the first syllable—"principles accepted on faith, as you said, a man cannot take a step, cannot draw a breath. *Vous avez changé tout cela*—you have changed all that. May God grant you good health and a general's rank, but as for us, we will merely look on and admire you, Messieurs *les*—what was that term you used?"

"Nihilists," Arcadii told him, enunciating the word clearly.

"Yes. Before we had the Hegelists, but now we have the nihilists. We'll see how you'll manage to exist in a void, in a vacuum; but right now please ring, brother Nicholai—it's time for my cocoa."

Kirsanov rang and called out, "Dunyasha!" But, instead of Dunyasha, it was Phenechka herself who appeared on the balcony. She was a young woman of twenty-three or so, all daintily white and soft, with dark hair and eyes, small red lips as plump as a child's and small, delicate hands. She had on a trim dress of printed calico; a new neckerchief of blue, folded in a triangle, rested lightly on her rounded shoulders. She was carrying a large cup of cocoa and, having placed it in front of Pavel Petrovich, became overcome with embarrassment—the warm blood surged in a wave of crimson under the delicate skin of her charmingly appealing face. She let her eyes drop and paused near the table, leaning lightly on her very finger tips. Apparently feeling awkward about having come, she at the same time seemed to feel that she had the right to do so.

Pavel Petrovich's eyebrows knit in a stern frown, while his brother seemed somewhat at a loss. "How d'you do, Phenechka," he said through his teeth.

"How d'you do, sir," she answered in a voice that was not loud yet resonant and, after a sidelong look at Arcadii, who smiled at her amiably, she left very quietly. Her walk was just a trifle waddling, but even this somehow became her.

For several seconds silence reigned on the balcony. Pavel Petrovich was sipping his cocoa—when he suddenly lifted up his head: "Here is M'sieu' the Nihilist himself, favoring us with his presence."

True enough, Bazarov was coming through the garden, stepping over the flower beds. His linen coat and trousers were muddied; a clinging marsh plant was wound about the crown of his old hat; he was holding in his right hand a small sack, in which was something alive and stirring. He quickly approached the balcony and greeted everybody with a nod: "How do you do, gentlemen; please excuse my being late for tea. I'll be back very shortly—I have to find a place for these fair captives."

"What's that you have there—leeches?" inquired Pavel Petrovich.

"No; they're frogs."

"Do you eat them or breed them?"

"Have to have them for experiments," Bazarov let drop negligently and went indoors.

"There, he's going to cut them up," Pavel Petrovich remarked. "He doesn't believe in principles, but he does believe in frogs."

Arcadii eyed his uncle with regret, and Nicholai Petrovich shrugged when no one was looking. Pavel Petrovich himself realized that his witticism had not scored and began talking about the management of the estate and about the new manager, who had called on him the evening before to complain about Thoma, a hired hand, who was "going in for debauchery" and getting all out of hand. " 'He's such a no-good ornery fellow,' he said among other things, 'that he's gotten himself a bad name everywhere; he'll stay on for a time here and then walk off over some foolishment.' "

6

Bazarov returned, seated himself at the table and quickly began on his tea. Both brothers watched him in silence, while Arcadii kept glancing stealthily now at his father, now at his uncle.

"Did you take a long walk from here?" Nicholai Petrovich asked at last.

"You have a small swamp hereabouts, close by the thicket of aspens. I started some snipe—five, I think; you can go ahead and slaughter them, Arcadii."

"Why, aren't you a hunter?"

"No."

"Physics is your particular study, isn't that so?" Pavel Petrovich inquired in his turn.

"Physics, yes; and natural sciences in general."

"They say the Germans have achieved great success in that field of late."

"Yes, we could go to school to the Nemtzi for such things."

Pavel Petrovich had used the term *Germans* in lieu of the common *Nemtzi* [tongue-tied ones] out of irony which, however, had been entirely wasted.

"Have you so high an opinion of the Nemtzi, then?" he inquired with exquisite politeness. He was beginning to feel a secret irritation. Bazarov's utter nonchalance went against the grain of Pavel Petrovich's aristocratic nature. This son of a sawbones was not only not cowed—he actually answered back, curtly and grudgingly, and there was something rude, wellnigh insolent, about the tone of his voice.

"Their scientists are a businesslike lot."

"Precisely, precisely. But then you probably do not have such a flattering estimate of the Russian scientists?"

"That's so, if you like."

"That is most laudable self-abnegation," Pavel Petrovich declared, sitting up straight and tossing his head back. "But how can this be, when Arcadii Nicholaievich was telling us only a little while ago that you accept no authorities whatsoever? That you do not believe in them?"

"But why should I accept them? And what am I going to believe in? If anybody talks sense to me I agree—and that's that."

"But what about the Nemtzi—do they always talk sense?" Pavel Petrovich managed to say, and his face took on an expression as impassive, as remote as if he had withdrawn for good to some height far above the clouds.

"Not all of them." Bazarov yawned a little as he answered; he obviously was unwilling to go on with the dispute. The uncle looked at his nephew, as if he wished to say "Your friend is certainly courteous, I must confess."

"As far as I am concerned," Pavel Petrovich resumed, not without a certain effort, "I don't favor the Nemtzi, sinner that I am. I am not as much as mentioning the Russian Nemtzi—everybody is aware what sort of birds they are. But even the Nemtzian Nemtzi go against my stomach. Those of an earlier period were halfway acceptable; at that time they had—well, a Schiller, let us say, or a Goethe. [He pronounced it *Gëtti*.] There, my brother is particularly well-disposed toward those two. But now they are all running to some sort of chemists and materialists—"

34

"A passable chemist is twenty times more useful than any poet," Bazarov cut in.

"So that's it," the other remarked and, as if he were falling asleep, raised his eyebrows by the merest trifle. "You do not recognize art, then?"

" 'The Art of Money-Making, or No More Hemorrhoids!' " Bazarov interjected with a disdainful smile.

"Just so, sir—just so. You deign to jest, I perceive. Consequently, you reject everything. So be it, then. That means you believe in science, and in science only?"

"I've already informed you that I don't believe in anything. And what is science—science in general? There is such a thing as science, in the same sense that there are trades, vocations; but such a thing as science in general simply has no existence."

"Very good, sir. Well, in the matter of other conventions accepted as part of social usage—do you adhere to the same negative tendency as far as they are concerned?"

"What is this—an official investigation?" asked Bazarov.

Pavel Petrovich turned a little pale. His brother considered himself bound to take a hand in the discussion:

"You and I will have a talk on this subject in greater detail sometime, my dear Evgenii Vassil'ich; we'll get to know your opinion and at the same time express ours. For my part I am very glad that you are taking up the natural sciences. I have heard that Liebig has made amazing discoveries in the fertilization of soils. You could help me in my agronomical work—you could give me some useful advice."

"I'm at your service, Nicholai Petrovich, but how

can we even think of coming near Liebig! You've got to learn your ABC's first and only then tackle a book, whereas we haven't laid our eyes on the first letter of the alphabet yet."

There, now, I can see you're a nihilist sure enough, Nicholai Petrovich reflected. "But just the same," he added aloud, "permit me to turn to you should the occasion arise. And now, brother, I believe it's time for us to go for a talk with the managing clerk."

Pavel Petrovich got up from his chair. "Yes," he let drop, without looking at anybody, "it is a calamity to live in a village for five years or thereabouts, withdrawn from the great minds! You'll turn into a fool among fools, sure as sure. You do your utmost not to forget the things they have taught you but—you come to with a start, and all that stuff turns out to be so much bosh, and you're informed that worth-while folks are no longer taken up with such trifles and that you, now, are nothing but old hat. What can one do! Evidently the youngsters are, for a fact, wiser than we."

Pavel Petrovich turned on his heels slowly and as slowly left; his brother set out after him.

"Say, is this uncle of yours always like that?" Bazarov imperturbably asked Arcadii, as soon as the door closed behind the two brothers.

"Listen, Evgenii, you treated him far too harshly, really," Arcadii commented. "You have offended him."

"There, do you think I'm going to start indulging these county aristocrats! Why, all that stuff is no more than vanity, dandified mannerisms, foppery! There, he should have kept on with his career in Petersburg, if that's his make-up. However, God be with him, for all of me! I've found a quite rare specimen of a water

36

bug, *Dytiscus marginatus*—are you familiar with it? I'll show it to you."

"I promised to tell you the story of—"

"The story of the bug?"

"There, enough of that, Evgenii. The story of my uncle. You'll see that he isn't at all the kind of fellow you imagine him to be. He's far more worthy of compassion than ridicule."

"I'm not arguing about that, but why are you so taken up with him?"

"One should be just, Evgenii."

"What is your premise for that?"

"No—you just listen—"

And Arcadii told him the story of his uncle.

7

Pavel Kirsanov had at first received his education at home, just like his younger brother Nicholai, and subsequently in the Corps of Pages. He had been distinguished from childhood for his remarkable good looks; in addition to that he was self-assured, given a little to mockery, and was somehow amusingly choleric—it was impossible not to like him. He began to appear everywhere as soon as he had been commissioned as an officer. He was spoiled by everybody and in turn he indulged himself; he actually played the fool, actually posed and postured—but even these things were becoming in his case. Women went mad over him, men called him a fop while envying him at heart. As explained before, he shared rooms with his brother, whom he loved sincerely, even though he did not resemble him in the least. Nicholai had a slight limp; his features were diminutive, pleasing, but rather melancholy; he had small dark eyes and his hair was thin and soft; he loafed willingly enough, but he was also willing to read, and he was timid in society. Pavel did not pass a single evening at home, was celebrated for his audacity and dexterity (it was he who had made gymnastics fashionable among the young men in society), and five or six French books marked the extent of his reading. In his twenty-eighth year he was already a captain; a brilliant career awaited him. But suddenly all this changed.

At that time Princess R——, a woman who has not been forgotten to this day, used to appear at infrequent intervals in St. Petersburg society. She had a well-brought-up, respectable, but rather foolish husband and no children. She was given to sudden departures for abroad, to sudden returns to Russia; on the whole she led a strange life. She had the name of a frivolous coquette, was infatuated with and devoted herself to pleasures of every sort, danced until she would collapse, went off into peals of laughter and joked with young men, whom she received during the forenoon in the semi-darkness of her drawing room, while her nights she spent in tears and prayer, unable to find peace anywhere, and often dashing about her room until the very morning, wringing her hands in melancholy or, all pale and chill, sitting bent over the Book of Psalms. Day would come and once more she was transformed into a lady in society. Anew she went out in her carriage, laughed, chattered, and seemed to throw herself in the path of anything which might afford her any distraction, no matter how slight.

She was strikingly well made; her braided hair, the color of gold and as heavy, fell to below her knees, yet no one would have called her a beauty: the only good feature about her whole face was her eyes, and yet not even the eyes themselves—they were gray and not at all large—but their look, swift and profound, carefree to the verge of bravado and pensive to the verge of dejection: an enigmatic look. There was a glow of something out of the ordinary in that look even while her tongue was babbling the most fatuous things. In matters of dress she had an exquisite taste.

Pavel Kirsanov met her at a ball, had danced a mazurka with her, during the course of which she had not said a single sensible word, and fell passionately in love with her. Accustomed to conquests as he was, it was not long before he attained his end in this case also, but the easiness of his triumph did not cool his ardor. On the contrary, he became still more agonizingly, still more strongly attached to this woman in whom, even at the moment of her irretrievable surrender, there seemed to remain something hallowed and inaccessible, to which no one could penetrate. What was nested in that soul, only God knows! It seemed as if she were under the sway of certain mysterious forces which were beyond even her own ken; they played with her as they willed; her intellect, which was none too great, could not overcome their whim. Her entire behavior confronted one with a succession of inconsistencies: the only letters which could have awakened justifiable suspicions on the part of her husband she had written to a man who was well-nigh a stranger to her, whereas her love had a haunting air of sadness about it; by now she did not laugh and did not jest with the one she chose; she listened to him and gazed at him in perplexity. At times, for the most part abruptly, this perplexity would change into icy horror; her face would assume a deathly and wild expression; she would lock herself in her bedchamber, and her maid, by putting her ear close to the keyhole, could hear her stifled sobs. More than once Kirsanov, on his way home after a love tryst, felt within him that rending and bitter vexation which rises in one's heart after a definite failure. "What more do I want?" he would ask himself, while his heart persisted in aching naggingly.

On one occasion he made her a present of a ring with a sphinx carved on the stone.

"What is this?" she had asked. "A sphinx?"

"Yes," he had replied, "and this sphinx is yourself."

"I?" she asked, and slowly raised her eyes to fix him with her enigmatic gaze. "Do you know, that is extremely flattering?" she had added with a smile that had no particular significance, yet her eyes still held the same strange gaze.

Things had been painful for Pavel even when Princess R—— was in love with him, but when she had cooled—and this had happened quite shortly—he almost went out of his mind. He tortured himself and was jealous, he would not leave her in peace, he dogged her steps wherever she went; she became bored by his importunate persecution and went abroad. He resigned from the army despite the pleas of his friends, despite the persuasions of his superiors, and set out on the trail of the princess; he passed four years in foreign lands, by turns in full pursuit of her or intentionally losing sight of her; he was ashamed of himself, he was indignant at his own pusillanimity—but there was no help for him. Her image, that incomprehensible, well-nigh meaningless yet captivating image, had let roots far too deeply within his soul. In Baden he had somehow come as close to her as he had been before; never yet, it seemed, had she loved him so passionately—yet a month later it was all over and done with: the flame had flared up for the last time and then expired forever. With a premonition of the inevitable parting, he desired to remain her friend at least—as if friendship were possible with a woman like that. She left Baden most secretively and from that time on consistently avoided Kirsanov.

He went back to Russia, made an attempt to pick up his old way of life where he had left off, but no longer could get back into the former groove. He wandered about from place to place as if he were a victim of slow poisoning; he still frequented society; he had preserved the ways of a man of the world; he could have been vain about two or three new conquests. However, by now he expected nothing extraordinary either from himself or from others and did not venture into anything. He aged, his hair turned gray; lounging evenings at his club in jaundiced boredom, engaging in an apathetic discussion in a circle of bachelors: such things became a necessity to him—a sinister symptom, as everyone knows. The thought of marriage never entered his head, of course.

Ten years went by in this manner, went by drably, fruitlessly, quickly—dreadfully quickly. Nowhere does time run by as fast as it does in Russia; in prison, we are told, it runs even faster. One day, while dining at his club, Pavel learned of the death of Princess R——.

She had died in Paris; her condition had bordered on madness. He had gotten up from the table and for a long while rambled through the club rooms, occasionally halting near the card players and standing there as if rooted to the spot, but he did not come home any earlier than usual. After some time had elapsed he received a small package addressed to him: it contained the ring he had presented to the princess. She had scored a cruciform mark over the sphinx and had left instructions to tell him that the unriddling of the enigma was to be found in the cross.

This occurred at the beginning of the year 1848, precisely at the time when Nicholai, having lost his wife, was coming to Petersburg. Pavel hardly ever saw his brother from the time the latter had settled down in the country: Nicholai's marriage had coincided with the first days of Pavel's acquaintance with the princess. Upon his return from abroad he had set out for his brother's place, intending to be his guest for two months or so, to be an admiring onlooker of his happiness, but had been able to last out only a week. The difference between the situations of the two brothers was too great. In 1848 this difference had lessened: Nicholai had lost his wife, Pavel had lost his recollections—after the death of the princess he tried to avoid thoughts of her. But consciousness of a life well spent stayed with Nicholai, his son was growing up before his eyes. Pavel, on the contrary, was a lonely bachelor on the threshold of that troubled, twilight time, a time of regrets that resemble hopes and of hopes that resemble regrets, when youth has gone by while old age has not yet arrived.

This was a harder period for Pavel than for anyone else: having lost his past, he had lost his all.

"I'm not inviting you to Maryino nowadays," Nicholai had told him on one occasion (he had given his estate the name of Maryino, in honor of his wife). "You found things dull there even when my wife was alive, but now you wouldn't know what to do; you would be so bored there, I think."

"At that time I was still foolish and restless," Pavel had answered. "Since then I have quieted down, even if I haven't grown any wiser. Now, on the contrary, I am ready to settle at your place for good, if you will allow me."

By way of answer Nicholai simply embraced him; but a year and a half went by after this talk before Pavel decided to carry out his intention. But then, having once settled in the country, he never left it, not even during those three winters which Nicholai had passed with his son in Petersburg. He took to reading, for the most part in English; in general, he arranged his whole life after English ways, rarely saw his neighbors or was seen by them, and left Maryino only to attend the election of a marshal of the local nobility, where he for the most part did not speak, although every now and then he would provoke and frighten the landed proprietors of the old school by his liberal pranks, yet avoided any close contact with the representatives of the new generation. Both the latter and the former deemed him too proud, yet both groups respected him for his excellent aristocratic manners, for what they had heard of his amatory conquests, for his splendid clothes and always putting up in the best room of the best hotel, for his generally dining well (there had even been an occasion when he had dined with the Duke of Wellington at the table of Louis Philippe), for his taking a dressing-case of sterling silver and a portable bath wherever he went, for his aura of some unusual perfume, strikingly on the *aristoi* side, for his playing whist like a master yet always losing; finally he was also respected for his irreproachable honesty. The ladies found him an enchanting melancholic, but then he did not mingle with the ladies.

"So you see, Evgenii," Arcadii declared as he came to the end of his story, "how unjust your judgment of my uncle is! I won't say anything about his having more than once come to my father's aid in times of trouble, giving him all his money—you may not know it, but they never divided the estate; however, he is glad to give a helping hand to anybody and, incidentally, he always intercedes for the peasants—even though, true enough, whenever he talks with them he wrinkles up his nose and sniffs eau de Cologne."

"That's easy to diagnose—it's his nerves," Bazarov broke in.

"Could be, but he has the kindest of hearts. And he's far from foolish. What useful counsels he has given me, especially . . . especially concerning women."

"Aha! He scalded himself with his own mug of milk, so he blows on somebody else's cold water. We're on to all that!"

"Well, to make it short," Arcadii continued, "he is profoundly unhappy, believe me; it is a sin to despise him."

"Why, who's despising him?" Bazarov retorted. "But just the same I would say that a fellow who has staked his entire life on the card of woman's love and who, when that card is trumped, goes all to pieces and sinks to such an extent that he's not fit for anything—a fellow like that is no man, no male. He's unhappy, you say—you ought to know best; but he's not shut of his

44

folly yet. I'm certain that, quite seriously, he imagines he's somebody worth while just because he reads that Galignani rag and once a month saves some mouzhik from getting flogged."

"Come, recall his education, the time in which he lived," Arcadii remarked.

"Education?" Bazarov caught at the word. "Every man must educate himself—well, just as I have done, for example. And as far as the time is concerned— why should I depend on it? It would be better if it depended on me. No, brother, all that is sloppiness, there's nothing in it! And what's this stuff about the mysterious relations between man and woman? We physiologists know what these relations are like. Just you bone up on the anatomy of the human eye: where are you going to find there that enigmatic look, as you put it? All that is romanticism, twaddle, dry rot, artiness. Let's better go and look that bug over."

And the two friends betook themselves to Bazarov's room, where some sort of a medico-surgical odor, with an admixture of the odor of cheap tobacco, had already managed to establish itself.

8

Pavel Petrovich did not stay long during his brother's talk with the managing clerk, a tall and gaunt fellow with a sweetish consumptive voice and the eyes of a knave, who answered all of Nicholai Petrovich's remarks with: "If you please, sir; that's a known fact, sir," and strove to represent the mouzhiks as thieves and drunkards. The estate, recently put on a new basis, was creaking like an ungreased wheel, cracking like homemade furniture of unseasoned wood. Nicholai Kirsanov was not despondent, but quite often he would sigh and fall into thought: he felt that things would not catch on without money, yet his money was almost all gone. Arcadii had told the truth: Pavel had helped his brother on more than one occasion; on more than one occasion, as he saw how the other struggled and cudgeled his brains trying to think how he might extricate himself, Pavel would saunter up to a window and, with his hands thrust in his pockets, mutter through clenched teeth: *"Mais je puis vous donner de l'argent,"* * and would give him money; but that day he did not have any himself and he had preferred to withdraw. He found the annoyances of managing an estate depressing; besides, it constantly seemed to him that his brother, despite all his application and love of work, did not tackle things in the proper manner, even though he himself would have been unable to indicate just where Nicholai was in error. My brother isn't practical enough, he reasoned to himself. People put things over on him. Nicholai, on the contrary, held the highest opinion of Pavel's practicality and always sought his advice. "I'm a soft, weak fellow," he would say, "I've spent all my life in the wilderness, while you haven't lived so much among people in vain; you have a thorough knowledge of them—you have the eye of an eagle." Pavel, whenever he heard such things, merely answered by turning his head away, but did not disillusion him.

* "But I can give you the money."

46

Having left Nicholai in his study, he walked through the corridor which divided the front part of the house from the rear and, on reaching a rather low door, halted for a moment in thought, tugged at his mustache and knocked.

"Who's there? Come in," came Phenechka's voice.

"It is I," Pavel Petrovich said, and opened the door.

Phenechka sprang up from the chair in which she had settled comfortably with her baby and, having transferred him to the arms of a girl who immediately carried him from the room, she hastened to adjust her neckerchief.

"Pardon me if I have disturbed you," Pavel Petrovich began, without looking at her. "I merely wanted to make a request of you. They're sending somebody to town today, I believe—please give orders to buy some green tea for me."

"Right, sir. How much do you wish to buy?"

"Why, half a pound should suffice, I suppose. But you have made a change here, I notice," he added, after a quick glance around him which glided over Phenechka's face also. "Those curtains, now," he remarked, perceiving that she did not understand him.

"Yes, sir—the curtains. Nicholai Petrovich was kind enough to give them to me, but they were hung up quite a while back."

"Yes, and it's quite a while since I've been here. You've a very pleasant place here now."

"All through Nicholai Petrovich's kindness," Phenechka got out in a whisper.

"Do you find this better than the small wing you had before?" Pavel Petrovich asked amiably but without as much as a hint of a smile.

"Of course it's better, sir."

"Whom have they put in your former quarters?"

"The laundresses are there now."

"Ah!"

Pavel Petrovich fell silent. He'll be leaving now, Phenechka was thinking; but he did not leave and she remained standing before him stock-still, twiddling her fingers hesitantly.

"Why did you have your little one carried away?" Pavel Petrovich broke his silence at last. "I'm fond of children—do let me see him."

She turned all red from embarrassment—and from delight. She feared Pavel Petrovich, who practically never spoke to her.

"Dunyasha," she called out, "please bring Mitya here." Phenechka addressed everybody in the house in the politest terms. "Or no—better wait; I've got to put something on him." She headed for the door.

"It doesn't matter, really," Pavel Petrovich remarked.

"I'll be right back," Phenechka answered, and nimbly slipped out.

Pavel Petrovich was left alone and this time he looked about him with particular attentiveness. The small, rather low room in which he found himself was very neat and cozy. It smelt of the recently painted floor, of camomile and melissa. Ranged along the walls were chairs with lyre-shaped backs—these had been bought long ago in Poland by the late general himself, during a campaign; in one corner stood a high, small bedstead under a muslin canopy, close to an iron-bound trunk with a rounded lid. In the corner opposite, a lampad was glowing before a large, dark holy image of Nicholai the Worker of Miracles; a tiny porcelain egg, suspended on a red ribbon attached to the nimbus, hung upon the breast of the saint; glass jars, translucently

48

green, filled with jam made last year, stood on the window sills; on their paper covers, carefully tied down, Phenechka herself had written GOOSEBERRY in large letters but misspelling the word a little; Nicholai Petrovich was especially partial to this jam. A cage with a bobtailed siskin hung on a long cord close to the ceiling; the bird was constantly chirping and hopping, and the cage was constantly swinging and shaking; hempseed pattered lightly as it fell on the floor. Above a small commode, on the wall space between two windows, were hanging some quite atrocious photographic portraits of Nicholai Petrovich in various poses, taken by an itinerant artist; there, too, hung a photograph of Phenechka herself, which was an utter fiasco: some eyeless face or other was smiling in a strained way from within a small dark frame—it was impossible to make out anything more; while above this depiction of Phenechka General Ermolov, in a Circassian cloak of felt, was scowling awesomely at distant Caucasian mountains, from under a small pincushion of silk in the shape of a shoe which came right down over his forehead.

Five minutes passed; one could hear whispering and sounds of fussing in the adjoining room. Pavel Petrovich picked up a much soiled book from the commode —it was an odd volume of Massalsky's *Archers of the Czar*—and turned a few pages. The door opened at last and Phenechka entered with Mitya in her arms. She had put a tiny red smock with a lace collar on him, and combed his hair and run a moist cloth over his face; he was breathing hard, straining his whole body and jerking his little arms, as all healthy children do, but his dandified smock had apparently made an impression on him and there was an air of satisfaction about the whole of his chubby little figure. Phenechka had put her own hair in order as well and had arranged her triangular neckerchief to better advantage, but she could well have left things the way they had been. For, after all, does the world hold anything more captivating than a comely young mother with a healthy baby in her arms?

"What a husky little fellow," Pavel Petrovich declared graciously and tickled Mitya's double chin with the tip of the long nail of his index finger; the baby stared at the siskin and chuckled.

"This is Uncle," said Phenechka, putting her face close to the boy and bouncing him lightly; Dunyasha in the meanwhile was most discreetly placing on the window sill a smoldering incense cone, with a copper coin under it.

"How many months is he, now?" Pavel Petrovich asked.

"Six months; he'll be in his seventh soon, on the eleventh of the month."

"Won't it be the eighth, Theodosia Nicholaievna?" Dunyasha interposed, not without timid hesitation.

"No, it will be the seventh—couldn't be otherwise!" The baby chuckled again, stared at the trunk, and suddenly made a fistful of his mother's nose and mouth. "You little mischief," Phenechka declared, without freeing her face.

"He resembles my brother," Pavel Petrovich commented.

"Whom else should he resemble?" Phenechka reflected.

"Yes," Pavel Petrovich continued, as though speaking to himself, "there is a resemblance, beyond all doubt." He regarded Phenechka attentively, almost sadly.

"This is Uncle," she repeated, but this time in a whisper.

"Ah, Pavel! So this is where you are!" They suddenly heard the voice of Nicholai Petrovich.

Pavel hastily turned and frowned, but his brother was looking at him so joyously, with such gratitude, that he could not help giving him a responsive smile.

"That's a glorious youngster you've got there," he said, and glanced at his watch. "I just dropped in about purchasing some tea—" And, having assumed an indifferent expression, he immediately left the room.

"Did he come on his own account?" Nicholai asked Phenechka.

"On his own account, sir; he just knocked and came in."

"Well, has Arcasha been here again?"

"He hasn't. Shouldn't I move into the wing, Nicholai Petrovich?"

"Why should you?"

"I wonder if that wouldn't be better at first."

"N-no," Nicholai Petrovich answered, not without hesitation, and rubbed his forehead. "This should have been done before. Greetings, pudgy," he said with sudden animation and, drawing close to the baby, kissed his cheek; then he bent over a little and let his lips touch Phenechka's hand, which showed as white as milk against the red of Mitya's little smock.

"Nicholai Petrovich! What are you doing?" she murmured, lowering her eyes, then raising them, ever so shyly. The expression in them was enchanting when she looked as if from deep within the sockets, and at the same time laughed tenderly and a trifle foolishly.

Nicholai Petrovich had first come to know Phenechka three years ago, when he had had occasion to put up for a night at an inn in a remote country town. He had been agreeably surprised by the cleanliness of the room given him, by the freshness of the bed linen. Does the lady of the house happen to be a German? the idea came to him; but the landlady turned out to be Russian, about fifty, neatly dressed, with a pleasantly comely, intelligent face and well spoken. He got to talking with her at tea; she proved very much to his liking. At that time Nicholai Petrovich had just moved into his new manor house and, since he did not want to have serfs about him, was looking for hired servants; the landlady in her turn complained that there were not many people passing through the town and that times were bad; he offered her the position of housekeeper—she accepted it. Her husband had died, a long time ago, leaving her only a daughter, Phenechka. Within two weeks Arina Savishna (which was the new housekeeper's name) came with her daughter to Maryino and moved into a small wing of the house. Nicholai Petrovich's choice turned out to be a fortunate one. Arina installed order in the household. No one ever spoke of Phenechka, who was seventeen at the time, and hardly anybody ever saw her; she lived very quietly, very unassumingly, and it was only on Sundays that Kirsanov might notice in the parish church, somewhere off to one side, the fine profile of her small white face. Thus more than a year went by.

One morning Arina appeared in his study and, after her customary low bow, asked him if he could not help her daughter, who had gotten a spark from the stove in her eye. Kirsanov, like all stay-at-homes, was a dabbler in medicine—he had even imported a small cabinet of homeopathic remedies. Arina was immediately bidden to bring the patient. On learning that the master wanted her to come Phenechka became thoroughly frightened; nevertheless she went along with her mother. Nicholai Petrovich led her over to a window and took her head in his hands. After a thorough examination of her reddened and inflamed eye he prescribed an eyewash which he compounded right then and there; then, tearing his handkerchief in strips, he showed how to apply the medicament. Phenechka, after having heard his instruction, was about to go, when her mother told her: "Do kiss the master's hand, you silly little thing!" Nicholai Petrovich did not give her his hand to kiss but, in his confusion, kissed her bowed head instead, where her hair was parted. Phenechka's eye got well soon enough, but the impression she had made on Kirsanov did not pass so quickly. That pure, gentle, timorously lifted face was constantly before his eyes; he felt that soft hair under his hands; he saw those innocent lips, slightly open and revealing small pearly teeth that gleamed moistly in the sun. He took to observing her with more attentiveness in church and made attempts to enter into conversation with her. At first she shied away from him, and once, with evening coming on, as she encountered him on a narrow footpath running through a field of rye she stepped aside into the tall thick grain and the growths of wormwood and cornflowers in order to avoid his seeing her. He caught sight of her little head as she peeped like some small wild creature out of the gold-tinted network of the growing wheat and gently called to her:

"Greetings, Phenechka! I'm not in the habit of biting people."

"Greetings," she answered in a whisper, without emerging from her covert.

Little by little she began to get accustomed to him, although she still turned timid in his presence. When Arina, her mother, died suddenly from cholera, what was Phenechka to do, where was she to turn? She had inherited from her mother common sense, sedateness and a love of orderliness; yet she was so young, so lonely; Nicholai Petrovich was so kindhearted, so modest . . . There is no need to tell the rest.

"So my brother did come in to see you, just so? He knocked and came in?"

"Yes, sir."

"Well, that's fine. Here, let me rock Mitya a little."

And Kirsanov started tossing him almost up to the ceiling, to the vast delight of the tot and the by no means slight uneasiness of the mother, who stretched out her arms to the bare little legs at his every flight ceilingward.

As for Pavel Petrovich, he returned to his artistic study, tastefully papered in neutral gray, with weapons arranged against a bright-hued Persian rug, with furniture of walnut upholstered in dark-green velveteen, with a Renaissance bookpress of old black oak, with bronze statuettes on the magnificent desk, with a fireplace. He cast himself on the divan, put his hands behind his head, and lay thus without stirring, his gaze fixed on the ceiling in something very like despair. Whether it was because he wanted to conceal from the very walls that which his face betrayed, or for some other cause, he got up, released the fastenings which kept back the heavy hangings over the windows, and again threw himself onto the divan.

9

Bazarov in his turn made Phenechka's acquaintance on the same day. He had been walking through the garden with Arcadii and explaining to him why certain of the young trees, particularly the young oaks, had done so poorly.

"You should have planted silver poplars here, mostly, and firs, and lindens, maybe, adding some black loam to the soil. That arbor, now, has caught on well," he added, "because the acacia and lilac bushes are good-natured fellows and don't demand much care. Hold on! Why, there's somebody in there."

Phenechka was sitting in the arbor, together with Dunyasha and Mitya. Bazarov stopped, while Arcadii nodded to Phenechka as if he had known her a long time.

"Who is that?" Bazarov asked him as soon as they had gone past. "What a pleasing little thing!"

"Why, whom are you talking about?"

"You know very well. Only one of them was pleasing."

Arcadii made it clear in a few words, and not without embarrassment, who Phenechka was.

"Aha!" Bazarov exclaimed. "Obviously, your father has good taste. I like your father, I swear! He's a grand fellow. However, we ought to get acquainted," he added, and started back for the arbor.

"Evgenii!" the other called after him in alarm. "Be as careful as you can, for God's sake!"

"Don't get excited," Bazarov told him. "Us city slickers have been around and seen things." He doffed his cap as he came up to Phenechka. "Allow me to introduce myself," he began, bowing politely. "I'm a friend of Arcadii Petrovich, and quite harmless."

Phenechka had gotten up from the bench and was looking at him without saying anything.

"What a marvelous baby!" Bazarov kept right on. "Don't worry, now—I've never put the evil eye on anybody yet. Why are his cheeks so red? Cutting his teeth —is that it?"

"Yes, sir," Phenechka confirmed. "He's cut four already, and now his gums are swollen again."

"Let's see the fellow, now—and don't be afraid: I'm a doctor." Bazarov picked up the baby which, to the surprise of both Phenechka and Dunyasha, did not offer the least resistance and was not frightened. "I see, I see—nothing wrong, everything in order; he'll have good choppers. If anything happens, let me know. And you yourself, are you enjoying good health?"

"I am, thank God."

"Thank God—that is the best thing of all. And you?" Bazarov added, addressing Dunyasha. The girl, who was a great stickler for propriety in the chambers of her masters but would laugh her head off outside the gates, could merely give something between a snort and a guffaw in answer. "There, that's splendid. And here is your mighty knight."

Phenechka took the baby into her arms. "How quietly he behaved with you," she remarked in a low voice.

"Children always behave with me," Bazarov informed her. "I have a certain knack for that."

"Children have a feeling for those as loves them," Dunyasha commented.

"Yes, that's true enough," Phenechka confirmed.

56

"Why, even Mitya won't let some people handle him, not for anything."

"Well, now, would he come to me?" asked Arcadii who, after having stood for some time at a distance, now approached the arbor. He coaxed Mitya to come to him, but the latter threw his head back and started mewling, to Phenechka's extreme embarrassment.

"I'll do better some other day, when he's had time to get used to me," Arcadii remarked indulgently, and the two friends withdrew.

"What's her name, now?" asked Bazarov.

"Phenechka—Theodosia, that is," Arcadii answered.

"And her patronymic? One should know that also."

"Nicholaievna."

"*Bene*. The thing I like about her is that she's not overembarrassed. Somebody might, I suppose, condemn her precisely for that. What bosh! What's there to be embarrassed about? She's a mother—well, she's in the right."

"She is, certainly," Arcadii remarked, "but my father, now—"

"And he's in the right, too," Bazarov cut him short.

"Well, no. I don't consider him right."

"An extra little heir evidently goes against our grain?"

"How is it you're not ashamed to suppose me capable of such notions!" Arcadii objected warmly. "It isn't from that point of view that I consider my father in the wrong; I'm of the opinion that he ought to marry her."

"Oho-ho!" Bazarov let drop imperturbably. "How very magnanimous we are! You still attribute significance to marriage—I didn't expect that from you." The friends took a few steps in silence. "I have looked

57

your father's whole place over," Bazarov resumed. "The livestock is poor and the horses are on their last legs. The buildings aren't up to snuff, either, and the hands look like out-and-out sluggards, while the managing clerk is either a fool or a swindler—I haven't quite made out which, so far."

"You're certainly in a harsh mood today, Evgenii Vassilievich."

"And the mouzhiks, those little darlings, will bamboozle your father sure as shooting. You know the proverb: The mouzhik can gobble up God Himself."

"I'm beginning to agree with my uncle," Arcadii remarked. "You decidedly have a poor opinion of Russians."

"Most important, that! The only good trait about a Russian is that he has a most atrocious opinion of himself. The only important thing is that two times two makes four, while everything else is all bosh."

"And is nature bosh?" Arcadii uttered, gazing pensively at the bright checkerwork of the fields lying in the distance, under the beautiful and soft light of the sun, which was by now quite low.

"And nature, too, is bosh—the way you conceive it. Nature is no temple but a workshop, and man is the worker therein."

At that very instant the lingering sounds of a violoncello came floating toward them from within the house. Someone was playing Schubert's "Expectation" with feeling, even though with an unpracticed hand, and the delectable melody spread mellifluously through the air.

"What's that?" Bazarov was amazed.

"That's my father."

"Does your father play the cello?"

"Yes."

"Say, how old is your father?"

"Forty-four."

Bazarov broke into hearty laughter.

"What do you find so funny?"

"Oh, please! A man of forty-four, a paterfamilias, living in these backwoods—and he plays the cello!"

Bazarov kept on laughing; but on this occasion Arcadii, despite all the reverence he felt for his preceptor, did not as much as smile.

10

About two weeks went by. Life at Maryino flowed along much as usual: Arcadii sybaritized, Bazarov worked away. Everybody in the house had become accustomed to him, to his easygoing ways, his laconic and abrupt speech. To Phenechka especially he had become so much like one of the household that one night she had him awakened when Mitya went into convulsions; Bazarov had come and, half-yawning, half-joking as usual, had sat up with her for a couple of hours and relieved the baby. Pavel Petrovich, though, had come to loathe Bazarov with all his soul: he considered him arrogant, brazen, a cynic, a plebeian; he suspected that Bazarov had no respect for him, that he all but held him in contempt—him, Pavel Kirsanov! Nicholai Petrovich was somewhat apprehensive about the young "nihilist" and had doubts as to whether his influence on Arcadii was a beneficial one, but he listened to his talks willingly and willingly attended his experiments in physics and chemistry. Bazarov had brought his microscope along and would fuss with it for hours at a stretch. The servants also had become attached to him, even though he twitted them: they felt that, when you came right down to it, he was a man and brother and not one of the masters. Dunyasha giggled readily enough when he was around and would cast meaningful sidelong glances at him whenever she dashed by like a little hen partridge; Peter, a fellow extremely conceited and stupid, with forehead perpetually wrinkled from strain, a fellow whose worth consisted, all in all, of his air of civility, his being able to read by syllables and his frequent cleaning of his small frock coat with a little brush—even he would smirk and brighten the moment Bazarov bestowed any attention upon him; the urchins about the place ran after the "doc" like so many puppies. Procophich, that old man, was the only one who had no liking for him; he served him at table with a surly air, referred to him as "knacker" and "scalawag" and maintained that Bazarov with those side whiskers of his looked like nothing else but a pig stuck in a bush. Procophich, after his fashion, was no less an aristocrat than Pavel Petrovich.

The best days of the year—the first days of June— set in. The weather was consistently fine; true, there was a remote threat of cholera recurring, but the people inhabiting this particular province had by now become accustomed to its visitations. Bazarov would get up very early and set out for a hike of two or three miles; not for the sake of pleasure, however, since he could not abide idle jaunts, but to collect herbs and insects. Now and then he would take Arcadii along. On the way back they would usually get into an argument—

with Arcadii most often winding up as the loser even though he had more to say than his companion.

On one occasion their return had been somehow long delayed; Nicholai Petrovich came out into the garden to meet them and, as he came abreast of the arbor, he suddenly caught the voices and quick steps of the two young men. They were following a path on the other side of the arbor and could not see him.

"You don't know my father sufficiently well," Arcadii was saying.

Nicholai Petrovich held his breath.

"Your father is a kindhearted fellow," Bazarov declared, "but he's a has-been—his act is over."

The father was all ears. Arcadii did not answer anything.

The has-been stood there without stirring for two minutes or so and then plodded homeward.

"A couple of days ago I came upon him reading Pushkin," Bazarov went on. Do explain to him, please, that this sort of thing is utterly useless. After all, he isn't a little boy; it's time to abandon all this twaddle. Why should he hanker to be a romantic in this day and age! Give him something worth while to read."

"What should I give him?" asked Arcadii.

"Why, Büchner's *Stoff und Kraft** for a starter, I think."

"That's what I think," Arcadii remarked with approval. *"Stoff und Kraft* is written in popular language."

"And that's how you and I happened to find ourselves among the has-beens," Nicholai Petrovich was saying the same day after dinner to his brother, sitting in the latter's study. "Our act is over. Oh, well—Ba-

* *Matter and Force.*

61

zarov may be right, at that; one thing does hurt me, however—I had hopes, precisely now, of getting on close and friendly terms with Arcadii, yet it turns out that I have been left behind; he has advanced and we can't understand each other."

"Come, just how has he advanced? And what makes him so very different from us by now?" Pavel Petrovich exclaimed impatiently. "It's that seigneur, that nihilist, who has stuffed his head with all this. I abominate this wretched little pillroller; he's simply a charlatan, to my way of thinking. I feel certain that, with all his frogs, he hasn't made much headway even in physics."

"No, don't say that, brother—Bazarov is intelligent and knowing."

"And what disgusting self-conceit!" Pavel again broke in.

"Yes," Nicholai commented, "he is conceited. But it looks as if one couldn't do without that. There's only one thing I can't grasp. I'm doing everything, it seems, not to fall behind the times; I've arranged things for the peasants, I have started a farm—why, they actually style me a Red all over the province; I read, I study, I strive—on the whole—to keep up with the demands of the times, yet they're saying my act is over. There, brother, I myself am starting in to think that it is over, sure enough."

"But why?"

"Well, here's why. Today I was sitting reading Pushkin. It happened to be "The Gypsies," I remember. Suddenly Arcadii walked up to me and without a word, his face betraying a compassion that was ever so tender, took the book away from me ever so gently, as if I were a baby, and placed another one before me, a

German one. Then he smiled and left—and carried Pushkin off with him."

"Well, now! But just what sort of a book did he give you?"

"This one." And Nicholai Petrovich drew Büchner's celebrated brochure, a copy of the ninth edition, out of his coattail pocket.

Pavel Kirsanov emitted a rumbling "Hm!" as he turned the book in his hands. "Arcadii is concerned about your education. Well, now, did you make a try at reading it?"

"I certainly did."

"And what was the upshot?"

"Either I'm stupid or all this is twaddle. Probably I'm stupid."

"You haven't forgotten your German, have you?" asked Pavel.

"I understand German."

Pavel again turned the book in his hands and glanced at his brother from under his brows. There was a short silence between them.

"And, by the way," Nicholai began, evidently desirous of shifting the conversation, "I've received a letter from Kolyazin."

"Matvei Ilyich?"

"The very same." He's in town on an inspection tour of the province. He has become a bigwig now and writes me that, as a kinsman, he desires to see us and invites both of us, as well as Arcadii, to visit him in town."

"Are you going?" asked Pavel.

"No. What about you?"

"No; I'm not going either. No great need to drag oneself forty miles or more for a mouthful of cranberry

sauce. *Mathieu* wants to show himself in all his glory
before us; to the devil with him. Let the incense the
whole province will be burning before him suffice him;
he'll manage to do without ours. And what a grand
personage—a Privy Councilor! If I had gone on in the
service, staying in the stupid harness, I would have
been an adjutant general by now. Besides, you and I
are has-beens."

"Yes, brother; the way things look it's time to get
measured for a coffin and fold one's hands on one's
breast," Nicholai commented with a sigh.

"Well, I'm not giving in so fast," his brother muttered. "I have a premonition that that pillroller and I
are going to tangle yet."

Tangle they did that same day, at evening tea. Pavel
Kirsanov came down into the drawing room all set
for battle, irritated and determined. All he was waiting
for was a pretext for falling upon the enemy, but for a
long time the pretext did not materialize. Bazarov generally had little to say in the presence of the "little
Kirsanov ancients," as he dubbed both brothers, while
on this evening he felt out of sorts and drank off cup
after cup of tea in silence. Pavel Petrovich was being
utterly consumed by impatience; his wishes found fulfillment at last.

The talk turned to one of the neighboring landed
proprietors. "Trash; a wretched little aristocrat," Bazarov, who had met this fellow in Petersburg, commented apathetically.

"Permit me to ask you," Pavel Petrovich began, and
his lips started quivering, "according to your conceptions the words 'trash' and 'aristocrat' have one and
the same significance?"

"I said 'wretched little aristocrat,'" Bazarov let drop, lazily sipping and swallowing some tea.

"Precisely so, sir; yet I suppose that you hold to the same opinion of aristocrats as of wretched little aristocrats. I consider it my duty to declare to you that I do not share that opinion. I venture to say that everybody knows me as a liberal and a man who loves progress; but it is precisely for that reason that I respect aristocrats—the real ones. Recall, my dear sir"—at these words Bazarov looked up and eyed Pavel Petrovich —"recall, my dear sir," the speaker repeated acrimoniously, "the English aristocrats. They do not yield an iota of their rights, and therefore respect the rights of others; they demand the fulfillment of the obligations due them, and therefore they themselves fulfill *their* obligations. The aristocracy has given freedom to England and it supports that freedom."

"We've heard that song, many's the time," Bazarov retorted. "However, what do you wish to prove by that?"

"What I want to prove by *that there*"—Pavel Petrovich, whenever he was in an angry mood, intentionally resorted to such turns of speech, even though he knew well enough that they were not grammatically permissible; this whim evinced a vestige of the traditions of the time of Alexander I: some of the gallants of that day, on the infrequent occasions when they spoke their native tongue, used *that there,* while others preferred *this here,* as if to say they were Russians from 'way back, and grandees on top of that, having the license to disdain rules laid down by scholars—"what I want to prove by that there is that without a feeling of one's own worth, without respect for one's own self

—and in an aristocrat these two feelings are thoroughly developed—there is no firm basis for the social *bien public,* the public good, the social structure. Personality, my dear sir, that's the main thing; man's personality must be as firm as a rock, for everything is built upon it. I know very well, for example, that it pleases you to find amusement in my habits, my dress—my personal neatness, if it comes to that; all this, however, emanates from a sense of self-respect, from a sense of duty—yes sir, yes sir: duty. I live in the country, in the backwoods, but I do not let myself sink, I respect the man within me."

"Just a moment, Pavel Petrovich," Bazarov spoke up. "So you respect yourself and sit there twiddling your thumbs. What good does that do the *bien public?* You still would be doing the same thing, even if you didn't respect yourself."

Pavel Petrovich paled.

"That's something else entirely. I am not at all constrained to explain to you at present why I sit twiddling my thumbs, as it pleases you to express it. All I want to say is that aristocracy is a principle, and that it is solely immoral or frivolous people who can live without principles in our time. I told that to Arcadii the day after his arrival, and I repeat it to you now. Didn't I say that, Nicholai?"

Nicholai nodded.

"Aristocracy, liberalism, progress, principles," Bazarov was saying in the meantime. "My, what a batch of foreign—and useless—words! No Russian needs them, even gratis."

"What does he need then, according to you? To hear you tell it, why, we're outside humanity, outside its laws. The logic of history, if you please, demands—"

"Why, what do we need that logic for? We manage even without it."

"How so?"

"Why, just so. You have no need of logic, I trust, to pop a hunk of bread in your mouth when you feel hungry? Who are we to bother with those abstractions!"

Pavel Kirsanov flung up his hands. "I don't understand you after this. You're insulting the Russian people. I don't understand—how is it possible not to acknowledge principles, rules? By virtue of what do you act, then?"

"I've already told you, dear uncle, that we don't acknowledge authorities," Arcadii broke in.

"We act by virtue of that which we acknowledge to be useful. At the present time repudiation is the most useful of all. We repudiate."

"Everything?"

"Everything."

"What! Not only art, poetry . . . but also—one dreads to say it—"

"Everything," Bazarov repeated with inexpressible calm.

Pavel Petrovich stared at him. He had not expected this; as for Arcadii, he actually glowed with satisfaction.

"However, permit me to say something," Nicholai Petrovich spoke up. "You're repudiating everything, or, to put it more exactly, you're demolishing everything. But then, it is necessary to be constructive as well."

"That, now, is no business of ours. The ground must be cleared, first of all."

"That's what the present state of the people de-

67

mands," Arcadii added with a pompous air. "We are obligated to fulfill these demands; we haven't the right to indulge in personal egoism."

Bazarov, it seemed, found this last phrase displeasing; there was a whiff of philosophy—of romanticism, that is—about it, since Bazarov dubbed philosophy, too, as romanticism; however, he did not deem it necessary to controvert his youthful disciple.

"No, no!" Pavel Kirsanov exclaimed with unrestrained impulsiveness. "I don't want to believe that you gentlemen have a true knowledge of the Russian people, that you are representatives of its needs, its aspirations! No, the Russian people is not such as you imagine it. It considers its traditions sacred; it is patriarchal, it cannot live without faith—"

"I'm not going to argue against that," Bazarov cut him short. "I am even prepared to agree that *as far as that goes* you are right."

"Well, if I am right—"

"But, just the same, that doesn't prove a thing."

"Precisely—that doesn't prove a thing," Arcadii echoed, with the assurance of an experienced chessplayer who had anticipated an apparently dangerous move of an opponent and therefore had not been at all at a loss.

"Just how doesn't it prove a thing?" muttered the astonished Pavel Petrovich. "You must be opposing your own people, in that case?"

"Well, and what if that is so?" Bazarov exclaimed. "Whenever it thunders the common folk think it's Elijah the prophet out for a ride through the sky in his chariot. Well, now—am I supposed to agree with them? And suppose the common folk are Russian, so what? Am I not Russian too?"

"No, you're not Russian—not after all you've just told me! I can't acknowledge you as a Russian."

"My grandfather ploughed the soil," Bazarov answered with a pride that bordered on superciliousness. "Ask any peasant you like—even one of your own—whom he would rather acknowledge as a fellow-countryman—you or me. Why, you don't even know how to talk to a peasant."

"Well, you talk to him—and hold him in contempt at the same time."

"What of that, if he deserves contempt! You disparage my attitude, yet who told you that it isn't accidental in my case, that it wasn't provoked by that self-same national spirit in the name of which you are contending so strenuously?"

"Oh, to be sure! As if there were any great need of nihilists!"

"Whether there is need of them or no is not up to us to decide. Why, you too consider yourself as not useless."

"Gentlemen, gentlemen—please, no personalities!" Nicholai Petrovich called out and rose from his seat.

Pavel Kirsanov smiled and, putting a hand on his brother's shoulder, made him sit down again. "Don't be alarmed," he remarked. "I shan't forget myself, precisely as a consequence of that sense of dignity which this gentleman, this doctor gentleman pokes such cruel fun at. Allow me to ask you," he went on, addressing Bazarov once more, "are you possibly thinking that your teaching is a novelty? You imagine so in vain. The materialism you are preaching has already been all the rage, more than once, and turned out to be insolvent—"

"Another foreign word!" Bazarov cut him short. He

was turning rancorous and his face had taken on a coppery and coarse hue. "First of all, we aren't preaching a thing—that's not one of our ways—"

"What is it you're doing, then?"

"Well, here's what we're doing. Hitherto, still quite recently, we used to say that our bureaucrats took bribes, that we had neither roads, nor commerce, nor real justice—"

"Why, yes, yes—you're denouncers: that's the term, I believe. I, too, am in agreement with many of your denunciations, but—"

"However, in time we wised up to the fact that blather, nothing but perpetual blather about our social sores wasn't worth the effort, that it led to nothing but banality and doctrinarism; we perceived that even the clever fellows among us, the so-called vanguard people and denunciators, weren't good for anything, that we were taken up with twaddle, spouting about some art or other, about unconscious creativeness, about parliamentarism, about the legal profession, and about the devil knows what else, when the real business at hand has to do with our daily bread, when the crassest superstition is suffocating us, when all our stock-issuing companies are going up the chimney solely because it turns out that there aren't enough honest men to go around, when that very emancipation which the government is going to such bother about will hardly be of any benefit to us, since our mouzhik is eager to rob his own self if only it will enable him to stupefy himself with rotgut at a pothouse."

"Exactly," Pavel Petrovich interposed. "Exactly; you've become convinced of all this and have resolved not to take on anything seriously yourselves."

"And we resolved not to take on anything," Bazarov

70

repeated dourly. He had suddenly become vexed with himself: why had he become so expansive before this seigneur?

"But only to go in for abuse?"

"And to go in for abuse."

"And that's what they call nihilism?"

"And that's what they call nihilism," Bazarov repeated once more, this time with especial rudeness.

Pavel Kirsanov puckered up his eyes slightly. "So that's how things stand!" he uttered in a strangely calm voice. "Nihilism is bound to help in everything that's wrong, and you—you!—are our redeemers and heroes. So! But why are you tongue-lashing others now—even though they may be the same sort of denouncers as yourselves? Aren't you going in for the same sort of blather as everybody else?"

"Whatever else we may be guilty of, this is one sin of which we're innocent," Bazarov got out through clenched teeth.

"Well, then? Are you taking action, or what? Are you getting ready to act?"

Bazarov did not answer anything. Pavel Petrovich plainly shuddered but immediately controlled himself. "Hm! Taking action, wrecking," he continued. "Yet how can one wreck without as much as knowing why?"

"We wreck because we are a force," Arcadii remarked. Pavel Petrovich gave his nephew a look and smiled slightly. "Yes, and a force simply does not give any accounting of itself," Arcadii declared, straightening up.

"You poor unfortunate!" Pavel Petrovich vociferated; he was utterly incapable of restraining himself any longer. "If you would only reflect just *what* it is you're supporting in Russia by your blatant sententious-

71

ness! No, this could make an angel lose his patience. Force! You'll find force even in the savage Kalmuck, even in the Mongol, but what's the good of it to us? It is civilization that we hold dear—yes, yes, my dear sir; we hold dear its fruits. And don't tell me those fruits are trifling: the last dauber, *un barbouilleur,* or the professor who gets five kopecks for pounding a piano all evening—why, even they are more useful than you, because they are representatives of civilization and not of naked Mongolian force! You imagine that you are in the vanguard, but where you really belong is squatting in a Kalmuck tent. Force! And finally, my forceful gentlemen, the fact remains that there are only four and a half of you, all in all, whereas there are millions of the others who won't allow you to trample down their most sacred beliefs, who will crush you!"

"If they crush us, that will be that. Only thing is, you may have another guess coming. There aren't as few of us as you seem to think."

"What! Are you thinking, in all seriousness, that you can come out on top—come out on top against all the people?"

"It took only a kopeck candle to burn down all of Moscow," Bazarov retorted.

"Exactly, exactly. Pride, almost satanic, first; then jeering. There, that's what infatuates youth, there's what vanquishes the callow hearts of schoolboys! There, take a look—there's one of them sitting right beside you; why, he's all but worshiping you—feast your eyes on him." Arcadii turned his face away and assumed a deep frown. "And by now this pestilence is widespread. In Rome—so they've told me—our artists won't as much as set foot in the Vatican. Raphael they

72

consider as but little short of an ass because, it seems, he is authoritative, yet they themselves are so impotent and sterile that they are abominable, while their own imagination cannot reach beyond some Girl at a Fountain, no matter what you do to them! And even that girl is drawn most execrably. Fine fellows, according to you, aren't they?"

"According to me," Bazarov retorted, "Raphael isn't worth a sou marquee, and as for those artists, they're no better than he is."

"Bravo, bravo! Just listen, Arcadii, that's how young people of today should express themselves! And, if one stops to think of it, how can they do otherwise than follow you! Formerly young people were faced with having to study; they were averse to becoming known as ignoramuses; so, like it or not, they worked hard. But now all they have to do is to say 'Everything in the world is bosh!'—and that does it. The young people rejoiced. And for good cause—up to that time they had been simply blockheads, but now they have, all of a sudden, become nihilists."

"There, now, your vaunted sense of personal dignity has failed you," Bazarov observed phlegmatically, while Arcadii brightened altogether and his eyes glittered. "Our disputation has gone too far. Apparently it would be better to break it off. As for me, I'll be ready to agree with you," he added as he stood up, "whenever you confront me with even one factuality in our present way of life, either domestic or social, which would not provoke total and merciless repudiation."

"I'll confront you with millions of such factualities!" Pavel Kirsanov exclaimed. "Millions of them! Why, take the village commune, for example—"

A chill smile distorted Bazarov's lips. "Well, as far as the village commune is concerned," he said, "you'd better have a talk with your own brother. The way things look, he has by now had a real taste of the village commune, mutual responsibility, temperance and suchlike pretty doodads."

"The family, then—the family, as one finds it among our peasants!" Pavel Petrovich was by now shouting.

"And that question too, I opine, it would be better for your own sake not to go into in detail. You've heard, I guess, about patriarchs who have the first go at their daughters-in-law? You listen to me, Pavel Petrovich—give yourself time for a couple of days; you're hardly likely to come up with anything right off. Go over all our social classes and give quite a bit of thought to each one, and in the meantime Arcadii and I will—"

"Mock at everything!" Pavel Petrovich broke in on him.

"No; we'll be cutting up frogs. Come on, Arcadii; we'll be seeing you, gentlemen!"

The two friends left the room. The brothers were left by themselves, and all they could do at first was to exchange occasional glances.

"There," Pavel Kirsanov began at last, "there is modern youth for you! There they are—our heirs!"

"Our heirs," his brother echoed with a despondent sigh. Throughout the dispute he had been sitting as if on a bed of live coals and could only cast furtive and pained glances at his son from time to time. "Do you know what I've recalled, brother? I had a quarrel once with our dear mother; she kept screaming, wouldn't listen to me. Well, now, I told her at last:

'You are incapable of understanding me; you and I, now, belong to two different generations.' She was horribly hurt by that, whereas I thought to myself, What can one do? The pill is a bitter one, yet it must be swallowed. Well, our turn has come now, and our inheritors are in 'a position to say to us 'You now don't belong to our generation; go ahead and swallow that pill!' "

"You're really too magnanimous and unassuming," Pavel Kirsanov retorted. "I, on the contrary, am convinced that you and I are considerably more right than these young *gentlemen,* even though we do, possibly, express ourselves in somewhat antiquated language, *vieilli,* and do not possess their impudent self-reliance. And how pompous the young people of today are! If you happen to ask one of them 'What wine do you want—red or white?' he answers in a bass and with a face as grave as if all Creation were regarding him at that moment 'A preference for red wine is a habit of mine!' "

"Don't you want some more tea?" asked Phenechka, with her head in the doorway: she had hesitated about entering the drawing room as long as the voices issuing from it had sounded disputatious.

"No; you can tell them to remove the samovar," Nicholai Petrovich answered and got up to meet her. Pavel Kirsanov bade him *"Bon soir!"* abruptly and withdrew to his study.

11

Half an hour later Nicholai Petrovich was on his way
to the garden, seeking his favorite arbor. He had been
overcome by cheerless reflections. He had had his first
clear realization of the disunity between him and his
son; he had a premonition that with every day it would
become greater and greater. Therefore it had been in
vain, during his winters in St. Petersburg, for him to
have sat for days at a time poring over the latest works
of literature; in vain had he lent an attentive ear to the
conversations of the youngsters, in vain rejoiced whenever he contrived to put in a word of his own during
their heated discussions. My brother maintains that
we're right, he reflected, and, putting all vanity aside,
it does seem to me that they are further from the
truth than we, yet at the same time I feel they have
something back of them which we have not, some sort
of superiority over us. Youth? No, it isn't youth alone.
Doesn't their superiority consist of their having fewer
traces of seigniory than we? He let his head sink and ran
his hand over his face. But—to reject poetry? he again
reflected. To have no feeling for art, for nature?

With that he looked about him, as if he wanted to
grasp how one could possibly have no feeling for nature. Evening was coming on by now; the sun had already screened itself behind a grove of aspens situated
about a third of a mile from the garden; the shadow
of this grove stretched endlessly across the still fields.
A most ordinary little mouzhik was trotting on a small
white nag along the dark narrow path that closely
skirted the grove; one could see all of him clearly—

all of him, to the very patch on his shoulder, even though he was riding in the shade; there was something pleasing about the distinctness with which one saw the flashing of the little nag's legs. The sun's rays for their part were making their way into the grove and, penetrating its thickets, flooded the trunks of the aspens with such warm light that they were beginning to look like those of pines, with their leafage showing blue, while a pale-blue sky, tinged a faint rose by the sunset glow, soared above them. The swallows were winging high; the wind had died down altogether; belated bees buzzed lazily and drowsily among the lilac blossoms; a swarm of midges rose in a pillar above a lonely branch that stretched far into space. My God, how fine all this is! Nicholai reflected, and some favorite lines came to his lips, but at this point he recalled Arcadii, and *Stoff und Kraft*—and fell silent; however, he still sat on, still went on yielding himself to the melancholy and delectable play of his solitary musings. He liked to indulge in an occasional reverie; country life had developed this tendency of his. Had it been so very long ago that he had been in a reverie, much the same as now, as he waited for his son at that small inn? Yet since then a change had come about; their relations, at that time still vague, had by now become definite—and how definite! His late wife again rose up in his imagination—not as he had known her during the course of many years, however, not as the kindly, home-loving mistress of a household but as a young girl, slim-waisted, her gaze innocently searching, and with hair tightly braided and surmounting a neck as slender as a child's. He recalled his first sight of her. He had been still a student at that time. He had encountered her on the staircase of the house where he

77

lived and, happening to jostle her, had turned around with the intention of apologizing, but had merely managed to mumble *"Pardon, monsieur,"* whereat she had inclined her head, smiled slightly and then, as if suddenly frightened, had dashed away and, at the turn of the stairs, she had given him a quick glance, assumed a grave air, and blushed. After that had come the first timid calls, words half-spoken, smiles half-smiled, perplexity and tristesse, and impulses; then, finally, that breath-taking rapture . . . Whither had all that sped? She had become his wife; he had been happy as but few on earth ever are. But, he reflected, those delectable first moments—why could they not live an eternal, an immortal life?

He was not trying to make clear to himself what he was thinking, but he longed to retain that beatific time through something more powerful than memory, he was desirous of sensing anew the nearness of his Maria, to feel her warmth and breath, and he was already imagining that, overhead—

"Nicholai Petrovich," Phenechka's voice came from somewhere near him, "where are you?"

He was startled. He felt neither pained nor conscience-stricken. He had never admitted even the possibility of any comparison between his wife and Phenechka, yet he regretted the latter's notion of searching for him. Her voice instantly reminded him of his gray hair, his advancing years, his present reality. The enchanted world into which he had already stepped, which was already rising from the waves of the past, had stirred—and vanished.

"Here I am," he answered. "I'll come later; you go ahead." There you have them, the thought flitted through his head, those traces of seigniory, now . . .

Phenechka peered into the arbor where he was and, without a word, disappeared, while he noticed with amazement that night had come on since he had first plunged into his reverie. Everything around him had become dark and still, and Phenechka's face as it glided before his eyes was ever so wan and small. He stood up and was about to start for home, but his heart, so profoundly moved, would not quiet down within his breast, and he took to pacing the garden slowly, his eyes, by turns, either fixed in deep thought on the ground before him or raised to the sky where the stars were by now swarming and twinkling to one another. He walked for a long time, until he was almost fatigued, yet the disquiet within him, some sort of searching, indeterminate, tristful disquiet, still refused to abate. Oh, how Bazarov would jeer at him if he were to learn what was going on within him just then! Arcadii himself would condemn him. He, a man of forty-four, an agronomist and a man of property, was on the verge of tears, of tears without rhyme or reason —why, that was a hundredfold more reprehensible than playing the violoncello!

He continued his pacing and could not find the resolution to enter the house, that peaceful and cozy nest which was regarding him so invitingly with all its lit-up windows; he had not the strength to part with the darkness, with the garden, with the sensation of the fresh air on his face and with this tristesse, this disquiet.

At a turn of the path he encountered Pavel. "What's wrong with you?" the latter asked. "You're as pale as an apparition; you're unwell—why don't you lie down?"

Nicholai explained in a few words the psychical state he was in and left him. Pavel walked on until he came to the end of the garden and he, too, fell into deep thought; he, too, raised his eyes to heaven. However, nothing was reflected in his splendid dark eyes except the light of the stars. No born romantic, he, and his gallantly dry soul, misanthropic after the French manner, was incapable of indulging in reveries.

"You know what?" Bazarov was saying that same night to Arcadii. "A magnificent notion has popped into my head. Your father was talking today about an invitation he'd gotten from that illustrious kinsman of yours. Your father won't go, so suppose the two of us dash over to town—for this great man has invited you also. Just see what a fine spell of weather we're having; well, we'll take a ride, look the town over. We'll knock about for five or six days, and that's that!"

"And you'll come back here then?"

"No; I have to go on to my father's. As you know, his place is twenty miles from the town we're going to. It's a long time since I've seen him and my mother—I should try to please the old folks. They're a good lot, my parents, particularly my father—a most amusing fellow. After all, I'm their only child."

"And will you be staying with them long?"

"I don't think so. Things will be dull, I guess."

"But will you drop in on us on your return trip?"

"Don't know. I'll see. Well, is it a go? Let's set out!"

"If you like," Arcadii let drop in an indolent tone. He was, at heart, exceedingly delighted with his friend's plan but had considered himself in duty bound to mask his reaction. He wasn't a nihilist for nothing!

The next day he left with Bazarov for the town of ————. The young people at Maryino regretted their going: Dunyasha actually had a good cry. But the two little ancients breathed more easily.

12

The town for which our friends had set out was under the jurisdiction of a governor of the youngish variety, a progressive fellow and, at the same time, a despot —a phenomenon which occurs over and over again in our land of Russia. During the first year of his administration he had succeeded in quarreling thoroughly not only with the Marshal of Nobility in his province, a retired second captain of the Horse Guards who ran a stud farm and was noted for his hospitality, but also with the officials on his own staff. The dissensions springing up because of this finally took on such proportions that the ministry in Petersburg found it necessary to send a trusted person with instructions to straighten everything out on the spot. The choice of those in authority had fallen upon Matvei Ilyich Kolyazin, the son of that same Kolyazin under whose guardianship the Kirsanov brothers had at one time found themselves. He, too, was of the youngish sort, that is, he had passed his fortieth year not so long ago but already had his eye set on becoming a statesman and displayed a star on either breast—although, truth to tell, one was merely a foreign star, and of a poorish sort. Like the governor whom he had come here to judge he was held to be a progressive fellow and, since he was already a Very Important Person, did not resemble the majority of persons of importance. He had the highest opinion of himself; his self-conceit knew no bounds, yet he conducted himself simply, looked on with approval, listened with condescension, and laughed with such good nature that, at first, he might actually have gained the reputation of "one fine fellow." On important occasions, however, he could—as the saying goes—kick up the dust. "You can't do without energy," he would say at such a time, *"l'énergie est la première qualité d'un homme d'état."* Yet with all that he was usually left holding the bag, and any pettifogger who was at all experienced could saddle and ride him.

Matvei Ilyich mentioned Guizot, as both historian and statesman, with great respect and strove to impress upon each and every person that he himself could not be numbered among the routinaires and moss-grown bureaucrats, that he did not let a single significant manifestation of public life escape his attention. He was very well versed in all such catchwords. He even kept an eye on the development of contemporary literature—with, it is true, a nonchalantly grandiose air, just as a mature person, on encountering a street procession of urchins, may occasionally fall in with it. In reality he had not progressed a great deal beyond those politicos of Alexander I's day who, when preparing to attend a soirée at the mystico-literary salon of Mme. Svyechina, who was residing in St. Petersburg at that time, would go through a page of Condillac's philosophy in the morning. The only difference was that he employed other dodges, more in keeping with the times. He was an adroit courtier, a great schemer, and nothing more; he did not know what was what in administrative matters, he had no intellect, but he did know how to run his own affairs—nobody could saddle and ride him when it came to such things and that, in the upshot, is the main thing.

Kolyazin received Arcadii with that amiability which befits an enlightened dignitary—we will go further and say that he met him with playfulness. He was amazed, however, on learning that the kinsmen whom he had invited had stayed behind in their village. "Your father always was an odd chap," he commented, juggling the tassels of his resplendent lounging robe, and turning abruptly to a young clerk whose long uniform frock coat was most discreetly buttoned to the last button, he called out with an air of preoccupation: "What now?" The young man, whose lips had become stuck together from his prolonged silence, stood up and regarded his chief with perplexity. Matvei Ilyich, however, having succeeded in stumping his subordinate, was no longer paying any attention to him. Our dignitaries are, on the whole, fond of stumping their subordinates; the devices to which they resort for the attainment of this end are rather varied. The following one, among others, is much used—*is quite a favorite,* as the English say: the dignitary will suddenly fail to comprehend the simplest words, will be afflicted by deafness. He will ask, for example: "What day is this?"

"It's Friday today, Your Ex-ex-ex-cellency," he is told with the utmost deference and much stammering.

"Eh? What? What's all this? What are you talking about?" the grandee keeps asking with a strained expression.

"Today is Friday, Your Ex-ex-cellency."

"How? What? What's this about Friday? What Friday?"

"Friday, Your Ex-ex-ex-cellency—a day of the week."

"Well, I must say! Are you presuming to teach me?"

Matvei Ilyich was, after all, a dignitary, even though he was rated as a liberal.

"I advise you, my friend, to pay a visit to the Governor," he said to Arcadii. "I'm advising you to do so, you understand, not because I adhere to the antiquated notions about the inevitability of paying one's respects to those in authority, but simply because the Governor is a decent fellow; at the same time you probably wish to become acquainted with the society in these parts —for you are no bear, I hope? Then, too, he is giving a grand ball, day after tomorrow."

"Will you attend the ball?" Arcadii asked.

"He's giving it in my honor," Kolyazin remarked casually, almost deploringly. "Do you dance?"

"I do—but badly."

"That's unfortunate. There are some pretty little things in town; then, too, it's a shame for a young man not to dance. Here, again, I'm saying this not because of any antiquated notions; I don't at all suppose that a man's intelligence should be localized in his feet, but Byronism is mirth-provoking; *il a fait son temps*— Byron's day is over."

"But then, dear uncle, it isn't at all because of Byronism that I refrain—"

"I'll introduce you to the local young ladies; I'm taking you under my wing," his uncle interrupted him and broke into complacent laughter. "You'll find that a warm spot, eh?"

A flunky entered and announced the arrival of the Chairman of the Administrative Department, an old man with mawkish eyes and wrinkled lips, who was extraordinarily fond of nature, particularly on a summer's day when, according to him, "Every little bee exacts a little bribe from every little flower." Arcadii left.

He found Bazarov at the inn where they had put up, and spent a great deal of time in persuading him to come along to the Governor. "There's nothing to be done!" Bazarov declared at last. "Once you put your hand to the plough you can't beg off. We've come to look the landed gentry over—let's look them over, then!"

The Governor received the young men cordially; he did not ask them to be seated, however, nor did he take a seat himself. He was perpetually bustling and on the go; come morning, he would don a tight uniform frock coat and an exceedingly stiff cravat; he never finished a meal or drained a glass—always the busy administrator. In his province they had nicknamed him Bourdaloue—not after the celebrated French Jesuit pulpit orator, however, but hinting at *bourda,* or over-fermented small-beer. He extended invitations to Kirsanov and Bazarov to attend his ball and two minutes later invited them a second time, by then considering them brothers and calling them Kaisarov.

They were walking back from the Governor's when suddenly a man of no great stature, wearing a short coat of a cut that denoted the professional Slavophile, even though it was a garment of Hungarian origin, jumped out of a passing droshky and, with a shout of "Evgenii Vassil'ich!" dashed toward Bazarov.

"Ah, it's you, Herr Sitnikov," Bazarov remarked disdainfully, striding over the sidewalk. "What fates have brought you here?"

"Imagine, I'm here by pure chance," the other answered and, turning to the droshky and waving his arms, called out: "Follow us, now!— My father had a matter to be attended to here," he resumed, skipping over some water running in the gutter, "and so he asked me to go. Today I learned of your arrival and have already paid you a call." (The friends, on getting back to their room, actually found a card there with the corners correctly bent, bearing the name of Sitnikov—in French on one side and, on the other, in Slavonic script.) "You're not coming from the Governor, I hope?"

"No use your hoping; we've just come from him."

"Ah! I'll also call on him in that case. Evgenii Vassilievich, do introduce me to your . . . to this gentleman."

"Sitnikov, Kirsanov," growled Bazarov, walking right on.

"I'm very much flattered," Sitnikov began, sidling along, smirking, and hastily pulling off his really far too elegant gloves. "I've heard a very great deal— I'm an old acquaintance of Evgenii Vassil'ich and, I may say, a disciple of his. It is to him that I am indebted for my regeneration."

Arcadii regarded this disciple of Bazarov's. The small but on the whole pleasing features of his slicked-down face betrayed a disquieted and stolid tension; the little eyes, which seemed to have been thumbed in, had an intense and restless look and his laugh, too, was restless—some sort of abrupt, xylophonic laughter.

"Would you believe it," he continued, "the first time I heard Evgenii Vassil'ich declare in my presence that one ought not to recognize any authorities, I experienced such rapture . . . just as if my eyes had been opened! 'Here,' it occurred to me, 'I have at last come upon a man!' Incidentally, Evgenii Vassil'ich, you absolutely must call on a certain lady here who is perfectly able to understand you and who would consider your visit a gala occasion. You've heard of her, I think?"

"Who is she?" Bazarov asked unwillingly.

"Kukshina, *Eudoxie*—Evdoxia Kukshina. A remarkable nature, hers; she's *émancipée* in the true sense of the word, a woman in the vanguard. You know what? Let's all go over to her place right now. She lives just a step or two from here. We'll lunch there. You haven't had your lunch yet, have you?"

"Not yet."

"Well, that's splendid. She has separated from her husband, you understand; she isn't dependent on anybody—"

"Is she pretty?" Bazarov interposed.

"N-no, you couldn't call her that."

"Then why the devil are you enticing us to her place?"

"There, now, you are a wag, really. She'll stand us a bottle of champagne."

"So that's it! One can spot a practical man right off. Incidentally, your father is still a liquor-tax farmer?"

"Yes, he still is." Sitnikov spoke fast and laughed squealingly. "Well, now—are we going?"

"I don't know, really."

"You wanted to see people—go ahead," Arcadii remarked in a low voice.

"And what about yourself, M'sieu' Kirsanov?" Sitnikov chimed in. "Do come along, too—we can't go without you."

87

"But how can we all crash in on her at the same time?"

"It doesn't matter! Kukshina is a wonderful person."

"There'll be a bottle of champagne?" asked Bazarov.

"Three bottles!" Sitnikov exclaimed. "That I'll guarantee."

"With what?"

"My own head."

"Your father's purse would be more acceptable. However, let's go."

13

The aristocratic mansionette with a Moscow air about it which was the residence of Avdotia (or Evdoxia) Nikitishna Kukshina was situated on one of the recently burned-out streets of the town: it is common knowledge that our provincial capitals undergo a conflagration every five years. On the door, above a visiting card tacked on at an angle, a visitor could barely see a bellpull, while in the vestibule the callers were met by a female in a lace cap who might have been either a servant or a lady's companion—obvious indications, these, of the progressive aspirations of the mistress of the house.

"Is that you, *Victor?*" a high-pitched voice issued from an adjoining room. "Come in!"

"I'm not alone," Sitnikov announced, shedding, with a flourish, his Russo-Magyar short coat, under which there turned out to be something in the nature of a coachman's baggy jacket or a *paletot-sac,* and tossing a lively look at Arcadii and Bazarov.

"It doesn't matter," the voice responded. *"Entrez."*

The young men entered. The room they found themselves in looked more like a study than a drawing room. Papers, letters, bulky Russian periodicals (their pages for the most part uncut) lay strewn over the dusty table; the eye caught the whiteness of half-smoked cigarettes scattered all over the place. On a leather divan a lady was half-reclining—still young, flaxen-fair, somewhat disheveled—in a silk dress that was not quite tidy, with big bracelets on her stubby arms and a lace fascinator perched on her head. She arose from the divan and, negligently drawing a velvet jacket lined with yellowed ermine over her shoulders, lazily drawled, "How d'you do, Victor," and clasped Sitnikov's hand.

"Bazarov, Kirsanov," Victor spoke brusquely, trying to ape Bazarov.

"You're most welcome," Kukshina responded and then, staring at Bazarov with her rounded eyes between which a diminutive retroussé nose reddened forlornly, added, "I know you," and clasped his hand as well.

Bazarov made a wry face. There was nothing outré about the small and unimpressive figure of this emancipated woman, yet her facial expression affected the beholder unpleasantly. One involuntarily wanted to ask her "What's wrong—are you hungry? Or down in the dumps? Or losing heart? What are you so wound up about?" She too, even as Sitnikov, was perpetually downhearted. She was most unconstrained in her speech and movements yet at the same time clumsy; she evidently considered herself a good-hearted and simple creature, yet for all that, no matter what she was doing, it invariably struck one that that was the very thing she had been reluctant to do; the result in her case seemed, every time, to have been brought about "on purpose," as children say—not simply, that is, not naturally.

"Yes, yes, Bazarov—I know you," she repeated (she was addicted to the habit, peculiar to ladies in Moscow and the provinces, of calling men by their last names from the first day of making their acquaintance). "Do you want a cigar?"

"A cheroot is fine, in its way," chimed in Sitnikov, who had already contrived to sprawl out in an easy chair with one of his legs raised high, "but you might give us some lunch—we're dreadfully hungry—and issue orders about putting up a baby bottle of champagne in our honor."

"Sybarite!" Evdoxia declared, and broke into laughter. (Whenever she laughed her upper gum became bared.) "He is a sybarite—isn't that so, Bazarov?"

"I do love the comforts of life," Sitnikov pontificated. "That does not hinder me from being a liberal."

"No, but it does, it does!" Evdoxia exclaimed and, nevertheless, gave orders to her handmaiden to see not only about serving lunch but the champagne as well. "What do you think about it?" she added, addressing Bazarov. "I feel certain you share my opinion."

"Why, no," Bazarov contradicted her. "A piece of meat is preferable to a piece of bread, considered even chemically."

"Ah, are you taking up chemistry? Chemistry is a

passion of mine. I've even invented a certain plastic material, all by myself."

"A plastic material? You?"

"Yes, I. And do you know what it was intended for? For dolls' heads—but unbreakable ones. After all, I'm practical too. But it isn't altogether ready yet; I still have to read up on it in Liebig. Incidentally, have you read Kislyakov's article on female labor in the *Moscow News*? Please read it, do. For you are interested in feminism, aren't you? And schools also? What does your friend do? What's his name?"

Madame Kushina *dropped* her questions lackadaisically, without pausing for any answers: spoiled children talk much the same way to their nannies.

"My name is Arcadii Nicholaievich Kirsanov," Arcadii spoke up, "and I'm not doing anything."

"Now this is charming!" Evdoxia broke into pealing laughter. "Come, don't you smoke? Do you know, Victor, I am displeased with you?"

"Whatever for?"

"I am told you've taken to praising George Sand again. She's really nothing more than a reactionary! How could one possibly compare her with Emerson? She has no ideas at all about education, or physiology—or anything. I feel certain she hasn't as much as heard about embryology—yet can you think of doing without such knowledge in our day?" Evdoxia actually threw up her hands at the very idea. "Ah, what an amazing article Ellisevich has written on that point! A gentleman of genius, no less!" (Evdoxia was constantly using *gentleman* for *man*.) "Bazarov, sit here beside me on the divan. You may not know it, but I am dreadfully afraid of you."

"Why should you be, if I may be so curious?"

"You are a dangerous gentleman—you are so critical. Ah, my God—I find it funny: talking like some landed proprietress from the backwoods! But then, I really am a landed proprietress. I manage my estate personally, and my clerk Erothei is, if you can imagine such a thing, an amazing type, just like Cooper's *Pathfinder*—there's something so unsophisticated about him! I've settled here for good—it's an unendurable town, isn't it? However, what can one do?"

"A town like any other town," Bazarov commented phlegmatically.

"The things it is interested in are all so petty— that's what is so dreadful. Up to now I used to spend my winters in Moscow; but now M'sieu' Kukshin, my lawful spouse, is in residence there. And besides, Moscow right now . . . really, I don't know—it, too, is no longer what it used to be. I'm thinking of taking a trip abroad; last year I was actually all set to go."

"To Paris, of course?" asked Bazarov.

"Paris—*and* Heidelberg."

"Heidelberg? Why go there?"

"Come, now! That's Bunsen's town!" Bazarov was stumped for an answer. *"Pierre* Sapozhnikov . . . do you happen to know him?"

"No, I don't."

"Really, now! *Pierre* Sapozhnikov . . . why, you can always find him at Lydia Hostatova's."

"I don't know her either."

"Well, it was he who took it upon himself to be my traveling companion. Thank God, I am free, I have no children. . . . *Thank God*—what a thing for me to say! Still, it doesn't matter, really." Evdoxia rolled a cigarette with fingers stained dark-brown by tobacco, licked the edge of the paper with her tongue, sucked

92

at the cigarette to see if it drew and lit it. The servant entered with a tray. "Ah, here's lunch at last! Care for a bite? Open the bottle, Victor—that's your department."

"So it is, so it is!" Sitnikov mumbled, and again broke into squealing laughter.

"Any pretty little things here?" Bazarov asked, finishing his third glass.

"There are," answered Evdoxia, "but they're all so frivolous. There's *mon amie* Odintsova, for instance —she's not at all bad-looking. It's a pity her reputation is—well, sort of . . . However, that would make no difference, but then she has no independent views whatsoever, there's no breadth to her—nothing of that sort. Our whole system of education requires change. I have already considered the matter; our women receive a very poor education."

"You won't accomplish anything with them," Sitnikov chimed in. "One should feel contempt for them, and contempt, utter and absolute, is what I do feel for them." The opportunity of feeling contempt and expressing it afforded a most gratifying sensation to Sitnikov; he was especially severe in attacking women, having no suspicion that in the space of a few months it would be his fate to grovel before his wife merely because she had been born Princess Durdoleossova. "Not one of them would be capable of comprehending our conversation; not one of them is worth being discussed by serious men like ourselves!"

"Why, it isn't at all necessary for them to comprehend our conversation," Bazarov declared.

"Whom are you talking about?" Evdoxia interrupted.

"About the pretty little things."

"What? That means, then, that you share Proudhon's opinion?"

Bazarov straightened up haughtily: "I don't share anybody's opinions; I have opinions of my own."

"Away with all authorities!" Sitnikov raised his voice, rejoicing at the chance of speaking up in the presence of a man upon whom he fawned with such servility.

"But Macaulay himself—" Kukshina was about to say something.

"Away with Macaulay!" thundered Sitnikov. "Are you sticking up for these silly little females?"

"No, not for silly little females, but for the rights of women, which I have vowed to defend to the last drop of my blood."

"Down with—" but at this point Sitnikov stopped short. "Why, I'm not denying those rights," he managed to say.

"No, I can see you're a Slavophile!"

"No, I'm not a Slavophile! Although, naturally—"

"No, no, no—you *are* a Slavophile! You follow the precepts of *Domostroi*, that bible of domestic tyranny. All you need is a lash in your hand!"

"The lash isn't a bad thing," Bazarov commented, "but right now we've come to the last drop—"

"Last drop of what?" Evdoxia interrupted him.

"Of champagne, most estimable Nikitishna—of champagne, and not of your blood."

"I cannot remain indifferent when I hear women assailed," Evdoxia continued. "It's dreadful—dreadful! Instead of assailing them you'd better read Michelet's book, *De l'amour*. It's marvelous! Gentlemen, let us talk of love," Evdoxia added, allowing an arm to drop languorously on a rumpled divan cushion.

A sudden silence ensued.

"No, why talk of love," Bazarov declared. "On the other hand, you mentioned Odintsova just now. You said that was her name, I believe? Who is this great lady?"

"She's delightful, delightful!" Sitnikov squeaked. "I'll introduce you. Clever girl, money to burn, a widow. Regrettably enough, she is still not sufficiently advanced; she should become more closely acquainted with our Evdoxia. I drink to your health, *Eudoxia!* Let's clink our glasses! *Et toc, et toc, et tin-tin-tin! Et toc, et toc, et tin-tin-tin!*"

"Victor, you're a scamp!"

The luncheon was a protracted affair. The first bottle of champagne was followed by another, a third, and even a fourth. Evdoxia chattered without pausing for breath; Sitnikov echoed her. They discussed at great length whether marriage was a prejudice or a crime, and whether people were born equal or not. And of just what, properly speaking, does individuality consist? Things finally came to the point where Evdoxia, all flushed from the wine she had imbibed and thrumming with her spatulate-nailed fingers on a grand piano that was all out of tune, launched into song in a hoarse voice: gypsy songs first, and then Seymour-Schiff's sentimental ballad, "Drowsy Granada Slumbers," while Sitnikov bound a scarf about his head and, when it came to the passage:

> Let my lips and thine, adored,
> Blend into a kiss of fire—

play-acted the swooning lover.

Finally Arcadii could not take any more of it. "Gentlemen," he commented aloud, "this has turned into something very like Bedlam."

Bazarov, who had been merely interjecting some word of mockery into the conversation at infrequent intervals, devoting himself to the champagne for the most part, now yawned loudly, stood up and, without saying goodbye to the hostess, left the house with Arcadii. Sitnikov followed them spryly.

"Well, now? Well, now?" he kept asking, fawningly trying to run ahead of his companions, now from the right, now from the left. "A remarkable personality, just as I said. That's the sort of woman we ought to have more of! She is, after her own fashion, a highly moral phenomenon."

"And is that establishment of your old man's also a highly moral phenomenon?" asked Bazarov, jabbing his finger in the direction of a pothouse which they were passing at that moment.

Sitnikov again broke into his squealing laughter. He was exceedingly ashamed of his origin and was uncertain whether he ought to feel flattered or insulted by Bazarov's unexpected familiarity of speech.

14

The Governor's ball was given a few days afterward. Kolyazin was, truly, the "hero of the occasion." The Marshal of Nobility for the province informed all and sundry that the guest of honor had come solely as a mark of respect for him, the Marshal of Nobility, while the Governor, even during the ball, even when he was standing stock-still, kept right on "getting things done." Kolyazin's affability of demeanor was equaled only by his courtliness. He was benign to everybody—to some with a shade of aversion, to others with a shade of deference; he spread himself out *"en vrai chevalier français"* before the ladies and was incessantly going off into full-bodied, sonorous and unvarying laughter, such as was fitting and proper for a dignitary. He patted Arcadii on the back and "dear nephew"-ed him loudly; bestowed on Bazarov (who was clad in a rather outmoded frock coat) an absent-minded yet condescending glance (sidelong, letting it glide across his cheek) and a vague yet amiable lowing sound in which one could barely catch "I . . ." and ". . . quite"; offered Sitnikov a finger and smiled to him—but with his head averted before he had done; even for Kukshina, who showed up at the ball without any crinoline and in soiled gloves—even for Kukshina he had an *"Enchanté!"*

The guests were past all counting, and there was no dearth of male dancing partners; the civilians were mostly wallflowers but the military danced zealously, particularly one who had passed all of six weeks in Paris, where he had picked up sundry daring expletives in the nature of *"Zut!," "Ah fichtrrre!," "Pst, pst, mon bibi!"* and the like. These he pronounced perfectly, with true Parisian *chic*, but at the same time he confused his tenses and used *absolument* in the sense of *absolutely*—in short, he expressed himself in that Great Russian-French dialect which Frenchmen laugh at so much when they do not feel any need to assure our sort that we speak their language like angels—*"comme des anges."*

Arcadii danced poorly, as we already know, while

Bazarov did not dance at all; they made their stand in a corner, where they were joined by Sitnikov. With his face expressing a contemptuous sneer as he let drop his venomous comments, he was looking about him insolently and seemed to be having a really delightful time. Then his face underwent a sudden change and, turning to Arcadii, he remarked with what seemed like confusion: "Odintsova has arrived."

Arcadii turned around for a look and saw a woman of tall stature in a black gown who had stopped in the doorway of the ballroom. He was struck by the dignity of her bearing. Her bare arms lay gracefully along her svelte waist; ethereal sprays of fuchsia gracefully fell from her gleaming hair upon her sloping shoulders; her radiant eyes looked calmly and intelligently— calmly, precisely, and not pensively—from under her slightly prominent white forehead, and a barely perceptible smile hovered on her lips. Some sort of kindly and gentle power emanated from her face.

"Do you know her?" Arcadii questioned Sitnikov.

"Intimately. Do you want me to introduce you?"

"Why not—but after this quadrille."

Bazarov also turned his attention to Odintsova. "Who in the world is that?" he wanted to know. "She doesn't resemble the rest of the females here."

After waiting till the quadrille was over Sitnikov brought Arcadii over to Odintsova, but it seemed quite doubtful that he was intimately acquainted with her: he himself became all tangled up in his lines, while she for her part regarded him with a certain perplexity. However, her face took on a cordial look when she caught Arcadii's family name. She asked him if he was the son of Nicholai Petrovich Kirsanov.

"Precisely."

"I've seen your father on two occasions and have heard a great deal about him. I'm very happy to make your acquaintance."

At that moment some adjutant or other dashed up to her and asked her for a quadrille. She consented.

"Why, do you dance?" Arcadii asked with deference.

"I do. But what makes you think I don't? Or do I strike you as too old?"

"Oh, please—that's unthinkable. . . . But since you do dance, allow me to ask you for a mazurka."

Odintsova smiled condescendingly. "By all means," she said, and bestowed on Arcadii a look that was not exactly superior but of the sort which married sisters bestow on their rather young brothers. She was but little older than Arcadii—going on twenty-nine—yet he felt like a schoolboy, like a freshman in her presence, just as if the difference in their ages were far more considerable. Kolyazin approached her with a regal air and ingratiating speeches. Arcadii stepped aside but kept on watching her: he did not take his eyes off her even during the quadrille. She chatted just as unconstrainedly with her dancing partner as with the grandee, turning her head and her eyes quietly and breaking into quiet laughter once or twice. Her nose —like the noses of almost all Russians—was a trifle bulbous, and her complexion was not altogether clear; for all that Arcadii decided that he had never encountered a woman so alluring. The sound of her voice would not leave his ears; the very folds of her gown, it seemed, fell differently from those of other women, more gracefully and amply, while her movements were, at the same time, more flowing and natural.

Arcadii felt a certain timidity at heart as, at the

99

first sounds of the mazurka, he was preparing to sit the dance out beside his partner and, while trying to begin a conversation with her, could only keep running his hand over his hair and was unable to find a single word to say. But he did not remain timid and agitated for long; Odintsova's tranquility was communicated to him also: not a quarter of an hour passed before he was talking to her unconstrainedly about his father, his uncle, his own life in Petersburg and in the country. She listened to him with polite sympathy, slightly unfolding and folding her fan. His chatter was interrupted whenever she was asked for a dance—Sitnikov, among others, asked her twice. She would come back, resume her seat and take up her fan, her breast rising and falling no faster than before, while Arcadii again fell to chattering, permeated with the happiness of finding himself in her proximity, of speaking to her as he took in her eyes, her lovely brow, all of her endearing, impressive and intelligent face. She herself did not say much, yet her words evinced a knowledge of life; from certain comments of hers Arcadii concluded that this young woman had already come to experience a great deal emotionally and to think over many things.

"Who was the man you were standing with," she asked him, "when M'sieu' Sitnikov brought you over to me?"

"Oh, so you did notice him?" Arcadii asked in his turn. "He has a fine face, hasn't he? That was Bazarov, a certain friend of mine."

Arcadii launched into talk about this "certain friend" of his. He talked about him in such detail and was so transported that Odintsova turned toward him and looked at him attentively. In the meantime the mazurka was coming to an end. Arcadii felt sorry about parting with his dancing partner: he had spent almost an hour with her so pleasantly! True, during all that time he had constantly felt as if she were condescending to him, as if it behooved him to be grateful to her—however, young hearts are not oppressed by such feelings.

The music ceased.

"Merci," said Odintsova, rising. "I have your promise to call on me; you may as well bring your friend with you. I'll find it extremely curious to see a man who has the temerity not to believe in anything."

The Governor approached Odintsova, announced that supper was ready and with a care-haunted face offered her his arm. As she was leaving she turned around for a last smile and nod to Arcadii. He made her a low bow, followed her with his eyes (how graceful her waist seemed to him, with the grayish sheen of black silk apparently poured over it!) and, as he reflected, She has already forgotten my existence at this very moment! he felt a certain refined humility in his soul.

"Well, now?" Bazarov asked him as soon as Arcadii had returned to their coign. "Did you enjoy yourself? A certain high-born gent was telling me just now that this lady is 'My-my-my!' But then the gentleman himself seems to be a nincompoop. Well, is she truly 'My-my-my!' in your opinion?"

"I don't fully understand that definition," Arcadii retorted.

"Come, now! What an innocent fellow!"

"In that case, I fail to understand this gentleman of yours. Odintsova is, indisputably, very much of a darling, but her demeanor is so cold and austere that—"

"Still waters—you know!" Bazarov put in quickly.

"She's cold, you say. That's precisely what the piquancy consists of. After all, you're fond of frozen sweets."

"Could be," Arcadii muttered. "I can't judge about that. She wishes to make your acquaintance and has asked me to bring you along when I call."

"I can imagine how you painted me! However, you did the right thing. Bring me along. No matter who she may be—simply a provincial celebrity or an *emancipée* after the style of Kukshina; she's got a pair of shoulders on her the like of which I haven't laid my eyes on in a long time."

Arcadii winced at Bazarov's cynicism but—as it so often happens—what he reproached his friend for was not the precise thing he found displeasing about him.

"Why don't you want to admit that there is freedom of thought among women?" he asked in a lowered tone.

"Because, brother, according to what I have observed, among women it is only the freaks who think freely."

With that the conversation ended. Both young men left immediately after supper. Kukshina sent a laugh after them that was nervously rancorous yet not without hesitancy: her vanity had been deeply wounded because neither of them had paid any attention to her. She remained at the ball later than all the other guests and when it was going on four in the morning danced a polka-mazurka with Sitnikov to the very end, an edifying spectacle which served as the finishing touch to the gubernatorial gala.

15

"Let's see what group of Mammalia this person belongs to," Bazarov was saying the next day as he and Arcadii were going up the staircase of the hotel at which Odintsova was staying. "My nose tells me there's something out of the way here."

"I'm amazed at you!" Arcadii exclaimed. "You—you, Bazarov!—sticking to that narrow morality which—"

"What a strange fellow you are!" Bazarov nonchalantly cut him short. "Really, don't you know that for fellows like me 'out of the way' means, in our dialect, 'everything is just dandy'? There's something to be gained here, that means. Weren't you yourself telling me today that she had made a queer marriage? Although, in my opinion, marrying a wealthy old man is not in the least a queer business but, on the contrary, a sensible one. I don't believe the talk of the town but I like to think, as our cultured Governor puts it, that the talk is not wide of the mark."

Arcadii made no reply and tapped on the door of the suite. A young flunky in livery brought the two friends into a spacious room, atrociously furnished, like all rooms in Russian hotels, but with flowers placed all over it. In a short while Odintsova herself appeared in an unassuming morning dress; she seemed still younger in the light of the spring sun. Arcadii introduced Bazarov and noted with secret wonder that his friend seemed to be ill at ease, whereas their hostess remained utterly calm, just as she had been the evening before. Bazarov himself grew aware that he was not at ease and became vexed by the fact. I'll be hanged! Scared by a female! the thought came to him and, sprawled out in an easy chair every bit like Sitnikov, he began talking with overdone jauntiness while she never took her radiant eyes off him.

Anna Odintsova was the daughter of Serghei Nicholaievich Loktev, widely known as an Adonis, an adventurer, and a gambler, who after keeping the ball rolling and creating a stir in Petersburg and Moscow for fifteen years, wound up by losing his shirt gambling and was driven to settling in the country, where he died soon afterward, leaving a microscopic estate to his two daughters—the twenty-year-old Anna and the twelve-year-old Katerina. Their mother, who came from a princely but impoverished line, had died in Petersburg when her husband had been still in his prime. Anna's situation after the death of her father was an extremely difficult one. The brilliant education she had been given in Petersburg had not prepared her to cope with the cares of household and estate management or the dullness of existence in the country. She knew absolutely nobody in the entire district and there was no one to whom she could turn for counsel. Her father had done his best to avoid having anything to do with his neighbors—he despised them in his fashion and they despised him in theirs. Still, she did not lose her head and at once sent off an invitation to a sister of her mother's, Princess Avdothea Stepanovna Kh——, an evil-tempered and arrogant crone who upon moving into her niece's house took over all the best rooms for herself, snarled and groused from morning to night, and would not go for a walk even in the garden unless she was attended by the only serf she owned, a morose flunky in worn-out livery of pea-green trimmed with light-blue galloon and sporting a cocked hat. Anna patiently endured all of her aunt's maggots, little by little undertook the education of her sister, and apparently had already become resigned to withering away in the backwoods.

Fate held, however, a promise of something else for her. She happened to strike the eye of a certain Odintsov, an exceedingly rich man of forty-six, an eccentric, a hypochondriac, bloated, ponderous, and soured yet, on the whole, neither stupid nor ill-natured; he fell in love with her and proposed. She consented to be his wife; for his part he lived with her for six years and, on his death-bed, made certain that she would come into all his property. For about a year after his death Anna Sergheievna never left her village; after that she went abroad with her sister but stayed only in Germany for a while, grew nostalgic and came back to live in her beloved Nikolskoe, which lay at a distance of twenty-five miles or so from the provincial capital. On this estate she had an excellently furnished, magnificent house, and a splendid garden with conservatories—the late Odintsov never denied himself anything.

Anna Sergheievna appeared in town only rarely, mostly on matters of business, and even then not for long. She was disliked in the province; there had been a frightful uproar over her marrying Odintsov, and every possible sort of wild and improbable tale was told about her; it was maintained that she had lent a hand to her father in his exploits as a cardsharp, and that even her trip abroad had not been an idle one but undertaken out of necessity to conceal certain unfortunate consequences of . . . "You understand what?" the talebearers would conclude in in-

105

dignation. "She's been through thick and thin," they said of her, while a well-known provincial wag would usually add: "And through the mill." All these slanders found their way to her, but she let them in one ear and out the other: she was of an independent and quite determined character.

Odintsova was leaning against the back of her armchair as she sat with one hand resting on the other and listened to Bazarov. He was talking away at quite a rate, contrary to his wont, and was obviously striving to entertain the lady—something which again surprised Arcadii. He could not decide whether Bazarov was gaining his purpose or not. It was difficult to surmise from Anna's face what impression he was making; it maintained the same unvarying expression, cordial and refined; her splendidly beautiful eyes were alight with attentiveness, but an attentiveness that was halcyon. Bazarov's posturing during the first few minutes of his visit had made an unpleasant impression upon her, like a bad odor or a harsh sound; but she had immediately perceived that he felt ill at ease, and this had actually flattered her. Only that which was vulgar repelled her; vulgarity, however, was something of which no one would have accused Bazarov.

That was to be a day of incessant surprises for Arcadii. He had expected that Bazarov would broach his convictions and views to Odintsova, since she was a woman of intelligence and had herself evinced a desire to listen to a man "who has the temerity not to believe in anything." Instead of that, however, Bazarov discoursed on medicine, on homeopathy, on botany. It became evident that Odintsova was not wasting her time in seclusion: she had read some worth-while books and expressed herself in impeccable Russian. She brought the conversation around to music but, perceiving that Bazarov had no regard for the arts, she most unobtrusively reverted to botany, even though Arcadii had just embarked on a disquisition concerning the significance of folk melodies. Odintsova was still treating him as a younger brother: apparently what she appreciated about him was the geniality and simpleheartedness of youth—and that was all. For more than three hours did the conversation keep up, leisurely, many-sided and animated.

The two friends at last arose and began saying goodbye. Anna Sergheievna regarded them cordially, extended her exquisite white hand to each and, after brief reflection, uttered with an uncertain yet pleasing smile: "If you aren't afraid of being bored, gentlemen, come and visit me at Nikolskoe."

"Oh, please, Anna Sergheievna!" Arcadii exclaimed. "I would esteem that particularly good fortune—"

"And you, M'sieu' Bazarov?"

Bazarov merely bowed—and Arcadii was faced with his last surprise: he noticed that his friend was blushing.

"Well?" Arcadii questioned him when they were outside. "Is it still your opinion that she's 'My-my-my'?"

"Really, who knows what she's like! Just see what an icicle she has turned herself into!" Bazarov retorted and, after a brief silence, added: "She's a duchess, a regal personage. All she needs is a long train to her gown and a crown on her head."

"Our duchesses don't speak Russian as well as she does," Arcadii remarked.

"She's been through the school of hard knocks, brother; she knows how bitter our bread tastes."

"But just the same she's a delight," Arcadii declared.

"What an opulent body!" Bazarov went on. "What a star for dissection at an anatomical theater!"

"Drop that, Evgenii, for God's sake! It's absolutely unseemly—"

"There, don't get angry, you softy. I told you, she's first class. We'll have to go out to her place."

"When?"

"We might as well start day after tomorrow. What would we be doing here, now? Guzzling champagne with Kukshina? Listening to that liberal grandee who's your kinsman? So we'll just dash over there, day after tomorrow. Incidentally, my father's patch of ground is not so far from there, either. For this Nikolskoe is on the road to ————, isn't it?"

"It is."

"*Optime!* Excellent! No use dilly-dallying: dilly-dallying is only for fools—and those who are much too clever. An opulent body, I tell you!"

Three days later the two friends were rolling along the road to Nikolskoe. The day was radiant and not too warm, and the well-fed hired horses raced along in unison, lightly switching their plaited and clubbed tails. Arcadii kept his eyes on the road and, without knowing why, was smiling.

"Congratulate me!" Bazarov suddenly exclaimed. "Today is the twenty-second of June, the day of the saint I'm named after. Let's see how well my guardian angel will take care of me. Today they're waiting for me at home," he added, lowering his voice. "Well, they'll wait a while longer—it's no great matter!"

108

16

Odintsova's countryseat stood on a sloping, exposed knoll, not too far from a church built of yellow stone, with a green roof, white columns and an alfresco painting above the main portal, representing the Resurrection of Christ, done in an "Italian" style. A swarthy warrior in a morion, sprawled out in the foreground, was especially remarkable because of his rounded contours. Behind the church an extensive settlement stretched along in two rows of huts, with an occasional chimney peeping out above a straw-thatched roof. The manor house was built in the same style as the church, the style familiar to us as Alexandrine; this house was of the same yellow tint, but painted, and also had a green roof, and white columns, and a pediment with an escutcheon. The provincial architect had erected both structures with the approval of the late Odintsov, who could not tolerate any frivolous and arbitrary (as he put it) innovations whatsoever. The house was closely flanked by the dark trees of an old-fashioned garden; an avenue of closely trimmed firs led up to the entrance.

Our friends were met in the vestibule by two stalwart flunkies in livery, one of whom immediately dashed out for the major-domo. The latter, a corpulent man in a black frock coat, put in a prompt appearance and led the guests up a staircase covered with rugs to a special room, already furnished with two beds and all the accessories for dressing. It was evident that order reigned throughout the house: everything was clean, everywhere there was a certain discreet fragrance, of the same sort as in ministerial reception halls.

"Anna Sergheievna requests you to be kind enough to come to her in half an hour," the major-domo informed them. "Are there any orders you would care to give me in the meantime?"

"There will be no orders whatsoever, my most estimable friend," Bazarov answered, "unless you'll be so good as to bring me a small glass of vodka."

"Right, sir," said the major-domo, not without some perplexity, and withdrew, his boots creaking.

"What *grand genre!*" Bazarov commented. "That's what they call it in your vocabulary, I think? A duchess, and that's all there is to it."

"A fine duchess," Arcadii contradicted, "when, to begin with, she has invited two such high and mighty aristocrats as ourselves to stay with her!"

"Especially me, a future pillroller and the son of a pillroller—and the grandson of a sexton. For you know that I'm a sexton's grandson, don't you? Like Speransky," * he added after a short pause and with his lips twisted. "However, say what you will, she's self-indulgent, this high-born lady—oh, she is that, and how! Should we put on full dress, perhaps?"

Arcadii merely shrugged—however, he too felt a trifle uneasy.

Half an hour later Bazarov and Arcadii came down to the reception room. It was a spacious, lofty chamber, furnished with luxury but without any particular taste. Ponderous expensive furniture was ranged in the usual prim array along the walls which were covered with cinnamon-brown paper arabesqued in gold—the late

* Count M. M. Speransky (1772-1839); well-known statesman.

Odintsov had secured it from Moscow, through a certain wine dealer who was his friend and agent. A portrait was hung over a divan placed centrally along one of the walls, and its subject, a bloated man with tow-colored hair, seemed to be eyeing the guests inimically. "Must be the late massa himself," Bazarov whispered to Arcadii, and then added, wrinkling his nose: "Maybe we'd better make tracks?"

But at that moment the lady of the house entered. She had on a light dress of barège; her hair, combed back smoothly behind her ears, bestowed a girlish expression on her pure and fresh face.

"I am grateful to you for keeping your word," she began. "I hope you can stay for a while; things aren't so bad here, really. I'll introduce you to my sister—she plays the piano well. That doesn't matter to you at all, M'sieu' Bazarov—but you, M'sieu' Kirsanov, do like music, I believe. In addition to my sister I have an old aunt living with me, and a certain neighboring squire drives over occasionally for a game of cards—and there you have our entire social circle. And now let us be seated."

Odintsova had delivered all of this speech with particular precision, just as if she had gotten it down by heart; then she began conversing with Arcadii. Her mother, it turned out, had known Arcadii's, and had even been her confidante at the time she had been in love with Arcadii's father. Arcadii spoke fervently about his dead mother; Bazarov in the meantime took to examining sundry albums. What a quiet little fellow I've become! he reflected.

A beautiful wolfhound bitch ran into the room, her nails pattering on the floor, while right behind her

111

came a girl of eighteen, black-haired and swarthy, with a rather round yet pleasing face and small dark eyes. She was holding a flower-filled basket.

"And here's my Katya," said Odintsova, with a motion of her head in the direction of the girl. Katya curtsied slightly, found a seat near her sister and began sorting her flowers. The wolfhound bitch, whose name was Fifi, walked up to each guest in turn and thrust her cold muzzle into his hand, wagging her tail as she did so.

"Did you pick all those by yourself?" asked Odintsova.

"Yes, I did," Katya answered.

"Is aunt coming to tea?"

"She is."

Whenever Katya spoke she had a most endearing smile, shy and ingenuous, and her upward look was somehow amusingly stern. Everything about her still had the greenness of youth: her voice, and the peach down over all her face, and her pink hands with the babyish marks on their palms, and her shoulders, which were just a mite of a trifle too narrow. She was forever blushing and breathing rapidly.

"You're looking those pictures over only out of politeness, Evgenii Vassil'ich," Odintsova began, turning to Bazarov. "You don't find them entertaining. Better move closer to us and let's discuss something."

Bazarov drew closer. "What's your pleasure as to the subject, ma'am?" he asked.

"Whatever subject you wish. I'm warning you that I'm a dreadfully argumentative woman."

"You?"

"Yes, I. You seem to find that surprising. Why?"

"Because, as far as I can judge, you have a calm and

112

cold temperament, whereas one has to be carried away in order to be argumentative."

"How have you managed to learn what I am like in so short a time? In the first place, I'm impatient and insistent—you'd better ask Katya; and, in the second, I'm very easily carried away."

Bazarov gave Anna Sergheievna a long look. "Could be," said he. "You're the best judge of that. And so, you're in a mood for a discussion. By all means. I was looking through your album of views in Saxon Switzerland, and you remarked to me that I could not find that entertaining. You said that because you don't suppose I have any understanding of art—and as a matter of fact I haven't; yet these views might have interested me from a geological standpoint—from the standpoint of mountain formation, for example."

"Pardon me. As a geologist you would prefer to have recourse to a book, to some specialized work, and not to a picture."

"One picture will show me vividly something which a book would take all of ten pages to explain."

Anna Sergheievna was silent for a space. "And so you honestly and truly haven't even a jot of artistic appreciation?" she observed, placing her elbows on a table and by that very movement bringing her face closer to Bazarov. "Yet how can you manage without it?"

"But what's the need for it, if I may ask?"

"Why, you need it to learn what people are like and to study them, if for nothing else."

Bazarov smiled a little. "In the first place, that's what worldly wisdom is for; and, in the second, let me inform you that studying isolated individuals isn't worth the effort. All people resemble one another in both body and soul; in each one of us the brain, the spleen, the heart, the lungs are arranged in the same way, and the moral qualities, so called, are precisely the same in all: the slight variations are absolutely of no significance. A single human exemplar suffices to form a judgment concerning all the rest. People are as uniform as trees in a forest: no botanist would go to the trouble of studying each individual birch."

Katya, who had been leisurely matching the flowers, lifted her eyes to Bazarov with a look of incomprehension and, meeting his cursory and careless glance, crimsoned to her very ears. Anna shook her head.

" 'Trees in a forest,' " she repeated. "Therefore, according to you, there is no difference between a foolish man and an intelligent one, between a good man and one who is evil?"

"No, there is a difference, even as there is between a sick person and one in good health. The lungs of a consumptive are not in the same state as yours and mine, even though they are constructed alike. We have an approximate knowledge of the origin of bodily maladies; moral disorders, however, have their origin in bad upbringing, in all sorts of idle notions with which the heads of people are stuffed from their very childhood—in the hideous state of society, to put it briefly. Reform society, and there won't be any maladies."

Bazarov was saying all this with the air of one reflecting at the same time: "You can believe me or not —it's all one to me!" He was slowly running his long fingers through his side whiskers, while his eyes were darting from corner to corner of the room.

"And it is your contention," Anna observed, "that when society has mended its ways there will be no more of either the foolish or the evil?"

114

"In properly organized society it will at least be absolutely immaterial whether a man is foolish or intelligent, evil or good."

"Yes, I understand: everybody will have a perfectly standardized spleen."

"Just so, my dear madam."

"And what is your opinion, Arcadii Nicholaievich?" Odintsova addressed Kirsanov.

"I agree with Evgenii," he replied.

Katya gave him a look from under frowning brows.

"Gentlemen, you astonish me," Odintsova declared, "but we'll discuss this further later on. Right now, however, I hear my aunt coming for her tea; we will have to spare her ears."

Anna's aunt, Princess Kh——, a wizened and tiny woman with a face clenched into a little fist and with fixedly staring malicious eyes under a gray scratch wig, came in and, barely bowing to the guests, lowered herself into a roomy velvet-upholstered easy chair in which no one but she had the right to sit. Katya placed a stool under her feet; the crone did not thank her, did not as much as give her a look, merely moving her arms a little under the yellow shawl which covered almost all of her puny body. The princess loved yellow: she had vivid yellow ribbons even on her cap.

"How did you sleep, Aunt?" Odintsova inquired, raising her voice.

"That dog is here again!" the crone growled by way of answer and, having noticed that the bitch had taken a couple of hesitating steps in her direction, she shouted: "Get away—get away!" Katya called to Fifi and opened the door for her; the bitch joyously dashed out, expecting to be taken for a walk, but, left to herself outside the door, fell to scratching upon it and whining from time to time. The princess frowned; Katya was about to step outside—

"Tea ready, I believe?" Odintsova spoke up. "Let us go, gentlemen; please come along for tea, Aunt."

The princess got up from her easy chair without a word and was the first to leave the reception room; all the others set out after her for the dining room. A page in livery noisily drew back from the table an easy chair, as sacredly the princess' as the other and lined with cushions, into which the princess lowered herself; she was the first to whom Katya, who was pouring, handed a cup blazoned with a coat-of-arms. The crone put honey in her cup (she deemed it both sinful and extravagant to drink tea with sugar, even though she never laid out as much as a kopeck for anything) and suddenly asked in a hoarse voice and mispronouncing the title: "And what does *Preence* Ivan write?"

No one answered her. It did not take Bazarov and Arcadii long to surmise that nobody paid any attention to what she said, even though she was treated with deference. They keep her around *for* to make themselves important, Bazarov reflected. Seeing *as how* it's princely spawn.

After tea Anna suggested going for a stroll, but it started to drizzle and the entire company, with the exception of the princess, went back to the reception room. Their card-loving neighbor, whose name was Porphyrii Platonych, drove up—a stout little, gray little man, with stubby little legs that looked just as if they had been turned on a lathe—a most polite and amusing fellow. Odintsova, who was confining her conversation more and more to Bazarov, asked him if he wouldn't care to have an old-fashioned go at preference. Bazarov consented, saying that it behooved him

116

to prepare himself betimes for the duties that lay ahead of him as a country general practitioner.

"Be on your guard," Anna Sergheievna remarked, "Porphyrii Platonych and I will trim you. As for you, Katya," she added, "do play something for Arcadii Nicholaievich—he loves music, and we'll have a chance to listen too."

Katya drew up to the grand piano reluctantly and Arcadii, although he truly loved music, followed her just as reluctantly: it struck him that Odintsova was brushing him off—and yet, like every young man of his age, he already felt a certain vague and enervating sensation, not unlike a premonition of love, forming in his heart.

Katya raised the top of the piano and, without looking at Arcadii, asked him in a low voice:

"What shall I play for you?"

"Whatever you wish," Arcadii answered apathetically.

"What kind of music do you prefer?" she asked again, without changing her attitude.

"Classical," Arcadii replied, without changing his tone.

"Do you like Mozart?"

"I like Mozart."

Katya got out Mozart's *Sonata-Fantasia in C Minor*. She played extremely well, even though a trifle austerely and drily. Without taking her eyes off the notes and with her lips pressed together tightly she sat motionless and erect, and only toward the conclusion of the piece did her face burst into a glow, while a small lock of her loosened hair fell over one of her dark eyebrows.

Arcadii was especially struck by the last part of the

sonata, that part wherein, amid the captivating gaiety of the carefree air, there suddenly arise transports of such woeful, well-nigh tragic mournfulness. Yet the thoughts aroused in him by the sounds of Mozart's music had no connection with Katya. As he looked at her all he thought was: Why, this young lady doesn't play so badly, and she herself isn't so bad-looking.

Having finished the piece Katya asked, "Enough?" without removing her hands from the keys. Arcadii assured her that he dared not impose on her any further, tried to start a conversation about Mozart, and asked whether she had chosen this sonata or if someone had recommended it to her. Katya answered him in monosyllables, however: she *hid,* withdrawing into herself. Whenever this happened she did not emerge again soon; her very face on such occasions assumed an obstinate, almost stolid expression. She was not shy, exactly, but rather mistrustful and a trifle cowed by her sister, who had educated her—an attitude which Anna, naturally, did not even suspect. In the end Arcadii, by way of a face-saving gesture, had to call the returned Fifi over to him and to pat her head while he smiled upon her benevolently. Katya busied herself with her flowers again.

Bazarov in the meanwhile was being penalized, time after time. Anna played cards like a master; Porphyrii Platonych could also give a good account of himself. Bazarov lost in the end; the sum was not a significant one, but just the same he could not consider the loss quite pleasant.

At supper Anna again brought the conversation around to botany. "Let's go for a walk tomorrow morning," said she to Bazarov. "I want to learn from you the Latin names and the properties of the field flowers."

"What would you want the Latin names for?" Bazarov asked her.

"One must have order in all things," she answered.

"What a marvelous woman Anna Sergheievna is!" Arcadii spoke up when he and his friend were at last in the seclusion of the room assigned to them.

"Yes," Bazarov responded, "a female with brains. Yes, and she's seen plenty in her life!"

"Just what do you mean when you say that, Evgenii Vassil'ich?"

"I mean well, Arcadii Nichola'ich, father of mine, I mean well! I'm convinced she manages her estate excellently too. However, it isn't she who's a wonder but that sister of hers."

"What? That swarthy little thing?"

"Yes, that swarthy little thing. There's the one who's dewy, and untouched, and timorous, and silent, and everything you like. There's the one worth taking in hand. Out of this one you could make whatever you liked, but the other one is a shopworn article."

Arcadii made no reply to Bazarov, and each lay down to sleep with his head filled with thoughts of his own.

Anna Sergheievna, in her turn, was thinking of her guests that evening. She had taken a liking to Bazarov because of the absence of any flirtatiousness in him and the very harshness of his judgments. She perceived in him something new, which she had never happened to encounter before—and she was curious.

She was quite a strange being. Lacking any prejudices whatsoever, lacking even strong convictions of any sort, she never retreated in the face of anything and was not advancing in any particular direction. She saw many things with clarity, many things interested her—and nothing satisfied her completely; but then, she could hardly be said to desire complete satisfaction. Her mind was searching and, at the same time, apathetic: her doubts were never lulled to forgetfulness and never attained the stature of alarm. If she had not been wealthy and independent she might have thrown herself into the fray, might have come to know passion. But life held only ease for her, even though there were times when she felt ennui, and she kept on passing day after day at a leisurely pace and experiencing perturbation only at rare intervals. Rainbow hues would at times burst into glow even before her eyes, but she found repose when they expired and felt no regret about them. Her imagination soared even beyond the bounds of that which by the canons of ordinary morals is considered permissible, but even at such times her blood coursed as placidly as ever through her enchantingly graceful and composed body.

There were times when, on emerging from a scented bath all warm and languorous, she would succumb to reveries about the insignificance of life, its misery, its toil and evil. Her soul would become filled with instantaneous daring, would seethe with noble yearning —but let a slight draft blow through a half-closed window, and there would Anna Sergheievna be, all shrunk into herself and complaining, almost angry, and there was just one thing imperative for her at that moment: not to have that nasty wind blowing on her.

Like all women who had failed to know love, she was longing for something without herself knowing precisely what. Properly speaking she was not really longing for anything, even though it seemed to her that she desired everything. She had been barely able to abide the late Odintsov (whom she had married out of calculation, although she probably would not have consented to be his wife if she had not thought him a kindhearted person) and had acquired a secret aversion for all men, whom she could not picture to herself otherwise than slovenly, heavy and flabby, impotently importuning creatures. On one occasion, somewhere abroad, she had met a young handsome Swede with a chivalrous look to his face, with honest blue eyes under an expansive brow; he had made a strong impression on her—but this had not hindered her from going back to Russia.

"A strange fellow, this doctor!" she mused, lying in her magnificent bed, on lace-trimmed pillows, under a coverlet of silk. Anna had inherited from her father something of a tendency towards luxury. She had loved her erring but kindhearted father very much, while he deified her, joking with her amiably as if she were an equal, confiding in her fully, and seeking her advice. Her mother she hardly remembered.

"He's strange, this doctor!" she repeated to herself. She stretched, smiled, clasped her hands behind her head, then let her eyes skim a couple of pages of a silly French novel, dropped the book to the floor—and fell asleep, all clean and cool, on clean and fragrant linen.

The following morning, immediately after breakfast, Anna set out to botanize with Bazarov and did not return until just before lunch; Arcadii had not gone anywhere and had spent about an hour with Katya. He had not been bored in her company, and she herself had offered to repeat for him the sonata she had played yesterday; but when Odintsova returned at last, when he caught sight of her, his heart contracted momentarily. She was walking through the garden with a some-what tired step; her cheeks were scarlet and her eyes were glowing more vividly than usual under her round straw hat. Her fingers were toying with the slender stalk of some field flower, her light mantle had slipped down to her elbows and the broad gray ribbons of her hat were clinging to her bosom. Bazarov was walking be-hind her, as self-assured and indifferent as ever, but his expression, for all its cheerfulness and kindliness, was not to Arcadii's liking. With a "Hello!" muttered through clenched teeth Bazarov went to his room, while Odintsova shook Arcadii's hand absent-mindedly and also went past him.

"Hello. . . ." Arcadii reflected. Why, haven't we al-ready seen each other today?

17

Time (as everybody knows) at times flies on the wings of a bird and at others crawls like a worm, but man is particularly well off when he actually does not notice whether it passes fast or slowly. It was in precisely such a state that Arcadii and Bazarov spent fifteen days at Odintsova's. This was partly due to the orderliness she had established both in her household and in her life. She adhered to this orderliness strictly and compelled others to submit to it. Everything during the course of the day was performed at a set time. In the morning, at eight exactly, all gathered for tea; from tea until luncheon everyone followed his or her bent; the lady of the house herself was busied with the manager (the income of the estate was derived from quitrents paid by the serfs), with the major-domo, with the chief housekeeper. Before dinner all came together again for conversation or reading; the evening was devoted to strolling, cards, music; at half-past ten Anna Serghei-evna retired to her room, issued orders for the following day, and went to bed. This proportioned, somewhat pompous regularity in daily living was not to Bazarov's liking: "It's just as if you were rolling on rails," he maintained—the liveried flunkies, the decorous major-domos offended his democratic feeling. He opined that one might as well go the whole hog and dine the way the British do, in long tails and white ties.

He once had a plain talk with Anna on this subject. Her demeanor was such that no one felt any hesitancy in fully expressing his or her opinions before her. She heard Bazarov out and then declared: "From your point of view you're right, and in this instance I am acting the grand lady; but one can't live in the country without orderliness—one would be overcome with en-nui." And she kept right on doing things in her own way. Bazarov grumbled, yet life at Odintsova's was so easy for him and Arcadii precisely because everything in her house was "rolling along on rails."

For all that, a change had come about in both young men from the very first days of their stay in Nikolskoe. Bazarov, toward whom Anna was evidently well disposed, though she rarely agreed with his views, began to evince an uneasiness to which he had hitherto been an utter stranger: he easily became irritated, was grudging in his speech, wore an angry look and could not sit still in one spot, just as if something were egging him on. As for Arcadii, who had definitely decided to himself that he was in love with Odintsova—he had begun to yield to a gentle despondency. However, this despondency did not hinder him from a rapprochement with Katya; it even helped him to get on affectionate, friendly terms with her. *She* does not appreciate me! Well and good! But here is a kind being who does not reject me, he reflected, and his heart partook anew of the sweetness of magnanimous feelings. Katya vaguely understood that he was seeking a certain consolation in her society and did not deny either to him or to herself the innocent pleasure of a half-shy, half-trusting friendship.

In the presence of Anna they did not converse with each other: under the keen eye of her sister, Katya always shrank into herself, while Arcadii, as it behooved a man in love, could hardly pay attention to anything else when in the proximity of the object of his love; yet he felt fine when he was alone with Katya. He felt that he was unable to interest Odintsova; he was timid and at a loss whenever he found himself alone with her, while she did not know what to say to him—he was too young for her. With Katya, on the contrary, he felt at home; his attitude toward her was tolerant, did not discourage her from voicing her impressions derived from novels and verse, from music and other trifles of the sort, neither noticing nor realizing himself that these "trifles" interested him as well. Katya, for her part, did not interfere with his indulgence in melancholy. Arcadii felt fine with Katya, Odintsova felt fine with Bazarov, and therefore things usually fell out that the two couples, after being together for a short while, would wander off in different directions—particularly during their walks. Katya *adored* nature and Arcadii loved it, even though he dared not admit it; Odintsova was quite indifferent to it, just as Bazarov was. The almost constant separation of our friends did not remain without consequences: the relationship between them began to change. Bazarov ceased discussing Odintsova with Arcadii, ceased even to disparage her "aristocratic goings-on"; true enough, he praised Katya just as before and merely advised an abatement of her proclivity to sentiment; however, his praises were hurried, his counsels dry and, in general, he talked with Arcadii considerably less than before. He seemed to be shunning him, seemed to be ashamed of him. . . .

Arcadii observed all this, but kept his observations to himself.

The real reason for all these "new" attitudes was a feeling inspired in Bazarov by Odintsova, a feeling which tormented and devilishly infuriated him and which he would have denied on the spot with contemptuous laughter and cynical invective had anyone hinted to him even in a roundabout fashion at the possibility of that which was going on within him. Bazarov was most partial to women and the beauty of women, but love in the ideal (or, as he expressed it, romantic) sense he called balderdash, unforgivable foolishness; chivalrous sentiments he considered as something in the nature of deformity or disease, and on more than one occasion had expressed his amazement as to why Schiller's Count of Toggenburg along with all the minnesingers and troubadours had not been clapped into a booby hatch.

"If you take a liking to a woman," he was wont to say, "try to get somewhere with her; but if it's no go— well, forget it, give her the go-by; she's not the only apple on the tree." Odintsova was to his liking: the widespread rumors concerning her, the freedom and independence of her thoughts, her indubitable predisposition for him—everything, it seemed, bade well for him; but he grasped quickly enough that he would not "get anywhere" with her, yet, to his amazement, it was beyond him to give her the go-by. His blood would be on fire if he as much as thought of her; he could have easily managed his blood but something else had got into him, something which he had never thought possible, something at which he had always poked fun, at which all his pride rebelled. In his discussions with Anna he proclaimed more than ever his indifferent contempt for everything of a romantic nature, but once he was alone, he became aware with indignation of the romantic mooncalf in himself. Whereupon he would head for the forest and walk about with great strides, breaking the branches that happened to be in his way and cursing both her and himself under his breath; or he would clamber up into the hayloft of a barn and, stubbornly keeping his eyes shut, would compel himself to sleep—something which naturally he did not always succeed in. Suddenly he would picture to himself that some day those chaste arms would twine themselves about his neck, that those proud lips would respond to his kisses, that those clever eyes would look deep into his with tenderness—yes, tenderness. And his head would start spinning, and for an instant he would forget his troubles—until indignation flared up in him once more. He caught himself in all sorts of "disgraceful" thoughts, as if some fiend were baiting him. Occasionally it seemed to him that Odintsova was also undergoing a change, that her facial expression betrayed a certain something, that, perhaps . . . But at that point he usually stamped his foot, or gnashed his teeth, or shook his fist in his own face.

And yet Bazarov was not so far off. He had overwhelmed Odintsova's imagination; she found him interesting and she thought a great deal about him. She was not bored when he was absent, did not wait for his appearance anxiously, but when he did appear she immediately became animated; she liked being left alone with him and liked talking with him, even when he made her angry or offended her taste, her refined ways. Her wish was, apparently, to put him to the test and at the same time to probe her own self.

One day, while strolling in the garden with her, he informed her abruptly in a morose voice that he intended to leave shortly for his father's place in the country. She paled, as if she had felt a stab at her heart, and such a stab that it made her wonder and for a long while afterward consider what it might signify. Bazarov had told her about his departure not at all with the idea of putting her to the test, of seeing what the outcome would be—he never "staged" anything. That day, in the morning, he had had an interview with Timotheich, his father's steward and his boyhood's mentor. This Timotheich, an astute little ancient who had had his share of hard knocks, with hair that had faded to the color of straw, a weather-beaten red face, and tiny teardrops in his puckered eyes, had unexpectedly bobbed up before Bazarov in his bobtailed peasant coat of grayish-blue cloth belted with a bit of leather and shod in boots dressed with axle grease.

"Ah, there—greetings, old-timer!" Bazarov had cried out.

127

"Greetings, Evgenii Vassil'ich, father of mine," the little ancient began and smiled for joy, from which his whole face became a network of wrinkles.

"What have you come after? Did they send you to fetch me—is that it?"

"Mercy, father of mine—how could that be?" Timotheich began to babble. (He recalled the strict injunction he had received from his master when he was leaving.) "We were on our way to town to attend to some business for the master and then we happened to hear about Your Honor, and so we turned in here, now, on our way, to look in on Your Honor, sort of . . . for otherwise how could we even think of disturbing you!"

"There, don't you lie," Bazarov cut him short. "Would this be the road you'd take to town, now?" Timotheich fidgeted and made no answer. "Is my father well?"

"Yes, sir—glory be to God."

"And my mother?"

"And Arina Vlassievna is well too, the Lord be thanked."

"They're expecting me, no doubt?"

The little ancient tilted his diminutive head to one side: "Ah, Evgenii Vassil'ich, what else should they be doing but expecting you, sir? As you believe in God, it fair broke my heart, watching your parents."

"Very well, very well—that'll do! Don't lay it on too thick. Tell them I'll be there shortly."

"Right you are, sir," Timotheich answered with a sigh.

Having left the house he pulled his brimmed cap over his ears with both hands, clambered into a wretched racing sulky and started off at a jog trot—not, however, in the direction of the town.

That same day, in the evening, Odintsova was sitting with Bazarov in her own room; as for Arcadii, he was pacing through the reception room and listening to Katya at the piano. The princess had retired to her apartment upstairs; she could not, in general, abide guests and, particularly, these "new giddy whipper-snappers," as she styled them. In the main rooms she merely sulked, but in her own apartment, before her maid, she at times went off into volleys of such invective that not only her cap but her scratch wig jigged on her head. Odintsova was aware of all this.

"How does it happen that you're getting ready to leave?" she began. "But what's become of your promise?"

Bazarov was startled. "What promise, ma'am?"

"You've forgotten? You wanted to give me a few lessons in chemistry."

"What can I do, ma'am? My father is expecting me; I can't delay any longer. However, you might read Pelouse *et* Frèmy, *Notions générales de Chimie*—it's a good book and clearly written. You'll find in it every·· thing you need."

"But, if you remember, you were assuring me that a book can't take the place of—I've forgotten just how you expressed it, but you know what I want to say. You remember?"

"What can I do, ma'am?" Bazarov repeated.

"Why should you leave?" asked Odintsova, lowering her voice.

He glanced at her. She had let her head rest against the back of her easy chair and had crossed her arms, bare to the elbows, on her breast. She seemed paler by the light of a single lamp with a paper shade of a perforated design. A voluminous white dress covered her completely with its soft folds; her feet were also crossed, and one could barely glimpse the tips of her slippers.

"But why stay?" Bazarov countered.

Odintsova turned her head a little. "How can you ask? Haven't you found your stay with me enjoyable? Or do you think you won't be missed here?"

"I'm convinced I won't be."

She was silent for a space. "You're wrong in thinking so. However, I don't believe you. You couldn't have been serious in saying that." Bazarov sat on without stirring. "Come, why are you keeping silent, Evgenii Vassilievich?"

"But what am I to say to you? On the whole, it isn't worth while to miss people—and that's particularly true when it comes to missing me."

"Why so?"

"I'm a sobersides, uninteresting. I don't know how to converse."

"You're angling for compliments, Evgenii Vassilievich."

"I don't make a habit of that. Don't you know yourself that the refined aspect of life—that aspect which you hold so precious—is beyond my reach?"

Odintsova nibbled at a corner of her handkerchief. "Think what you like, but I'll find things dull when you leave."

"Arcadii will stay on," Bazarov remarked.

Odintsova gave a slight shrug. "I'll find things dull," she repeated.

"Really? In any event, you won't find things dull for long."

"Why do you suppose that?"

"Because you told me yourself that you find things dull only when your orderly ways are disrupted. You have arranged your life with such impeccable regularity that there can be no place in it for dullness or yearning . . . or any painful emotions whatsoever."

"And you find that I am impeccable—that is to say, that I've arranged my life with such regularity?"

"And how! Why, here's an example: in a few minutes the clock will strike ten, and I actually know beforehand that you will drive me out."

"No, I won't drive you out, Evgenii Vassil'ich. You may remain. Open that window . . . I feel stifled, somehow."

Bazarov stood up and gave the window a push. It opened wide, suddenly and noisily; he had not anticipated the ease with which it would open—besides that, his hands were shaking. The dark, soft night peered into the room with its almost black sky, its faintly susurrant trees and the fresh fragrance of the pure air from the open spaces.

"Lower the blind and sit down," Odintsova bade him. "I want to have a chat with you before your departure. Tell me something about yourself—that's something you never talk about."

"I try to pick out worth-while subjects for our conversations, Anna Sergheievna."

"You're much too modest. However, I'd like to find out something about you, about your family, about your father for whose sake you are abandoning us."

Why is she saying such things? Bazarov wondered, and then went on aloud: "All that is not in the least entertaining, especially for you; we're obscure folk—"

"And I, according to you, am an aristocrat?"

Bazarov looked up at Odintsova. "Yes," he managed to say, with exaggerated brusqueness.

She smiled a little. "I see you know me but little,

131

even though you assert that all people resemble one another and that it isn't worth while to study them. I'll tell you my life some day—you must tell me yours first, however."

"I know you but little," Bazarov echoed her. "Perhaps you are right; perhaps every being really is an enigma. Why, take even you for example: you shun society, you find it depressing—and you have invited two students for a stay in your house. Why do you, with your intellect, with your beauty, live in the country?"

"How? How did you put it?" interposed with animation. "With my . . . beauty?"

Bazarov scowled. "It doesn't matter," he muttered. "What I wanted to say was that I don't rightly understand why you have settled down in the country."

"You don't understand that. . . . However, you do explain it to yourself in some fashion?"

"Yes. . . . My supposition is that you stay in the same place all the time because you have pampered yourself too much, because you're too fond of comfort, of convenience, and too indifferent to everything else."

Odintsova again smiled slightly. "You positively do not want to believe that I am capable of being carried away by anything?"

Bazarov gave her a look from under his brows. "By curiosity, perhaps; but by nothing else."

"Really and truly? Well, now I understand why we've become close friends; after all, you're just the same sort of person as I am."

"We've become close friends—" Bazarov uttered in a stifled voice.

"Oh! . . . Why, I'd forgotten that you want to go away."

Bazarov stood up. The lamp cast a dim light in the

middle of the dusky, fragrant, isolated room; every now and then the blind swayed, admitting currents of the perturbing freshness of the night; one could hear its mysterious susurration. Odintsova did not stir a limb, but a secret agitation was overcoming her little by little. It was communicated to Bazarov. He suddenly realized that he was alone with a young and lovely woman.

"Where are you going?" She spoke slowly.

He made no reply and sank on a chair.

"And so you consider me a tranquil, enervated, spoiled creature," she continued in the same voice, without taking her eyes away from the window. "But the one thing I do know about myself is that I am very unhappy."

"You—unhappy! For what reason? Can it be possible that you attach any significance to vile gossip?"

Odintsova frowned. She was vexed at his having taken that as her meaning.

"I don't find such gossip even amusing, Evgenii Vassil'ich, and I am too proud to let it upset me. I am unhappy because . . . there is no desire in me, no will to live. You're looking at me mistrustfully, you're thinking it's the 'she-aristocrat' talking, all in lace and sitting in a velvet easy chair. Why, I'm not at all concealing the fact: I love that which you call comfort, and at the same time I have little desire to live. Reconcile that contradiction as best you can. However, in your eyes all that is romantic nonsense."

Bazarov shook his head. "You're in good health, independent, wealthy—what else is there? What do you want?"

"What do I want?" Odintsova echoed, and sighed. "I'm very weary, I'm old; it seems to me I've been living a very long time. Yes, I'm old," she added, drawing the ends of her mantilla over her bare arms. Her eyes encountered Bazarov's and the faintest of blushes came over her cheeks. "There are already so many recollections in my past: life in Petersburg, riches, then poverty, then father's death, my marriage, then, in due course, the trip abroad . . . plenty of recollections, yet there's nothing to recall, and there's a long, long road ahead of me, yet there is no goal. . . . And I really have no wish to go on."

"Are you as disillusioned as all that?" Bazarov asked.

"No; but I am dissatisfied," Odintsova replied, pausing at each word. "It seems that if I could become strongly attached to something—"

"You long to fall in love," Bazarov interrupted her, "yet cannot do so—that's where your trouble lies."

Odintsova fell to examining the sleeves of her mantilla. "Am I really incapable of falling in love?" she wanted to know.

"Hardly! However, I shouldn't have called it trouble. On the contrary, it is the one to whom such a thing happens who really deserves commiseration."

"What thing?"

"Falling in love."

"And how do you happen to know that?"

"I've heard tell of it," Bazarov answered in irritation, and the thought came to him: You're coquetting; you're bored and teasing me because you've nothing to do, while I— and his heart was truly straining to break free from his breast. "Besides that, you are probably far too demanding," he declared, inclining his whole body forward and toying with the tassels on her easy chair.

"Could be. It's either all or nothing with me. A life for a life. If you've taken mine, give up thine—and do it without any regrets and for keeps. Otherwise better not begin."

"Well, why not?" Bazarov commented. "It's a fair enough stipulation, and I wonder why, so far . . . you have failed to find what you desired."

"Why, do you think it is easy to yield oneself fully to just anything at all?"

"No, it isn't—not if you go in for mulling things over, and marking time, and tacking on more and more to what you think you'll fetch—thinking yourself too precious. But to yield oneself without mulling things over is mighty easy."

"But how can one help thinking oneself precious? If I wouldn't fetch anything, who needs my devotion?"

"That's no longer one's concern; it's somebody else's concern to appraise one's value. The main thing is to know how to yield oneself."

Odintsova was no longer leaning against the back of her chair. "You speak," she began, "as if you had gone through all that."

"It happened to be appropriate to the discussion, Anna Sergheievna. All that kind of thing, you know, is not my line."

"You, however, would know how to yield?"

"I don't know. I don't want to boast."

Odintsova did not say anything and Bazarov fell silent. The sounds of the grand piano floated up to them from the reception hall.

"How is it Katya is playing so late?" Odintsova wondered.

Bazarov stood up. "Yes, it really is late now—time for you to retire."

"Wait a little—where are you hurrying . . . there's something I must tell you."

"What is it?"

"Wait a little," she said in a whisper. Her eyes were fixed on Bazarov; she appeared to be examining him intently.

He paced the room briefly, then suddenly approached her, hurriedly said "Goodbye" and, having squeezed her hand so hard that she almost cried out, left the room. She brought her crushed fingers up to her lips, blew on them and, springing up on the impulse of the moment from her easy chair, headed with rapid strides for the door, as if she wished to bring Bazarov back. A maid entered the room with a carafe on a silver tray. Odintsova stopped, bade her leave, sat down again, and again fell into deep thought. Her braid worked loose and, like a dark snake, slithered down to her shoulder. For a long while yet did the lamp burn in Anna's room, and for long stretches did she remain motionless, save that at rare intervals she would run her fingers over her arms, nipped at by the night chill.

As for Bazarov, he returned to his bedroom two hours later, all glum, his hair ruffled and his boots wet from the dew. He found Arcadii at the desk, holding a book and with his coat all buttoned.

"You haven't gone to bed yet?" he asked, with apparent annoyance.

"You were sitting a long while with Anna Sergheievna this evening," Arcadii remarked, without answering his question.

"Yes, I was sitting with her all the time you and Katerina Sergheievna were playing the piano."

"I wasn't playing it—" Arcadii was about to explain

and then fell silent. He felt tears welling up in his eyes, yet he did not want to start crying before his mocking friend.

18

The next day, when Odintsova appeared for morning tea, Bazarov sat for a long while bent low over his cup—and then, suddenly, he looked up at her. She turned in his direction, just as if he had nudged her, and it appeared to him that her face had grown slightly pale overnight. She shortly retired to her own room and reappeared only at luncheon. The weather was rainy since morning—going for a walk was out of the question. Everybody gathered in the reception room. Arcadii reached for the last issue of a certain periodical and started reading it aloud. The old princess, following her usual course, began by putting on an expression of astonishment, just as if he were up to something indecent, then fixed her eyes on him in a malevolent glare; he, however, did not pay any attention to her.

"Evgenii Vassilievich," Anna spoke up, "let's go up to my room—there's something I want to ask of ʹou. . . . You gave me the name of a certain manual yesterday—"

She stood up and went to the door. The princess looked about her with an expression which she meant to convey: "Look, look how amazed I am!" and again fixed her eyes on Arcadii, but the latter raised his voice and, having exchanged glances with Katya, near whom he was seated, went on with his reading.

Odintsova reached her study with quick strides. Bazarov followed her nimbly enough, without raising his eyes, but all that his ears caught was the delicate swishing and rustling of the silk dress gliding ahead of him. She sank in the same armchair she had sat in the previous evening and he took the same seat he had occupied then.

"Well, what is the name of that book?" she began after a short silence.

"Pelouse *et* Frèmy, *Notions générales—*" Bazarov answered. "However, I could also recommend to you Ganot, *Traité élémentaire de physiqué expérimentale.* In this work the illustrations are clearer, and in general this textbook is—"

Odintsova held out her hand. "You'll have to forgive me, Evgenii Vassil'ich, but it was not with the intention of discussing textbooks that I asked you to come here. I wanted to renew our talk of last night. You left so abruptly. . . . You won't find this boring?"

"I'm at your service, Anna Sergheievna. However, just what were you and I talking about last night?"

Odintsova gave Bazarov a quick, sidelong glance. "You and I were talking about happiness, I believe. I was telling you about myself. Incidentally, it was I who mentioned the word *happiness*. Tell me, why is it that even when we are enjoying something—music, for instance, or a fine evening, or a conversation with congenial people—why does all this seem rather an intimation of some immeasurable happiness, having an existence somewhere or other, than actual happiness—such happiness, that is, as we ourselves possess? Why is that? Or, perhaps, you feel nothing of the kind?"

"You know the proverb 'Things are fine where we are not,'" Bazarov countered. "Besides, you yourself told me yesterday that you are dissatisfied. As for me, you're right—such notions never enter my head."

"Do they strike you as ridiculous, perhaps?"

"No; but they never enter my head."

"Really? You know, I'd very much like to know what *you* think."

"What? I don't understand you."

"Look, I've long been wanting to have a frank talk with you. It is unnecessary to tell you—you're aware of it yourself—that you're not of the ordinary run of men; you're still young; your whole life is before you. For what are you preparing yourself? What future awaits you? What I mean to say is, what goal do you want to reach, where are you going, what's in your soul? In a word, who are you, what are you?"

"You surprise me, Anna Sergheievna. You know that I am taking up the natural sciences; as for who I am—"

"Yes, who are you?"

"I've already informed you that I'm a future country doctor."

Anna made a gesture of impatience. "Why do you say that? You yourself don't believe that. That's an answer Arcadii might give, but not you."

"But in what way does Arcadii—"

"Stop that! Is it possible for you to be satisfied with so modest a career, and aren't you yourself constantly maintaining that, as far as you are concerned, medicine does not exist? You—with your ambition—a country doctor! You answer me like that just to get rid of me, because you have no confidence at all in me. And yet, Evgenii Vassil'ich, do you know that I could understand you; I myself was poor and ambitious, even as you; I myself may well have gone through the same trials as you have."

"That's all very fine, Anna Sergheievna, but you will have to excuse me . . . I'm not used to expressing myself freely, and there is such a distance between us—"

"What distance? Are you going to tell me again that I'm a 'she-aristocrat'? Enough of that, Evgenii Vassil'ich; I've proven to you, I think, that—"

"And, even aside from that," Bazarov interrupted her, "who wants to talk and think of the future, which for the most part does not depend on us? Should a chance of accomplishing something turn up—fine; but if it shouldn't, one will at least have the satisfaction of not having indulged in idly talking about it beforehand."

"You call a friendly conversation idle talk? Or do you perhaps regard me, since I am a woman, as not worthy of your confidence? For you do despise all of us!"

"I do not despise you, Anna Sergheievna, and you know it."

"No, I don't know anything . . . however, let's suppose that I understand your unwillingness to talk about your future activity; still that which is going on within you now—"

"Going on within me!" Bazarov echoed her. "Just as if I were some sort of body politic or a social structure! In any event, this isn't at all interesting—and besides, can a man always speak out loud about all that is 'going on' within him?"

"Well, for my part I don't see why one can't speak freely about all that one has at heart."

"*You* can?" Bazarov asked.

"I can," Anna answered, after a slight hesitation.

Bazarov inclined his head. "You're more fortunate than I."

She regarded him with a questioning look. "Just as you like," she resumed, "but just the same something tells me that it was not in vain we met, that we're going to be good friends. I feel certain that this—how should I put it?—tension of yours, this reserve, will vanish in the end."

"So you have noticed the reserve—how else did you express it?—the tension in me?"

"Yes."

Bazarov got up and walked over to the window. "And you would like to know the reason for this reserve, you'd like to know what's going on within me?"

"Yes," Odintsova repeated, with a certain dread which was as yet incomprehensible to her.

"And you won't be angered?"

"No."

"No?" Bazarov was standing with his back to her. "Know, then, that I love you—foolishly, madly. There, you've succeeded in getting that out of me."

Odintsova held out her arms, but Bazarov had his forehead pressed hard against the window pane. He was gasping; one could see his whole body trembling. It was, however, not the tremor of youthful timidity not the delectable terror of a first declaration which possessed him: it was passion struggling within him, potent and painful—passion that resembled wrath and which was, perhaps, akin to it. Odintsova became both afraid of him and sorry for him.

"Evgenii Vassil'ich—" she managed to say, and there was the ring of uncontrollable tenderness in her voice.

He turned around quickly, devoured her with his eyes and, seizing her hands, drew her suddenly to his breast.

She did not free herself from his embraces at once, yet a moment later she was standing in a distant corner and watching Bazarov from there. He made an impulsive move toward her.

"You have misunderstood me," she whispered, spurred on by alarm. Apparently she would have screamed were he to take another step. He bit his lips and walked out.

Half an hour later a maid brought Anna a note from Bazarov; it consisted of just one line: "Must I leave today, or may I remain till tomorrow?" "Why leave? I did not understand you—you did not understand me," Anna wrote him in reply, while the thought occurred to her: I did not understand myself either.

She did not show herself until dinnertime but kept pacing back and forth through her room, pausing at infrequent intervals now before the window, now before the mirror, and slowly ran her handkerchief over her neck, on which she imagined she felt a burning spot. What had compelled her (to use Bazarov's expression) to "get at" his confidence, she asked herself, and hadn't she suspected something? "I'm at fault," she decided aloud, "yet I couldn't have foreseen this." She fell into deep thought from time to time and turned red as she recalled Bazarov's almost bestial face when he had rushed toward her.

"Come, is that really so?" she spoke suddenly, and stopped short, and gave a toss to her curls. She caught sight of herself in the mirror; her head, thrown back, with the half-closed, half-open eyes and lips mysteriously smiling, seemed to be telling her at that moment something of such a nature that she herself became embarrassed. . . .

"No," she decided at last, "God knows where this might have led to; one mustn't play around with a thing like that; tranquility is, after all, the best thing in the world."

Her tranquility remained unshaken; however, she was saddened and even cried a little bit, without herself knowing why—except that it was not because of any insult inflicted upon her. She did not feel herself insulted—if anything, she felt herself at fault. Under the influence of sundry vague emotions, the consciousness of life slipping away, a desire for something new, she had compelled herself to reach a certain limit, had compelled herself to peer beyond it—and had beheld beyond it, something that was not even an abyss but a void . . . or an amorphous hideousness.

19

Despite all her self-possession, despite her superiority to all prejudices, Odintsova nevertheless felt ill at ease when she appeared in the dining room. However, the dinner went quite well. Porphyrii Platonych arrived and told all sorts of anecdotes—he was just back from town. He informed them, among other things, that

Governor Small Beer had ordered those of his clerks who were assigned to special tasks to wear spurs, just in case he might dispatch them somewhere on horseback in a particular rush. Arcadii was discoursing to Katya in an undertone and was diplomatically making himself useful to the princess. Bazarov maintained a stubborn and morose silence. Odintsova looked at him a couple of times—not by stealth but directly at his face, which was grim and jaundiced, with the eyes cast down and with an imprint of contemptuous resolve on every feature—and she reflected: No . . . no . . . no. . . .

After dinner she went with all the others into the garden and, noticing that Bazarov wanted to speak to her, she took a few steps to one side and stopped. He approached her, but even at that point did not raise his eyes and spoke in a stifled voice:

"I must apologize to you, Anna Sergheievna. You could not be otherwise than wroth with me."

"No, I'm not angry at you, Evgenii Vassil'ich," Odintsova replied, "but I am hurt."

"So much the worse. In any event, I've been punished enough. My position—as you will probably concur—couldn't be more foolish. You wrote me: 'Why leave?' However, I cannot and I do not want to stay. Tomorrow I will no longer be here."

"Evgenii Vassil'ich, why are you—"

"Why am I leaving?"

"No, that isn't what I wanted to say."

"One can't bring back the past, Anna Sergheievna . . . and sooner or later this was bound to happen. Consequently, it is necessary for me to leave. I can conceive of but one condition upon which I could remain —but that condition can never come about. For—ex-

144

cuse my impertinence—you don't love me and will never come to love me?"

Bazarov's eyes glinted for an instant from under their dark brows. Anna did not answer him. I am afraid of this man! the thought flashed through her mind.

"Goodbye, ma'am," said Bazarov, as if he had guessed her thought, and started back for the house. Anna followed him in an exceedingly subdued mood and, calling Katya over to her, took her arm. She did not part from her until the very evening. She refused to play cards and for the most part kept breaking into half-smiles, which were not at all in keeping with her pale and perplexed face. Arcadii kept wondering and observing her the way all young men observe—that is, he constantly asked himself: What's the meaning of all this, now? Bazarov locked himself up in his room; he came back for tea, however. Anna felt an urge to say something kind to him but did not know how to begin a conversation with him.

An unexpected incident delivered her from the embarrassing situation: the major-domo announced the arrival of Sitnikov.

It is difficult to convey in words what a quail-hen figure the young progressive cut as he fluttered into the room. Although, with that obtrusiveness so characteristic of him, he had resolved on a trip into the country to visit a woman whom he hardly knew, who had never extended an invitation to him, but with whom, according to information he had collected, such clever and intimate people of his acquaintance were staying, he was nonetheless scared to the marrow of his bones and, instead of delivering the apologies and greetings he had previously drilled himself in, he mumbled some rubbish or other to the effect that Evdoxia, now—Kukshina, that is—had sent him to find out about the health of Anna Sergheievna, and that Arcadii Nicholaievich, too, had always spoken to him with the highest praise concerning. . . . With that he faltered and lost his head so completely that he plumped down on his own hat. Still, since no one kicked him out and Anna Sergheievna actually presented him to her aunt and sister, he recovered quickly enough and started chattering away at a great rate. The emergence of vulgarity can often serve a useful purpose in life: it relieves the tension of overtaut strings, it has a sobering effect on such emotions as self-assurance or self-forgetfulness by reminding them of its close kinship to them. With the coming of Sitnikov everything became somehow duller, emptier—and simpler; they all actually supped more substantially and went off to bed half an hour before the usual time.

"I can now repeat to you," Arcadii, lying in bed, was saying to Bazarov, who was also undressed by then, "the remark you once made to me: 'Why are you so downcast? Have you, perhaps, fulfilled some sacred duty?' "

For some time past a certain spuriously free-and-easy banter had become an accepted thing between the two young men, which can always be relied upon as a symptom of secret resentment or unvoiced suspicions.

"I'm leaving tomorrow to see my old man," Bazarov announced.

Arcadii raised himself a little and leaned on his elbow. He was both surprised and, for some reason, overjoyed. "Ah!" he commented. "And is that the reason why you are downcast?"

146

Bazarov yawned. "You'll age before your time if you get to know a lot."

"But what about Anna Sergheievna?" Arcadii persisted.

"Well, what about Anna Sergheievna?"

"What I am trying to say is, will she really let you go?"

"I didn't hire myself out to her."

Arcadii fell into thought; as for Bazarov, he lay down and turned his face to the wall. Several minutes passed in silence.

"Evgenii!" Arcadii called out suddenly.

"Well?"

"I'll go along with you tomorrow." Bazarov made no answer. "The only thing is, I'll go on home," Arcadii continued. "We'll set out together for the Khokhlovsky settlements and there you'll get horses from Phedot. It would be a pleasure to get to know your folks, but I'm afraid I'll be imposing both on them and on you. Surely, you'll come to us again afterwards?"

"I left all my things with you," Bazarov responded, without turning around.

But why doesn't he ask me why I'm leaving? And leaving just as abruptly as he? Arcadii reflected. But really, why am I leaving, and why is he? he went on with his meditations. He could give no satisfactory answer to his own questions, yet his heart was filling with some corrosive feeling. He sensed that it would be hard for him to break with this life to which he had become so used, yet at the same time he felt somehow awkward about staying on alone. Something or other has happened between them, he reasoned to himself. Why, then, should I hang around as an eyesore for her

147

after his departure? She'll become utterly fed up with me; I'll lose even what little regard she still has for me. He began to picture Odintsova to himself, then the features of another emerged little by little from behind the lovely visage of the young widow. "It's a pity about Katya, too!" he confided in a whisper to his pillow, on which a tear had fallen by now. . . . Suddenly he tossed back his hair and protested in a loud voice: "What the devil made that featherbrain Sitnikov honor us with a visit?"

Bazarov delivered his pronouncement only after tossing about a little on his bed: "I can see, brother, that you're still at the foolish stage. We just can't do without the Sitnikovs. Do understand this—I have need of such numskulls. After all, it isn't up to the gods to fire pots!"

Oho-ho! Arcadii reflected, and it was only then that the full extent of the Bazarovian bottomless pit of self-conceit was revealed to him in a split second. "So you and I are gods—is that it?" he asked. "That is, you are a god—but would I be the numskull, by any chance?"

"There, you're still at the foolish stage," Bazarov reiterated glumly.

Odintsova showed no special surprise when Arcadii told her the next day that he was leaving with Bazarov; she appeared absent-minded and tired. Katya looked at him with a serious air, without saying a word, while the princess actually crossed herself under the cover of her shawl, so that he could not help but notice her action; but as for Sitnikov, he was thrown into an absolute dither. He had just descended for lunch in a new and dandified get-up, this time not at all after the Slavophile fashion; the evening before he had astonished the valet who was put at his disposal by the great quantity of linen he had brought along—and here, all of a sudden, his boon companions were abandoning him! He took a few mincing steps, dashed this way and that like a harried hare at the edge of a forest—and abruptly, almost in panic, almost clamorously, declared that he intended to leave also. Odintsova made no move to detain him.

"I have a most comfortable carriage," added the unfortunate youth, addressing Arcadii. "I can give you a lift, while Evgenii Vassil'ich can take your tarantass —that way things will actually be more convenient."

"Come, now—it's altogether out of your way, and it's a long ride to my place."

"No matter, no matter! I've lots of time; besides, I have things to attend to over that way."

"In connection with liquor taxes?" asked Arcadii, by now with excessive contempt.

Sitnikov, however, was in such despair that, contrary to his wont, he did not as much as snigger. "I assure you my carriage is extremely comfortable," he mumbled, "and there will be plenty of room."

"Don't distress M'sieu' Sitnikov by refusing," Anna Sergheievna remarked.

Arcadii glanced at her and inclined his head gravely.

The guests left after lunch. As she was bidding goodbye to Bazarov, Odintsova held out her hand to him and said: "We'll see each other again—isn't that so?"

"I am at your command," Bazarov answered.

"In that case, we shall see each other."

Arcadii was the first to come out on the front steps; he clambered into Sitnikov's carriage. The major-domo was deferentially helping him get seated, but Arcadii could have beaten him with pleasure, or have broken into tears. Bazarov seated himself in the tarantass. When they finally got to the Khokhlovsky settlements Arcadii waited until Phedot, the keeper of the inn, had harnessed the horses and then, walking over to the tarantass, he said with his former smile: "Evgenii, take me along; I want to go to your place."

"Get in," Bazarov uttered through clenched teeth.

Sitnikov, who had been strutting around the wheels of his carriage as he whistled briskly, could only let his jaw drop on hearing these words, while Arcadii coolly got his things out of the carriage, seated himself next to Bazarov and, after a polite bow to his erstwhile traveling companion, called out: "Let 'er go!" The tarantass rolled away and shortly disappeared from view. Sitnikov, altogether confused, looked at his driver, but the latter merely kept flicking his short whip over the tail of the off horse. Thereupon Sitnikov jumped into the carriage and, after thunderously bidding two mouzhiks who happened to be passing by "Put your hats on!" started off on the tiresome drive to town, where he arrived very late and where, the following day, at Kukshina's, he had plenty to say about the two "nasty stuck-up creatures and ignoramuses."

As he was getting into Bazarov's tarantass Arcadii had squeezed his hand hard and for a long while refrained from speaking. Bazarov apparently had understood and appreciated both the handclasp and the silence. He had not slept at all during the night and had not smoked, and for several days had eaten almost nothing. His profile, gaunt by now, jutted morosely and harshly from under his cap, pulled low over his forehead.

"Tell you what, brother," he said at last, "let's have

a cheroot. And you might take a look—my tongue is yellow, isn't it?"

"It is that," Arcadii informed him.

"To be sure . . . there, even the cheroot has no flavor to it. The machine is all out of order."

"You have changed of late, for a fact," Arcadii commented.

"It's nothing—we'll get better soon! The only thing that bothers me is that my mother is so soft-hearted; if you don't grow a belly on you and eat ten times a day she gets all broken up. My father, though, isn't a bad sort; he's been places and had his full share of hard knocks. It's no use—I can't smoke," he added, and tossed the cheroot into the dust of the road.

"It's around twenty miles to your place, isn't it?" Arcadii asked.

"Around that. But better ask this sage," Bazarov indicated the mouzhik sitting on the box, one of Phedot's hired hands. But all the sage answered was "Who knows—nobody measures the miles around here," and resumed cursing the shaft horse in a low voice for "kicking with her jowl"—that is, jerking her head.

"Yes, yes," Bazarov began, "let this be a lesson to you, my youthful friend, an instructive example, as it were. The devil alone knows what tommyrot this is! Every mortal is dangling on a thread, a bottomless gulf may spread out under him any minute but, besides that, he thinks up all sorts of unpleasant things for himself, he messes up his own life."

"What are you hinting at?" Arcadii asked.

"I'm not hinting at anything—I'm coming right out with it: we've both behaved like utter fools. But what's the use of talking about it! However, as I noticed even

151

back in my clinic days, the fellow who resents his illness is bound to get the better of it."

"I don't quite follow you," Arcadii commented. "By the look of things you had nothing to complain about."

"Well, since you don't quite follow me, I'll let you in on something—the way I see it, a man is better off making little ones out of big ones on a road chain-gang than letting a woman get a real hold of even a finger-tip. All that sort of thing is"—Bazarov had almost come out with his pet phrase, "romantic bosh," but restrained himself and substituted "—nonsense. Right now you won't believe me, but I'm telling you: you and I fell into the society of women, and we found it pleasant; but leaving such society is as grand as throwing icy water over yourself on a sultry day. A man has no time for such trifling things; a man must be untamed, as an excellent Spanish proverb proclaims. Take you, now," he added, addressing the mouzhik up on the box, "you're a clever fellow—have you a wife?"

The mouzhik turned his flat, purblind face upon the two friends: "A wife, did you say? Sure. How else?"

"Do you beat her?"

"My wife, now? All sorts of things can happen. She don't get beaten without a reason."

"That's just dandy. Well now, does she beat you?"

The mouzhik began tugging hard at the reins. "What a thing to say, master. You're after having your joke, all the time." He evidently felt offended.

"Do you hear that, Arcadii Nicholaievich? Whereas in our case it's we who have been slapped down. That's what it means to be educated."

Arcadii laughed in a constrained fashion, while Bazarov turned away and did not open his mouth again for the rest of the way.

The twenty miles or thereabouts seemed all of forty to Arcadii. But the tiny hamlet where Bazarov's parents lived came into sight at last, on the slope of a gently rising knoll. Alongside the hamlet, in a copse of young birches, one could glimpse a small house thatched with straw, yet with a genteel look about it. Two mouzhiks with their hats on were standing near the first hut and quarreling. "You're a big swine," one was saying to the other, "but you act worse than a suckling pig." "And your old woman is a witch," the other retorted.

"From their unconstrained behavior, and the raciness of their speech," Bazarov commented to Arcadii, "you can judge that my father's mouzhiks aren't too downtrodden. Why, there he is himself, coming out on the steps of his abode. That means he must have heard the jinglebells. It's he, it's he—I recognize his figure. My—how gray he has turned, though, poor fellow!"

20

Bazarov leaned out of the tarantass, while Arcadii craned his neck from behind his companion's back and caught sight on the small porch of the genteel little house of a tall gaunt man with ruffled hair and a thin aquiline nose; his old military frock coat was unbuttoned. He was standing with his legs astride, smoking a long pipe and with his eyes puckered against the sun. The horses stopped.

"So you have favored us at last," Bazarov's father remarked, although his long-stemmed pipe was simply jiggling between his fingers. "There, come on out, come on out—let me kiss you," and he put his arms around his son.

"Gene, little Gene," they heard a woman's quavering voice. The door flew open and a roly-poly, squat little old woman in a white cap and a short striped blouse appeared on the threshold. She oh'd, swayed and would surely have fallen if Bazarov had not held her up. Her small plump arms instantly entwined his neck, her head rested upon his breast, and everything became hushed: the only thing one could hear were her broken sobs.

Old Bazarov was breathing hard and his eyes were puckering more than ever. "There, that'll do, that'll do, Arisha—stop it!" he spoke up, exchanging a glance with Arcadii, who was standing still near the tarantass, while the mouzhik up on the box actually turned his head away. "There's no need for that at all! Please stop it."

"Ah, Vassilii Ivanych!" the little old woman babbled. "I haven't seen him in ages, my own dear one, my darling, my own little Gene," and, without releasing him from her arms, she drew her tear-stained face, rumpled and overcome with emotion, away from Bazarov, gazed at him with eyes that were somehow both blissful and mirth-provoking, and again clung to his breast.

"Well, yes, of course, all this is in the nature of things," Vassilii Ivanych remarked, "only it would be better, really, if we went inside. There, Evgenii has brought a guest with him. Do excuse it," he added, addressing Arcadii, and scraped his foot a little. "You understand, it's a woman's weakness; and, too, there's

154

the heart of a mother—" yet his own lips and eyebrows were twitching and his chin quivered. Still, one could see that he wanted to control himself and to appear almost indifferent.

"Really, Mother, let's go in," said Bazarov, and he led the little woman, who was all overcome, into the house. Having seated her in an easy chair he once more hurriedly hugged his father and introduced Arcadii to him.

"Glad to make your acquaintance, with all my soul," Vassilii Ivanovich declared. "But you mustn't be too exacting; everything here is simple, on a military footing. Arina Vlassievna, do calm yourself, as a favor to me: why all this faint-heartedness? Our guest is bound to form a poor opinion of you."

"Father of mine," the little woman managed to say through her tears, "I haven't the honor of knowing your name and that of your father—"

"Arcadii Nichola'ich," her husband prompted her gravely in an undertone.

"Excuse me for being so foolish." She blew her nose and, inclining her head to the right and then to the left, carefully dried each eye in turn. "Do excuse me. I thought I'd die, that for all my waiting I would never see my da-a-a-arling—"

"Well, we've lived to see him after all, madam," old Bazarov put in quickly. "Taniushka." He turned to a barefooted girl of thirteen in a dress of vivid red calico, who was timorously peeping in around the edge of the door. "Bring your mistress a glass of water—on a tray, do you hear? And you, gentlemen," he added with a certain old-fashioned playfulness, "I would ask you, if you permit me, to step into the study of a retired veteran."

155

"Let me hug you once more, my little Gene," the mother moaned. Bazarov bent down over her. "Why, what a handsome fellow you've turned into!"

"Well, he may not be exactly handsome," the father remarked, "but as a man he's what they call *ommfé*.* And now I hope, Arina Vlassievna, that having satisfied your maternal heart, you'll see to satisfying the hunger of our dear guests—since, as you're aware, it would not do to feed nightingales on fables only."

The little crone got up from her easy chair. "Vassilii Ivanych, the table will be set this minute; I'll run over to the kitchen myself and order the samovar to be brought; everything will be ready—everything! Why, I haven't seen him, I haven't given him food or drink for all of three years—do you think it was easy for me?"

"There, mind, my little housekeeper, see to it— don't disgrace us. And you, gentlemen, I beg of you to follow me. And here's Timotheich, come to pay his respects to you, Evgenii. I guess he's overjoyed too, the old watchdog. Eh? Aren't you overjoyed, you old watchdog? Follow me, gentlemen, if you please." And old Bazarov bustled ahead, his slippers, trodden down at the heels, scuffing and flapping.

All his little house consisted of was six tiny rooms. One of them, the one to which he brought our friends, was styled the study. A desk (the legs thick), cluttered with papers so darkened by ancient dust that they had a smoke-cured look, took up the entire space between the two windows; hanging on the walls were Turkish muskets, quirts, a saber, two maps, anatomical charts of some sort, a portrait of Hufeland,† a monogram woven of hair and framed in black, and a diploma

* *Homme fait*—an impressive man.
† Christoph Wilhelm Hufeland (1762-1836); German physician.

156

under glass; a leather divan, with hollowed and torn spots here and there, was placed between two enormous closets of Carelian birch; books, small boxes, stuffed birds, jars, phials were crowded in disorder on shelves; a broken-down electrical contrivance stood in a corner.

"I warned you, my honored guest," Vassilii Ivanovich began, "that we're living here as if we were bivouacking—"

"Do stop—why are you apologizing?" his son cut him short. "Kirsanov knows very well that you and I are no Croesuses and that your place is no palace. The question is, where are we going to put him?"

"Mercy, Evgenii—I have an excellent little room for him in the small wing; he will be very well off there."

"So you've acquired a wing, have you?"

"But of course, sir—where the bathhouse is, sir," Timotheich volunteered.

"Alongside of the bathhouse, that is," Vassilii Ivanovich hastened to add. "After all, it's summer now. I'll run over there right away and see to everything—and in the meantime, Timotheich, you could bring in their things. And, of course, Evgenii, I'll place my study at your disposal. *Suum cuique*—to every man his own."

"Well, there he is! A most amusing codger and the kindliest," Bazarov added, as soon as his father had walked out. "Just such another oddity as yours, only of another sort. But he does chatter an awful lot."

"Your mother, too, seems a splendid person," Arcadii remarked.

"Yes, there's nothing mean about my mother. Wait till you see the dinner she'll set out for us."

"You wasn't expected today, father of mine—they

haven't provided any beef," observed Timotheich, who had just lugged in Bazarov's suitcase.

"We'll get along with something else—it's not a hanging matter. Poverty, so they tell us, is no disgrace."

"How many souls does your father own?" Arcadii asked suddenly.

"The estate is not his but mother's. There are fifteen souls, if memory serves me right."

"There are two and twenty in all," Timotheich volunteered, with displeasure in his voice.

They caught the flapping of slippers, and old Bazarov reappeared. "Your room will be ready for your reception in a few minutes," he proclaimed with an air of triumph. "Arcadii . . . Nichola'ich—is that the form you prefer? Well, here is your attendant," he added, pointing to a boy with short-cropped hair who had entered with him, clad in a blue kaftan that was out at the elbows and wearing boots that were obviously not his own. "Phedka, they call him. In spite of my son's prohibition, I still repeat—you mustn't be too exacting. The lad knows how to fill a pipe, though. You do smoke, of course?"

"I smoke cigars, mostly," Arcadii informed him.

"And that shows quite good judgment on your part. My own preference goes to cheroots, but in our isolated regions it is extremely difficult to get them."

"Come, that's enough of your pleading poverty," Bazarov interrupted him again. "Better sit down here on the divan and let me take a real good look at you."

Vassilii Ivanovich laughed and sat down. His face was very much like his son's, except that his forehead was narrower and not as high, while his mouth was a trifle wider; and he was incessantly fidgeting, shrugging as though his coat were cutting him under the armpits, blinking, coughing, and twiddling his fingers, whereas his son was distinguished by a certain nonchalant immobility.

"Pleading poverty!" echoed the father. "Don't get the notion, Evgenii, that I want to win the sympathy of our guest; as if to say: 'There, just see what a wilderness we're living in!' On the contrary, I opine that for a man of reason there is no such thing as a wilderness. At least I try, insofar as circumstances permit, not to become moss-grown, as they say, not to fall behind the times." He drew out of his pocket a fresh handkerchief of yellow foulard which he had had a chance to get on his way to Arcadii's room and, as he waved it about, continued: "I am not referring now to the fact, for example, that, not without sacrifices which I personally felt, I have changed the status of my serfs to that of tenants, and that I am letting them farm my own land on half-shares. I considered that my duty, a course of action which prudence itself dictates in this instance, although other landed proprietors are not even contemplating it. I am referring to the sciences, to education."

"Yes; I notice you have some issues of *The Friend of Good Health* lying there—and they aren't more than four years old," Bazarov remarked.

"An old comrade sends it to me out of friendship," the father commented hastily. "But we have, for example, a conception even of phrenology," he added, addressing himself, however, principally to Arcadii, indicating a small plaster cast of a head divided into numbered squares and standing on top of a closet. "Neither Schönlein nor Rademacher has remained unknown to us."

"What—do people in this province still believe iṅ Rademacher?" asked Bazarov.

Vassilii Ivanovich had a coughing spell. "In this province . . . Of course, gentlemen, you have superior knowledge; how could we ever keep up with you? For you have come to replace us. Even in my time a certain humoralist by the name of Hofmann, or a certain Brown with his vitalism, struck us as extremely laughable, and yet they had created a great stir once upon a time. Some newcomer has taken Rademacher's place for you; you bow down before him, yet in twenty years, as likely as not, he too will be laughed at."

"If it will make you feel any better," observed Bazarov, "I can tell you that nowadays we laugh at medicine in general and don't bend the knee before anybody."

"How is that possible? You want to be a doctor, don't you?"

"I do; but the one thing doesn't interfere with the other."

Old Bazarov poked his ring finger in his pipe, which still held some smoldering ashes. "Well, maybe, maybe— I'm not going to argue. After all, who am I? A retired army doctor, *volatoo;* * now I've turned into an agronomist. I served in your grandfather's brigade." He again turned to Arcadii. "Yes, sir, yes sir; many a sight have I seen in my time. And into what sorts of society haven't I been thrown, whom haven't I had to do with! I, I myself, the man whom you see before you now, felt the pulse of Prince Wittgenstein and of Zhukovsky the poet! As for those who were in the Southern Army, in the Fourteenth Regiment, you understand" —and at this Vassilii Ivanovich pursed his lips signifi-

* *Voilà tout*—that is all.

cantly—"I knew every last one of them. Well, naturally, I kept myself to myself; physician, stick to your lancet, and that's that! But your grandfather was a greatly respected person, a real military man."

"Own up—he was an out-sized blockhead," Bazarov commented lazily.

"Ah, Evgenii, what expressions you use! Do have some consideration. Of course, General Kirsanov did not belong to the number of those who—"

"There, drop him," Bazarov broke in. "As I was getting close to home I felt great when I saw your grove of birches—it has spread out gloriously."

Vassilii Ivanovich became animated. "Why, you ought to take a look at what a little garden I have now! I planted every last tree myself. I've got fruit trees, and berry bushes, and all kinds of medicinal herbs. No matter how clever you young gentlemen may try to be, old man Paracelsus uttered the sacred truth just the same: *in herbis, verbis et lapidibus.** As you surely know, I've retired from practice, yet twice a week or so I have occasion to go back to my old trade. They come for advice—and after all one can't just take them by the napes of their necks and chuck them out. Occasionally the poor turn to me for help. And besides, there are actually no doctors hereabouts. One of the neighbors here, a retired major, goes in for doctoring too, if you can imagine such a thing. I inquired about him: had he ever studied medicine? No, they told me, he hadn't; he doctors mostly out of philanthropy. Ha, ha—out of philanthropy! Eh? How does that strike you?" and he went on laughing.

"Phedka! Fill a pipe for me!" Bazarov called out grimly.

* Through herbs, words and stones (minerals).

"Then there was another doctor hereabouts, who had driven over to see a patient," his father went on in something very like desperation, "but the patient was already *ad patres,* with his fathers, you know; well, the servant wouldn't admit the doctor; 'Your services are no longer required,' he told him. The doctor hadn't expected this; he became all confused, and asked: 'Well, now, did your master hiccup just before his death?' 'He did that, sir.' 'And did he hiccup a lot?' 'Yes, a lot.' 'Ah, well, that's fine!'—and he made backtracks—" and he again broke into laughter.

The old man was the only one to laugh; Arcadii assumed a smiling expression; Bazarov merely drew deeply on his pipe. The conversation lasted in this manner for an hour or so; Arcadii found time to visit his room, which turned out to be the entry to the bathhouse but was very cozy and clean just the same. Finally Taniushka came in and informed them that dinner was ready.

Vassilii Ivanovich was the first to stand up. "Let us go, gentlemen! You will be magnanimous and excuse me if I have bored you. Let us hope the hostess will offer you entertainment that is better than mine."

The dinner, although it had been gotten together hurriedly, turned out to be very good, even copious; the wine alone was a trifle off, to put it plainly: an almost black sherry, which Timotheich had bought in town from a dealer he knew, it had a bouquet that was either coppery or resinous—it was hard to determine which; the flies, too, were annoying. At ordinary times a serf boy would drive them away with a large branch of greenery, but on this occasion Vassilii Ivanovich, apprehensive of censure by the younger generation, had dismissed him. Arina Vlassievna had found time to primp; she had donned a high cap with silk ribbons and a patterned shawl of light blue. She had another little cry as soon as she laid eyes on her little Gene, but this time her husband did not find it necessary to admonish her: she herself hastened to wipe away her tears, so that they might not spot her shawl.

The young men were the only ones who ate; the host and hostess had dined long before. Phedka, obviously encumbered by the novelty of boots, acted as waiter and was assisted by a woman with a masculine face and only one eye, by the name of Anphissushka, who fulfilled the duties of housekeeper, poultry-woman, and laundress. Old Bazarov paced up and down the room throughout the dinner and, with an utterly happy and even beatific mien, spoke of the grave apprehensions inspired in him by Napoleonic politics and the imbroglio of the Italian situation. His wife paid no attention to Arcadii, did not show any solicitude about his eating or drinking; propping up with a little fist her round face, to which her puffy, cherry-colored tiny lips, and the small birthmarks on the cheeks and over the eyebrows lent a very simplehearted expression, she never took her eyes off her son and kept sighing all the time; she was dying to find out for how long a stay he had come yet feared to ask him. There, now, suppose he says it's only for a couple of days? she thought, and her heart swooned.

After the roast old Bazarov disappeared for an instant and came back with an uncorked half-bottle of champagne. "Here," he exclaimed, "even though we dwell in a wilderness, we nevertheless have something to make merry with on important occasions!" He poured out three goblets and a small wineglass, toasted the health of "our inestimable guests," tossed off his goblet at one breath and compelled Arina Vlassievna to drain her glass to the very last drop. When, in due course, jams were brought to the table Arcadii, who detested anything sweet, nevertheless deemed it his duty to partake of four different sorts which were freshly made; all the more so because Bazarov had flatly turned them down and immediately lit a cigar. Then tea appeared on the scene, served with thick cream, butter and sweet pretzels, after which the old doctor led all of them into the garden to admire the beautiful evening.

As they were passing a bench he whispered to Arcadii: "This is the spot where I love to philosophize as I contemplate the setting of the sun; this befits an anchorite like me. And over there, a little further, I have planted several of the trees beloved by Horace—"

"What trees may they be?" asked Bazarov, who had happened to overhear him.

"Why, what else but . . . acacias."

Bazarov fell to yawning.

"It is time, I think, for our travelers to be in the arms of Morpheus," old Bazarov commented.

"That is to say, it's time to sleep!" Bazarov seconded him. "That's a sound notion. It's time, sure enough."

As he was saying goodbye to his mother he kissed her on the forehead, while she embraced him and blessed him on the sly by making the sign of the cross thrice behind his back. Vassilii Ivanovich escorted Arcadii to his room and wished him "That beneficently pleasant repose which I, too, used to enjoy at your happy age." And, actually, Arcadii did sleep very well in his bathhouse entry; it was redolent of mint, and two crickets behind the stove vied with each other in chirping soporifically. From Arcadii's room Vassilii Ivanovich headed for his study; where, perching on the divan at his son's feet, he was just getting ready to chat with him—but the latter got rid of him, saying that he wanted to sleep. However, he did not fall asleep until morning. With his eyes wide open he stared rancorously into the darkness. Memories of childhood held no sway over him and, besides, he had not yet had time to rid himself of his latest bitter impressions. As for Arina Vlassievna, she first had her sweet fill of prayer; then she held a long, long talk with Anphis-sushka, who was standing stock-still before her and, with her only eye fixed upon her mistress, transmitted to her in a conspiratorial whisper her own observations and surmises concerning Evgenii Vassilievich. The little old woman's head began to spin from joy, from the wine, from the cigar smoke; her husband attempted to talk to her but at last gave it up as a hopeless task.

Arina Vlassievna was a true Russian daughter of the petty nobility; by rights she should have lived a couple of centuries before, in the times of old Moscow. She was very devout and emotional: she believed in all sorts of omens, ways of telling fortunes, spells, dreams; she believed in holy innocents, in brownies, in wood demons, in unlucky encounters, in the evil eye, in folk remedies, in salt especially blessed on Holy Thursday, in the imminent end of the world; she believed that if the tapers did not go out during the all-night Mass on Easter Sunday there would be a bumper crop of buckwheat, and that a mushroom stops growing if the eye of man lights on it; she believed that the Devil loves to hang around watery places, and that every Jew has a small bloody spot on his breast; she went in dread of mice, of grass snakes, of frogs, of sparrows, of leeches, of thunder, of cold water, of drafts, of horses, of goats, of red-haired people and black cats, and considered crickets and dogs to be unclean beasts; she ate neither veal, nor pigeons, nor crayfish, nor cheese, nor asparagus, nor Jerusalem artichokes, nor rabbit meat, nor watermelons (because a watermelon when it is cut into reminds one of the head of John the Precursor), and as for oysters she could never speak of them without a shudder; she was fond of eating well—and was strict about fasting; she slept ten hours out of the twenty-four—and did not go to bed at all if her husband had as much as a headache; she had never read a book with the exception of that masterpiece of French sentimentalism, *Alexissa,* or the *Cottage in the Forest;* she wrote one letter in a year —or two, at most—but knew what was what when it came to running the household, or drying fruits and vegetables, and making jam, although she did not actually put her hand to anything and was, generally, unwilling to budge.

She was very kindhearted and, in her own way, not at all foolish. She knew that the world held masters who had to command and common folk who had to serve—and hence she disdained neither servility nor bows that amounted to prostrations, but she treated her dependents kindly and gently, would not let a single beggar leave empty-handed, and never condemned anyone, even though she did indulge in gossip now and then. In her youth her looks had been very appealing, she had played the clavichord and spoken a bit of French, but during the many years of wanderings with her husband, whom she had married against her will, she had lost her figure and forgotten both music and the French language. She loved and feared her son unutterably; she had left the management of the estate to her husband, and no longer concerned herself with anything; she oh'd, fluttered her handkerchief defensively and raised her eyebrows higher and higher in fright as soon as her old mate launched into talk about impending reforms and his own plans. She was inclined to hypochondria, was constantly awaiting some great calamity or other, and would break into tears the instant she merely recalled something sad. Women like that are now becoming scarcer and scarcer. God knows whether that is properly a matter for rejoicing!

21

On getting out of bed Arcadii opened the window, and the first sight to meet his eye was Vassilii Ivanovich. Wearing a Bokhara dressing gown with a handkerchief by way of a belt, the old man was earnestly digging in his vegetable garden. He noticed his young guest and, leaning on his spade, called out: "Greetings and good health! How did you sleep?"

"Splendidly," Arcadii told him.

"Well, as you see, here am I like some Cincinnatus, preparing a bed for late turnips. The time has come now—and thank God for that!—when every man must obtain his sustenance with the work of his own hands; there's no use in relying on others; one must toil oneself. And it turns out that Jean Jacques Rousseau is right. Half an hour ago, my dear sir, you would have beheld me in a different situation. Half an hour ago I— how had I best express it?—I was pouring laudanum into a certain country wife who was complaining of "the trots"—that's what they call it, but according to our terminology it's dysentery—and there was another for whom I extracted a tooth. I offered to etherize her, but she wouldn't consent. All this I do gratis—*en amateur*. However, that is nothing new to me, for I am a plebeian, *homo novis,* a newcomer—since, unlike my spouse, I am not descended from any ancient line. But perhaps you would like to come over here into the shade, to have a breath of the morning freshness before tea?"

Arcadii stepped out and walked over to him.

"Once more—welcome!" old Bazarov almost declaimed, placing his hand in a military salute against the greasy skullcap he was wearing. "You are, I know, accustomed to luxury, to pleasures, yet even the great ones of this world do not deem it beneath them to pass a short while under the roof of a cabin."

"Oh, please!" Arcadii protested vehemently. "What sort of a great one of this world am I? And I am not accustomed to luxury."

"Allow me, allow me," Vassilii Ivanovich rejoined with an amiable simper. "Even though I'm filed away as a back number now, I've knocked about the world a bit; I can tell a bird by its flight. Also, I'm a psychologist, after my own fashion, and a physiognomist. If I hadn't had that gift—for I'll venture to call it that—I would have perished long ago; a little man like me would have been simply lost in the shuffle. I will tell you this, without paying you any compliments—I sincerely rejoice at the friendship I notice between you and my son. I've just been to see him. He was up very early—according to his wont, as you are probably aware—and was dashing off for a ramble through the environs. Permit me to satisfy my curiosity—have you been acquainted long with my Evgenii?"

"Since last winter."

"Just so, sir. And permit me to ask you also—but wouldn't it be better if we sat down? Permit me to ask you as a father, in all frankness: What's your opinion of my Evgenii?"

"Your son is one of the most remarkable people I have ever met," Arcadii answered with animation.

The father's eyes suddenly opened wide and a faint flush mantled his cheeks. The spade fell out of his hands. "And so, you suppose—" he began.

"I feel certain," Arcadii said quickly, "that a great future awaits your son, that he will make your name famous. I became convinced of this the first time we met."

"How . . . how did it come about?" Vassilii Ivanovich barely managed to ask. An enraptured smile parted his thick lips and remained there.

"You want to know how we met?"

"Yes . . . and in general—"

Arcadii launched into his story and spoke of Bazarov with still greater enthusiasm than on that evening when he had danced a mazurka with Odintsova. The father listened and listened, blew his nose, kept rolling his handkerchief into a wad between his hands, coughed, ruffled his hair and finally could endure the strain no longer: he bent toward Arcadii and kissed him on the shoulder.

"You've made me utterly happy," he declared, without ceasing to smile. "I must tell you that I . . . deify my son; I won't comment on my old wife—everybody knows how mothers are!—but I dare not reveal my feelings before him, because he doesn't like that sort of thing. He's opposed to all emotional demonstrations; there are many who even condemn him for such firmness of character and perceive therein a sign of pride or insensibility; but such men as he do not have to be measured by an ordinary yardstick—isn't that so? Why, here's just one instance: another man in his place would have been extorting money from his parents all the time; but he, would you believe it, never took an extra copper from us in all his born days, by God!"

"He is a disinterested, honest person," Arcadii commented.

"Disinterested—precisely. But I not only deify him, Arcadii Nicholaievich, I am proud of him, and all my ambition consists of having the following words appear in his biography in due time: 'Son of an ordinary army doctor who, however, was capable of divining his nature at an early day, and who spared nothing for the sake of his education—' " Here the old man's voice broke. Arcadii pressed his hand hard. "What is your opinion?" Vassilii Ivanovich asked after a certain silence. "It won't be in the field of medicine, will it, that he will attain that celebrity which you prophesy for him?"

"Of course it won't be in the field of medicine—although even in that respect he will be one of the foremost scientists."

"In what field then, Arcadii Nicholaievich?"

"That is difficult to say at present, but he will be famous."

"He will be famous!" the old man echoed, and plunged into deep thought.

"Arina Vlassievna bade me ask you to come to tea," Anphissushka informed them as she passed by, bearing an enormous platter heaped with ripe raspberries.

Vassilii Ivanovich was startled out of his trance. "And will there be chilled cream for the raspberries?"

"There will be, sir."

"But chilled, mind you! Don't stand on ceremony, Arcadii Nichola'ich—take more. But how is it Evgenii is not coming?"

"I'm here," Bazarov's voice came from Arcadii's room.

Vassilii Ivanovich turned quickly. "Aha! You wanted to visit your friend, but you've come too late, *amice,* and we've already had an extensive conversation. Now we'll have to go in to tea; your mother is calling us. Incidentally, I'll have to have a little talk with you."

"What about?"

"There's a little mouzhik hereabouts; he's suffering from icterus—"

"Jaundice, you mean?"

"Yes, chronic and very obdurate icterus. I prescribed gentian root and St. John's wort for him, made him eat carrots and dosed him with soda, but all these are palliatives; we need something more drastic. And even though you deride medicine, I'm convinced you can give me worth-while advice. We'll talk about that later, but right now let's go in to tea." He sprang up spryly from the bench and began to sing the lines from *Robert le Diable:*

"One law, one law, one law we'll set before us—
    In joy, in joy, in joy to pass our life!"

"What remarkable vitality!" Bazarov commented as he left the window.

Midday had come. The sun behind its tenuous veil of unbroken whitish clouds was scorching. All things were hushed: the roosters alone were challengingly calling to one another in the village, arousing in everyone who heard them a strange sensation of somnolence and tedium, while somewhere on high, among the treetops, the incessant cheeping of a young hawk rang in plaintive appeal. Arcadii and Bazarov were lolling in the shade of a small hayrick, having put a couple of armfuls of rustlingly dry but still green and fragrant grass under them.

"That aspen," Bazarov broke the silence, "reminds me of my childhood; it's growing at the edge of a pit where a brick barn once stood, and at that time I felt certain that that pit and the aspen possessed a talismanic aura of their own; I never felt bored in their vicinity. What I did not understand at that time is that I wasn't bored because I was a child. Well, I'm grown up now—the talisman doesn't work."

"How much time have you spent here altogether?" Arcadii asked.

"Two years in a row; after that we came here from time to time. We led a nomadic life, traipsing from town to town, mostly."

"And has this house been standing a long time?"

"Yes, a long time. Grandfather—my mother's father —built it in his day."

"Who was he, this grandfather of yours?"

"The devil knows. A second major, or something of that sort. Served under Suvorov and was telling stories all the time about the crossing of the Alps. Lying his head off, probably."

"So that's why you have a portrait of Suvorov hanging in your parlor! For my part I love small houses like

172

yours; they're such old and warm little things, and there's a special aroma about them."

"Yes, there's a reek of icon-lamp oil about them, and of hart's-clover," Bazarov declared, yawning. "And what a world of flies there is in those darling little houses! Ugh!"

"Tell me," Arcadii began, after a brief silence, "were you treated harshly as a child?"

"You see for yourself what my parents are like. They're not strict folks."

"Do you love them, Evgenii?"

"I do, Arcadii!"

"They love you so much!"

For some time Bazarov kept silent. "Do you know what I'm thinking of?" he said at last, putting his hands behind his head.

"I don't know. What is it?"

"I'm thinking what a fine thing life on this earth is for my parents! Father, at sixty, is bustling about, talking about 'palliatives,' doctoring people, playing the magnanimous master to the peasantry—having himself a high time, in short; and my mother is well off, too: her day is so stuffed with all sorts of activities, and oh's and ah's, that she has no time to stop and come to her senses. Whereas I—"

"Whereas you—what?"

"Whereas I am thinking: Here am I, lying under a hayrick. The tiny narrow spot I'm taking up is so infinitesimally small by comparison with the rest of space, where I am not and which has nothing to do with me, and the portion of time which I may succeed in living through is so insignificant when confronted with eternity, wherein I was not and shall not be. Yet within this atom, this mathematical point, the blood is circulating, the brain is working, something or other yearns also to . . . What hideous incongruity! What trifles!"

"Allow me to point out to you: that which you're saying is applicable in general to all men—"

"You're right," Bazarov quickly agreed. "What I wanted to say was that they—my parents, that is—are taken up with things and don't trouble themselves about their own insignificance; it doesn't stink in their nostrils . . . whereas I—all I feel is tedium and malice."

"Malice? But just why malice?"

"Why? What do you mean, why? Come, have you forgotten?"

"I remember everything, but just the same I won't admit that you have any right to feel malice. You're unlucky, I grant you, but still—"

"Ah! Why, Arcadii Nicholaievich, I see that you have the same notions about love that all the ultra-modern young people have: 'Here, chick, chick, chick!' But the second the chick starts coming at you you take to your heels for all you're worth. I'm not built that way. However, enough of that. It's downright shameful to cry over spilt milk." He turned over on his side. "Aha! Here's a gallant ant, dragging a half-dead fly. Drag her along, brother—drag her along! Pay no attention to her resistance; avail yourself of your right as an animal not to acknowledge the sentiment of compassion—don't be like one of our sort, who breaks himself on the rack!"

"You ought to be the last one to talk like that, Evgenii! When did you break yourself on the rack?"

Bazarov lifted his head a little. "That's the only thing I'm proud of. If I haven't broken myself, then no petticoat is going to ruin me. Amen! *Finis!* You won't hear another word about this from me."

Both friends lay for some time in silence.

"Yes," Bazarov resumed, "man is a strange creature. When one gets a look, off to one side, sort of, and from a distance, at the dead-end life our 'fathers' lead here, what could be better, apparently? Eat, drink, and know that you're acting in the most regular, most sensible manner. But that's not the way things pan out— tedium will get you down. One wants to bother with people—even to curse them out, yet bother with them just the same."

"A man must arrange his life so that its every moment should be significant," Arcadii uttered reflectively.

"Who says so! The significant, even though it is false on occasion, is nevertheless sweet, yet one can become reconciled to the insignificant also; but when it comes to petty annoyances—petty annoyances, there's the rub!"

"Petty annoyances do not exist for a man as long as it is his will not to recognize them."

"Hm . . . That was a *commonplace in reverse* you just got off."

"What? What are you applying that term to?"

"Why, just this: to say, for instance, that enlightenment is a useful thing is a commonplace, but to say that enlightenment is harmful, that's a commonplace in reverse. It sounds classier, sort of, but substantially it's the very same thing."

"But what side is the truth on—where is it?"

"Where? I'll answer you like an echo: Where?"

"You're in a melancholy mood today, Evgenii."

"Is that a fact? The sun must have steamed me up—

and besides, one shouldn't eat so many raspberries."

"If that's the case, it's not a bad idea to take a snooze," Arcadii remarked.

"If you like; but don't you look at me—every man has a stupid face when he's asleep."

"But isn't it all one to you what people think of you?"

"I don't know what to tell you. A real man oughtn't to feel concerned over such a thing; a real man is one whom it's useless to think about, but whom one must either obey or hate."

"Strange! I don't hate anybody," Arcadii declared after brief reflection.

"Whereas I hate so many. You're a soft-hearted, wishy-washy creature—where do you get off hating anyone! You get cold feet, you have but little confidence in yourself—"

"And what about you," Arcadii interrupted him, "do you have confidence in yourself? Do you have a high opinion of yourself?"

Bazarov was silent for a while. "When I come up against a man who won't back water before me," he said, articulating every word, "it will be time to change my opinion of myself. To hate—that's the thing! There, for instance, you remarked today as you were going past the hut of our overseer Philip—it's such a fine, white hut—well, you remarked that Russia would attain perfection when every last mouzhik had a place just like that to live in, and that every one of us was in duty bound to help toward that end. But me, I've grown to hate this ultimate mouzhik, this Philip or Sidor, for whom I am in duty bound to strain every nerve and sinew, and who won't give me as much as a thank-you; and besides, what would I do with his

176

thank-you? Well, so he'll be living in that white hut, but I'll be pushing up the daisies—well, and what comes after that?"

"Enough of that, Evgenii. To hear the way you talk today, one cannot help but agree with those who reproach us with lacking principles."

"You're talking like your uncle. There are, in general, no such things as principles—you haven't wised up to that to this very day! But sensations actually exist. Everything depends on them."

"How so?"

"Why, just so. Take me, for example: I maintain a negative attitude—through the force of sensation. I find negation pleasant; that's the way my brain is constructed, and that's that! Why do I find pleasure in chemistry? Why are you fond of apples? Also through the force of sensation. It's all one whole. Beyond that men will never penetrate. It isn't everyone who will tell you that, and I won't tell you that a second time either."

"Well, now—is honesty, too, a sensation?"

"I should say so!"

"Evgenii!" Arcadii began in a lugubrious voice.

"Eh? What is it? That's not to your liking?" Bazarov brought him up short. "If you've decided to mow everything down, swing the scythe at your own legs too! However, we've philosophized enough. 'Nature wafts a slumbrous silence,' as Pushkin said."

"He never said anything of the sort," Arcadii objected.

"Well, if he didn't, he could—and should—have said it, being a poet. Incidentally, he must have done a stretch in the army."

"Pushkin never was a military man."

"Come, now—he has 'To war, to war—for Russia's honor fight!' on every page."

"What sort of cock-and-bull stories are you making up! Why, if you stop to think, it's out-and-out calumny!"

"Calumny! My, my, what a grave matter! What a word the man has thought of to scare me with! Whatever calumny you bring up against a man, he really deserves something twenty times worse."

"We'd better go to sleep!" Arcadii declared in a vexed tone.

"With the greatest of pleasure," Bazarov countered.

However, neither one of them was sleepy. Some sort of almost hostile feeling was taking possession of the hearts of both young men. Five minutes later they opened their eyes and exchanged glances in silence.

"Look," Arcadii said suddenly, "a dry maple leaf has torn loose and is falling to the earth; its flutterings bear an utter resemblance to the flight of a butterfly. Isn't that strange? The deadest and saddest of things bears a resemblance to the gayest and liveliest."

"Oh, Arcadii Nichola'ich, my friend!" Bazarov exclaimed. "I beg but one thing of you: don't go in for pretty talk."

"I talk the best I can. And, finally, this is despotism. An idea came into my head; why shouldn't I express it?"

"Just so; but just why shouldn't I express mine also? I find that pretty talk is indecent."

"What's decent, then? Bickering?"

"Eh-eh! Why, I see that you're really set on following in your uncle's footsteps. How overjoyed that idiot would be were he to hear you!"

"What did you call Pavel Petrovich?"

"I called him by his proper name—an idiot."

"Why, this is intolerable!" Arcadii exclaimed.

"Aha! Family pride spoke up in you," Bazarov commented calmly. "It persists most stubbornly in people, I've noticed. A man may be all set to renounce everything, to break with every prejudice—but to admit that his brother, let's say, who steals handkerchiefs is a thief: that's more than he can stand. And really, now: that's *my* brother—*mine!*—and he's no genius? Can such a thing be possible?"

"It was the simple feeling for justice which spoke up in me, and not at all a feeling of family pride," retorted Arcadii, flaring up. "But since that's a feeling which you don't understand, you're a stranger to that *sensation* and consequently you can't judge it."

"In other words, Arcadii Kirsanov is too lofty for me to understand; I genuflect and will say no more."

"Please, Evgenii, that'll do; we'll really wind up quarreling."

"Oh, Arcadii! Do me a favor: let's have an honest-to-goodness quarrel for once—till we're both laid out cold, till we exterminate each other."

"But at that rate, likely as not, we'll end up by—"

"By fighting?" Bazarov anticipated him. "Well, why not? Here, on the hay, in such an idyllic setting, far from the world and the gaze of men, it wouldn't be so bad. However, you wouldn't be able to handle me. I'd grab hold of your throat right off—"

Bazarov spread out his long and calloused fingers. Arcadii turned and, as though in jest, got set to resist. But his friend's face struck him as so sinister, the menace he imagined he saw in the smile that distorted the other's lips and smoldering eyes was so far removed from a jest, that Arcadii felt an involuntary timidity.

"Ah, so that's where you've gone to!" the voice of Vassilii Ivanovich sounded at that moment and the old army doctor appeared before the young men; he was clad in a homemade linen jacket and was wearing a straw hat, also homemade. "I've been looking and looking for you. However, you've chosen a fine spot, and are indulging in a splendid occupation. Lying on the *earth,* to be gazing up to *heaven.* Do you know, there's a certain peculiar significance about that!"

"I gaze up to heaven only when I want to sneeze," Bazarov growled and, turning to Arcadii, added in a low voice: "It's a pity he interrupted us."

"There, that'll do," Arcadii whispered and on the sly squeezed his friend's hand hard. "But no friendship can long sustain such shocks."

"I am contemplating you, my youthful companions," Bazarov was saying in the meantime, shaking his head and leaning his folded hands on some sort of a cunningly twisted stick of his own workmanship, with a carving of a Turk's figure by way of a knob, "I am contemplating you, and I cannot help but admire you. How much strength there is in you, how much youth in its very blossom, how many aptitudes, talents! You're simply . . . Castor and Pollux!"

"So that's where the man is heading—smack into mythology!" Bazarov commented. "One can tell right off you were a mighty Latinist in your day! Why, if I remember rightly, you won a silver medal for a composition in Latin—yes?"

"The Dioscuri, the Dioscuri!" Vassilii Ivanovich reiterated.

"Still, that will do, Father—don't get mushy."

"It's allowable, for once in a great age," the old man mumbled. "However, it was not for the purpose of paying you compliments that I sought you out, gentlemen, but for the purpose, first of all, of . . . I wanted to warn you, Evgenii. You're a clever fellow, you know people, and you know women and, consequently, you'll be tolerant. . . . Your mother wanted a thanksgiving service to celebrate your arrival. Don't imagine that I am asking you to attend this service—it's all over by now; but Father Alexei—"

"The hedge-priest?"

"Well, yes, the village priest; he's going to . . . dine with us. I didn't expect it, and actually advised against it, but somehow it came about of itself—he misunderstood me. Well, Arina Vlassievna, too. Besides, we consider him a very worthy and sensible man—"

"He's not going to eat my portion at dinner, I imagine?" asked Bazarov.

His father laughed. "Good gracious, what are you saying!"

"Well, that's the only demand I make. I'm ready to sit at the same table with any man."

Vassilii Ivanovich adjusted his hat. "I felt certain beforehand," he declared, "that you're above all prejudices. You take me, now, an old man going on sixty-two, yet I am free from them." He dared not confess that he himself had wanted the mass. He was no less pious than his wife. "As for Father Alexei, he was most desirous of making your acquaintance. He'll prove to your liking—you'll see. He has nothing against a little game of cards, actually, and—but this is just among ourselves—he even smokes a pipe."

"Well, why not? We'll settle down to humbug-whist after dinner and I'll trim him."

Old Bazarov laughed. "We'll see! You may have another guess coming."

"How is that? Unless you go back to your old tricks," Bazarov spoke with an odd emphasis.

The father's bronzed cheeks flushed dully. "How is it you aren't ashamed, Evgenii? . . . Let bygones be bygones. Well, yes—I'm ready to confess before this gentleman that this was a passion of mine in my youth, true enough, but I've surely paid a high price for it! How hot it is, though. Permit me to sit down with you. I'm not in your way, I hope?"

"Not at all," Arcadii assured him.

Vassilii Ivanovich, grunting, lowered himself into the hay. "Your present couch, my dear sirs, makes me recall my military, bivouacking life, dressing stations, also near some haystack like this somewhere—and we thanked God even for that." He sighed. "I've experienced so many, many things in my time. I might, for instance, tell you a curious episode during the black plague in Bessarabia, if you'll permit me—"

"For which you received the Vladimir Cross?" Bazarov chimed in. "We know, we know. By the way, how is it you aren't wearing it?"

"Why, I told you that I have no prejudices," muttered Vassilii Ivanovich (he had ordered the small red ribbon to be ripped off his coat only the previous evening) and launched into the story of the black plague episode. "Why, he's fallen asleep," he suddenly whispered to Arcadii, pointing to Bazarov and winking good-naturedly. "Evgenii, get up!" he added, raising his voice. "Let's go to dinner."

Father Alexei, a handsome and stout man with thick, painstakingly groomed hair, with an embroidered sash around his cassock of lilac silk, proved to be a person of exceeding adroitness and resourcefulness.

182

He lost no time in being the first to offer his hand to Arcadii and Bazarov, as if anticipating that they stood in no need of his blessing, and, in general, he conducted himself without constraint. He neither lost face himself nor trod on anybody else's toes; when the occasion arose he laughed at dog Latin and came to the defense of his bishop; drank off two small glasses of wine but refused a third; accepted a cigar from Arcadii but did not light up, saying that he would take it home.

The only thing that was not quite pleasing about him was the way he kept constantly raising his hand slowly and warily to catch the flies that lit on his face, and occasionally squashing them in the process.

He took his seat at the green baize table, evincing his pleasure in doing so in modulated terms, but wound up by taking Bazarov over for two roubles and fifty kopecks in paper money—they had not even a notion in Arina Vlassievna's house how to reckon silver coin. The mother was, as usual, sitting near her son (she did not play cards); as usual, she had her cheek propped up by a tiny fist, and would get up only to order some new refreshment to be served. She was afraid to caress Bazarov, and for his part he did not encourage her, did not invite her caresses; besides that, the father had earnestly cautioned her not to "bother" their son too much. "Young folks aren't any too fond of that sort of thing," he had kept telling her over and over. (It goes without saying what the dinner was like that day: Timotheich, in *propria persona,* had galloped off at dawn-glow after a special variety of Circassian beef; the village elder had ridden off in another direction after eelpouts, perch, and crawfish; country wives had garnered forty-two copper kopecks for the mushrooms alone.) But the mother's

183

eyes, directed undeviatingly at Bazarov, did not express devotion and tenderness only: one could also glimpse sorrow in them, mingled with curiosity and awe—one could glimpse in them a certain resigned reproach.

However, Bazarov was in no mood to analyze just what his mother's eyes might be expressing; he rarely addressed her, and then only with the briefest of questions. Once he asked to shake hands "for luck"; she laid her soft little hand ever so gently on his rough and broad palm.

"Well," she asked a little later, "didn't it help any?"

"Things have turned still worse," he answered her with a careless, mocking smile.

"He plays far too recklessly," Father Alexei declared, as if in regret, and stroked his beautiful beard.

"Napoleon's precept, Father—Napoleon's precept," Vassilii Ivanych chimed in, and led with an ace.

"And it was that very precept which landed him on the island of Saint Helena," Father Alexei declared, and trumped his ace.

"Would you care for some currant drink, little Gene?" asked Arina Vlassievna. Bazarov merely shrugged.

"No!" Bazarov was telling Arcadii the next day. "I'm leaving here tomorrow. It's boring; I want to work, but it can't be done here. I'm setting out for your village again; after all, I left all my prepared specimens there. At your place a man can lock himself in. For here my father keeps repeating to me: 'My study is at your disposal—nobody is going to interfere with you,' but he himself won't go a step from me. And besides, I feel conscience-stricken somehow, locking myself in from him. And then there's Mother, too. I hear her sighing on the other side of the wall, yet if I step out to see her I can't find anything to say to her."

"She'll be very much upset," Arcadii pointed out, "and so will he."

"I'll come back to them again."

"When?"

"Why, when I start out for Petersburg."

"I feel particularly sorry for your mother."

"How come? Has she gotten around you with berries, or what?"

Arcadii looked down. "You don't know your mother, Evgenii. She's not only an excellent person, she's very intelligent, really. This morning she chatted with me for half an hour—and so sensibly, interestingly."

"Expatiating upon me all the while, most probably?"

"We didn't talk about you exclusively."

"What you say is possible; as an outsider you can see things better. If a woman can keep up a conversation for half an hour, that is already a good sign. But I'll leave just the same."

"It won't be very easy for you to break the news to them."

"No, it won't be. The devil nudged me to tease my father today; a little while back he had ordered one of his tenant-serfs to be flogged, and he was very right in doing so—yes, yes, he was very right in doing so, because this mouzhik is the most dreadful thief and drunkard; the only thing was, my father absolutely had not expected that I had become cognizant of the business, as the phrase goes. He was exceedingly embarrassed, and now I'll have to upset him still further. Well, no matter! His wounds will heal soon enough."

"No matter!" Bazarov had said, but the whole day

went by before he could bolster up his resolution sufficiently to inform his father of his intention. Finally, when he was already saying good night to him in the study, he said casually, pretending to yawn: "Yes . . . I almost forgot to tell you—you might order our horses to be sent to Phedot's inn as a relay."

Vassilii Ivanovich was taken aback. "Why, is M'sieu' Kirsanov leaving us?"

"Yes, and I'm leaving with him."

The father spun and reeled where he stood. "You're leaving?"

"Yes . . . I have to leave. Please make arrangements about the horses."

"Very well—" the old man began to babble. "A relay of horses . . . very well . . . only . . . only . . . what's this all about?"

"I have to go to Arcadii's place for a little while. I'll come back here again, later on."

"Yes! For a little while. . . . Very good." He took out his handkerchief and, as he blew his nose, drooped almost to the ground. "Well, what can one do? This— all will be attended to. Here I was thinking you would be with us for . . . a somewhat longer stay. Three days. This . . . this, after three years, is rather short— rather short, Evgenii!"

"But I'm telling you that I'll be back soon. I find this unavoidable."

"Unavoidable. . . . Well, what can one do? One must fulfill one's obligations first of all. So you want the horses sent ahead? Very well. Arina and I didn't expect this, of course. Why, she has just wheedled some flowers out of one of her neighbors; she wanted to decorate your room with them." He did not even mention that each morning, when it was barely light, standing with only slippers on his bare feet, he held a consultation with Timotheich and, peeling off with trembling fingers tattered banknote after banknote, entrusted the old peasant with making sundry purchases, with particular emphasis on good things to eat and on red wine, the latter having proven, as far as one could observe, very much to the liking of his young guests. "Freedom—that's the main thing; it's a principle with me; one mustn't hamper people . . . one mustn't—" He suddenly fell silent and headed for the door.

"We'll be seeing each other again soon, Father, really we will."

But the father, without turning around, merely gestured hopelessly and walked out. When he came back to his bedroom he saw his wife in bed and began to pray in a whisper, so as not to awaken her. Nevertheless she awoke. "Is that you, Vassilii Ivanych?" she asked.

"It's me, mother of mine!"

"Have you come from little Gene? Do you know, I'm uneasy—does he find it comfortable sleeping on that divan? I bade Anphissushka to put your campaign pallet on his divan, and some new pillows; I would have given him our featherbed, only I remember he doesn't like to sleep on anything too soft."

"It's no great matter, mother of mine; don't trouble yourself. He's all right. Lord, have mercy on us sinners," he resumed his prayers in a low voice. Vassilii Ivanovich had spared his little old woman; he had not wanted to tell her, with the whole night ahead of her, what grief was awaiting her.

Bazarov and Arcadii left the next day. From the very morning the whole house was plunged in dejection; the crockery kept falling out of Anphissushka's hands; even Phedka was perplexed and wound up by removing his boots. Vassilii Ivanovich bustled about more than ever: he was evidently putting up a brave front, talking loudly and walking noisily; his face was haggard, however, and his glances glided past his son. Arina Vlassievna was weeping softly; she would have been utterly at a loss and unable to control herself if her husband had not devoted all of two hours early that morning to reasoning with her. But when Bazarov, after repeated promises of a return visit no later than a month hence, finally struggled free from the embraces restraining him and took his seat in the tarantass; when the horses started off, and the horses' bells broke into jingling, and the wheels began to turn, and the dust settled, and Timotheich, all hunched up and tottering as he walked, shuffled off to his cubbyhole; when the little old couple was left all alone in its house, which in its turn seemed to have suddenly shrunk into itself and grown decrepit—Vassilii Ivanovich, who had persisted for a few moments more in waving his handkerchief with a dashing air as he stood on the front steps, sank on a chair and let his head drop on his breast.

"He's forsaken us, he's forsaken us," he began to babble. "He's forsaken us; he became bored in our company. I'm all by myself now, all by myself like a single finger!" he repeated several times, and each time thrust forth his hand with the index finger isolated from the others. It was then that Arina Vlassievna drew near him and, placing her gray head against his gray head, told him: "What can a body do, Vassya! A son is a slice cut off the loaf. He's the same as a falcon: he felt like it, and he winged back to the

188

nest; he felt like it, and he winged away. But you and I are like brown autumn mushrooms that grow on a hollow tree: stuck there side by side and never budging from our places. I alone will remain unchanged for you through all time, just as you will for me."

Vassilii Ivanovich took his hands away from his face and embraced his wife, his mate, harder than he had ever embraced her even in their youth: she had consoled him in his grief.

22

Without speaking, except for exchanging insignificant remarks at rare intervals, our friends reached Phedot's inn. Bazarov was not altogether satisfied with himself; Arcadii was dissatisfied with him. Besides that he was experiencing in his heart that causeless melancholy which is familiar exclusively to very young people. The driver changed the team of horses and, having clambered up on the box, inquired: Should he turn to the right or, maybe, to the left?

Arcadii was startled. The road on the right led to the town and, from there, to his home; the road on the left led to Odintsova.

He glanced at Bazarov. "To the left, Evgenii?" he asked.

Bazarov turned away. "What's all this foolishness?" he muttered.

"I know it's foolishness," Arcadii answered. "But

where's the harm in it? Is this the first time we've done foolish things?"

Bazarov pulled his cap down over his forehead. "Do as you know best," he said at last.

"Go to the left," Arcadii called out.

The tarantass rolled off in the direction of Nikolskoe. But, having decided in favor of foolishness, the friends maintained silence still more stubbornly than before, and seemed to be actually sulking.

Judging merely by the major-domo's manner as he met them on the steps of Odintsova's residence, the friends could surmise that they had acted without judgment in yielding to the whim which had suddenly occurred to them. They were evidently not expected. They had to sit for quite a long while, with quite foolish faces, in the reception room. Odintsova finally came out to meet them. She welcomed them with her customary amiability, but was surprised at their speedy return and, insofar as one could judge from the deliberateness of her movements and words, was not excessively delighted thereby. They hastened to announce that they had only dropped in on their way and would go on to the town in four hours or so. She limited herself to a slight exclamation, requested Arcadii to remember her to his father, and sent somebody for her aunt. When the princess put in her appearance she seemed very sleepy, which lent even greater malevolence to the look on her wrinkled, aged face. Katya was not feeling well; she did not leave her room. Arcadii suddenly felt that he had desired to see Katya at least as much as Anna Sergheievna herself.

The four hours went by in inconsequential talk about one thing or another; Odintsova both listened

and spoke without a smile. It was only at the actual parting that her former friendliness apparently stirred in her soul. "I'm out of sorts at present," she said, "but don't you mind it and do come again—I'm saying this to both of you—at some later time."

Both Bazarov and Arcadii acknowledged this invitation by bowing in silence, got into their vehicle and, without making any further stops, rode on to Maryino, where they arrived safely the next day, at evening. During the whole trip neither one nor the other as much as mentioned Odintsova's name; Bazarov in particular hardly opened his mouth and kept staring off to one side, his eyes avoiding the road with a certain ferocious tension.

All those at Maryino were extraordinarily delighted at their coming. The prolonged absence of his son was beginning to make Nicholai Petrovich uneasy; he gave a little shout, jiggled his legs and bounced on the divan when Phenechka ran into his room, her eyes aglow, and announced the arrival of the "young masters"; Pavel Petrovich himself experienced a certain agreeable agitation and smiled condescendingly as he shook hands with the returned wanderers.

Much talk and many questions ensued; it was Arcadii who spoke for the most part, especially at supper, which lasted far beyond midnight. Several bottles of porter, just brought from Moscow, were served at the order of Nicholai Petrovich, while he himself embarked on such a spree that his cheeks took on a raspberry hue and he kept constantly breaking into laughter that was half-childish and half-nervous. The general animation spread even to the servants. Dunyasha kept dashing back and forth like a victim of charcoal fumes and was forever banging doors; while Peter, even when it was going on three in the morning, was still attempting to play a Cossack dance in waltz time. The strum of the strings had a plaintive and pleasing sound in the still air, but with the exception of a short *fioritura* at the very beginning nothing came off with the cultured valet: nature had denied him any musical ability, just as she had denied him every other.

Yet at the same time life at Maryino was not falling into any too smooth a pattern and poor Nicholai Petrovich was having a rough time of it. Difficulties at the farm multiplied with every day—dreary, senseless difficulties. The fussing with the hired hands was becoming unbearable. Some were asking either to be paid off or to have their wages increased; others absconded after pocketing advances on their wages; horses sickened; harness was used up as if consumed by fire; tasks were performed sloppily; a threshing machine that had been ordered from Moscow turned out to be useless on account of its ponderousness; another was ruined the first time it was used; half of the cattle sheds burned down because an old blind female farm-serf, who had wanted to fumigate her cow, had carried a burning brand in windy weather. True, according to what this same crone maintained, all this mischief had come about because the master had gotten the notion into his head of going in for making certain cheeses and milk products the likes of which nobody had ever seen. The manager had suddenly turned bone-lazy and grown lardy, as every Russian grows lardy when he latches on to a good thing. On catching sight of Nicholai Petrovich in the distance he would, in order to evince his zeal, shy a chip at a suckling pig trotting by or threaten some ragged urchin, but otherwise he just slept and slept.

The rent-paying mouzhiks did not bring the money in on the due dates; they stole timber; hardly a night passed without the watchmen catching the horses of the peasants grazing on the meadowlands of the "farm"—and at times they would capture the animals in pitched battle. Nicholai Petrovich had at first set a monetary fine for damages, but matters usually wound up with the horses, after they had been kept a day or two on the master's fodder, being returned to their owners. To top everything, the mouzhiks took to squabbling among themselves: brothers demanded a partition of their property: their wives could not abide in the one hut; all of a sudden things would come to a boiling point and a free-for-all would ensue, and all would get up on their hind legs, would gather on the run before the small porch of the office, barging in on the master, often with battered faces and far gone in drink, and demand justice and judgment; hubbub, screaming, sniveling feminine squeals intermingled with male cursing would fill the air. It was necessary to judge between the contending parties, to shout oneself hoarse, knowing beforehand that it was impossible, after all, to come to a just decision.

There was a shortage of hands for the harvesting— a neighbor who was a landowner in a small way, with a face as comely as comely could be, had contracted to furnish him with reapers at two roubles for each two and three-quarters acres reaped and had rooked him in a most conscienceless manner; his own peasant women were extorting unheard of wages, yet in the meantime the grain was falling from the ears; here they were behind with the mowing, and there the Council of Guardians was threatening and demanding prompt and full payment of interest due on the mortgage.

"I'm at the end of my rope!" Nicholai Petrovich had cried out in despair on more than one occasion. "To fight against them all by myself is impossible, to send for the district police officer is against my principles— yet you can't do a thing with them unless they fear you!"

"Du calme, du calme," was Pavel Petrovich's usual reaction to this, yet he himself was constantly humming, tugging at his mustache, and frowning.

Bazarov kept aloof from these "petty annoyances," and besides, as a guest, he had no occasion to meddle in the affairs of others. The day after his arrival at Maryino he buckled down to his frogs, his infusoria, his chemical compounds, and kept fussing with them all the time. Arcadii, on the other hand, deemed it his duty, if not actually to help his father, then at least to make a show of his readiness to help him. He would patiently hear him out and once offered him some bit of advice or other, not with the intent of its being followed but only to evince his concern. Husbandry did not arouse any revulsion in him: he even indulged with pleasure in reveries of working the land, but at that time other ideas had begun to swarm in his head.

Arcadii, to his own amazement, was constantly thinking of Nikolskoe. Formerly he would have merely shrugged had anyone told him that he could possibly get bored while under the same roof with Bazarov—and what a roof, at that: the parental one! Yet bored he was, actually, and longing to get away. He struck on the idea of hiking, to tire himself out, but even that did not avail. Once, while conversing with his father, he learned that the latter had several letters, rather interesting, which Odintsova's mother had at one time written to his late wife; and he would not leave his father alone until he got hold of these letters, for which Nicholai Petrovich had had to rummage through a score of sundry boxes and trunks. Having come into possession of these half-crumbled scraps of paper Arcadii appeared to have quieted down, just as though he had beheld a goal which it behooved him to attain. " 'I'm saying this to both of you,' " he was incessantly quoting to himself in a whisper. "She added that herself. I'll go, I'll go, the Devil take it!"

But then he would recall their last visit, the chill reception and the awkwardness he had felt even before that—and he would be overcome by timidity. The "maybe" mood of youth, the secret desire to try one's luck, to test one's mettle all by oneself, without the patronizing assistance of anyone, no matter who— these motives at last tipped the scale. Not even ten days had passed since his return to Maryino when, under the pretext of studying the operational methods of Sunday schools, he was off, racing for the provincial capital again and from there to Nikolskoe. Incessantly urging the driver on, he was rushing to his destination as a young officer rushes into battle: he felt frightened, and blithe, and impatience was suffocating him. "The main thing is not to think," he kept saying to himself, over and over.

The driver who had fallen to his lot happened to be a lad of spirit; he came to a halt before every tavern, saying as he did so: "How about a drop of something?" or: "Shouldn't I have a drop, now?" but then, having had his "drop," he did not spare his horses. And, at last, the high roof of the familiar house appeared. What am I doing? the question flashed through Arcadii's head. But come, there couldn't be any turning back now! The troika flew along as if the three horses were but one; the driver was whooping and whistling shrilly. By now the little bridge was rumbling under the hoofs and wheels, then the avenue of clipped firs was already advancing upon the troika. There was a fleeting glimpse of a woman's rose-colored dress amid the dark verdure, a young face peeped out from under the light fringe of a parasol. He recognized Katya and she recognized him. He ordered the driver to rein the horses, which had been going at a full gallop, sprang out of the carriage and walked up to her.

"It's you!" she called out, and little by little her whole face mantled. "Let's go to my sister—she's here, in the garden; she'll be delighted to see you."

Katya led him into the garden. Meeting her had struck him as an especially happy presage; he was as overjoyed to see her as if she were his kith and kin. Everything had come about so remarkably well; no major-domo, no formal announcement. At a turn of the path he saw Anna Sergheievna. She was standing with her back to him. On hearing footsteps she turned around, ever so slowly.

Arcadii became abashed all over again, but the first words she uttered reassured him at once. "Greetings, runaway!" said she in her even, kindly voice, and she walked toward him, smiling and puckering her eyes because of the sun and wind. "Where did you find him, Katya?"

"Anna Sergheievna," Arcadii began, "I've brought you something which you simply do not expect—"

"You've brought yourself—that is best of all."

23

After seeing Arcadii off with mocking regret and letting him see that he had not been taken in at all about the real purpose of the trip, Bazarov isolated himself completely: he was in a fever to work. He no longer carried on disputes with Pavel Petrovich, all the more so since the latter adopted too aristocratic a mien in his presence and expressed his opinions for the most part in mere sounds rather than words. On one occasion only did Pavel Petrovich launch upon a controversy with the "nihilist" about a problem in vogue at that time, concerning the rights of the Baltic noblemen; however, he himself stopped abruptly, declaring with icy politeness: "However, we are unable to comprehend each other; I, at least haven't the honor of comprehending you."

"Of course not!" Bazarov exclaimed. "Man is capable of comprehending everything: how the ether vibrates, and what's taking place on the sun; but when it comes to how another man can blow his nose in a way that differs from one's own—why, that's something beyond one's powers of comprehension."

"What, is that supposed to be witty?" Pavel Petrovich remarked inquiringly and went off to one side.

Still, now and then he requested permission to be present at Bazarov's experiments, and once actually put his face, washed with a superfine preparation and scented, close to the microscope for a look at a transparent infusorian gulping down a green mote of dust and fussily masticating it with some sort of extremely nimble cogs in its gullet. Nicholai Petrovich dropped in on Bazarov considerably more often than his brother; he would have come every day "to learn," as he put it, except that cares connected with running the estate were distracting him. He did not hinder the young scientist: taking a seat somewhere in a corner of the room he would look on attentively, permitting himself a discreet question at rare intervals. At dinner or supper he tried to bring the talk around to physics, geology or chemistry, since all other subjects, even those having to do with husbandry, to say nothing of political ones, might lead if not to conflicts then to mutual displeasure.

He conjectured that his brother's detestation of Bazarov had not diminished to any extent. One slight incident, among many others, confirmed his conjectures. Cholera had begun to appear here and there in the environs and had even "plucked" two people from Maryino itself. One night Pavel Petrovich had a quite severe attack. He went through torments until morning but would not resort to Bazarov's skill and, on seeing him the next day, in answer to the latter's question as to why the sick man had not sent for him, he said, still pale but already meticulously groomed and shaved: "Well, if my memory serves me right, you yourself were saying that you have no faith in medicine?"

Thus the days went by. Bazarov worked away persistently and grimly. But at the same time there was in Nicholai Petrovich's house one being to whom he did not exactly open his heart, yet with whom he was glad enough to talk. That being was Phenechka.

Most of the time he encountered her early in the morning, in the garden or the yard; he avoided dropping in at her room, and she had come to his door only once to ask him if it was all right to bathe

Mitya or no. She did not merely trust him, she was not merely unafraid of him—she was actually less restrained and more at ease in his presence than in that of Nicholai Petrovich himself. It was hard to say what this was due to; perhaps it was because she unconsciously sensed in Bazarov the absence of all that smacked of gentility, of that superiority which both attracts and frightens. In her eyes he was both excellent as a doctor and simple as a man. She attended to her baby without being embarrassed by Bazarov's presence; when her head suddenly began to go round and to ache she would accept a spoonful of medicine from his hand. Before Nicholai Petrovich she seemed to keep aloof from Bazarov: she acted thus not out of guile but from a certain sense of propriety. Of Pavel Petrovich she was more apprehensive than ever; for some time past he had taken to keeping an eye on her and would unexpectedly bob up behind her back, as though he had sprung up out of the ground, in that *suit* of his, with his inflexible, keen-eyed face and his hands stuck in his pockets. "It simply sends a chill right through you," she used to complain to Dunyasha, while the latter responded by sighing and at the same time thinking of another man "without feelings." Bazarov, without suspecting it himself, had become the *cruel tyrant* of her heart.

Bazarov was to Phenechka's liking, but she was to his liking as well. Even his face would change whenever he talked to her: it took on a serene, almost kindly expression, and a certain jocose attentiveness would be added to his wonted nonchalance. Phenechka was growing prettier with every day. There is an epoch in the life of young women when they suddenly begin to bloom and become full-blown, like summer roses;

such an epoch had come to Phenechka. Everything furthered it, even the prevailing sultriness of July. Clad in a light white dress she herself seemed whiter and lighter; suntan spared her, but the heat, which she could not avoid, spread a gentle glow over her cheeks and ears and, infusing her entire body with a soft indolence, found a dreamily languorous reflection in her very pretty eyes. She was practically incapacitated for any work; her hands were forever slipping into her lap. She could hardly walk and was constantly ohing and complaining with an amusing helplessness.

"You ought to go for a dip more often," Nicholai Petrovich told her. He had contrived a large bathhouse, covered over with canvas, in one of his ponds which had not yet dried up entirely.

"Oh, Nicholai Petrovich! Why, a body will die before coming to the pond—and a body will die before getting back from the pond! For there's no shade in the garden at all."

"That's true, about there being no shade," Nicholai Petrovich would answer, and he would take to worrying his eyebrows.

One day, about seven in the morning, as Bazarov was on his way back from a walk he came upon Phenechka in the lilac arbor; the bushes were through flowering long ago but were still thick and green. She was seated on a bench, with a white kerchief thrown over her head as usual; lying near her was a pile of roses, red and white, still wet with dew. He bade her good morning.

"Ah, Evgenii Vassilievich!" said she, lifting up the hem of her kerchief a trifle for a look at him, which move bared her arm to the elbow.

"What are you working at there?" asked Bazarov, sitting down beside her. "Making a bouquet?"

"Yes—for the breakfast table. Nicholai Petrovich loves it."

"But breakfast is still a long way off. What a slew of flowers!"

"I plucked them now, for it's going to be hot and a body won't be able to go out. This is the only time one can breathe. I've grown altogether weak from this heat. I'm afraid, really—will I be taken sick?"

"What sort of a notion is that! Let me feel your pulse." He took her hand, found the evenly pulsing vein, but did not even bother counting the beats. "You'll live to be a hundred," he declared, releasing her hand.

"Ah, God keep me from it!" she exclaimed.

"Why not, now? Don't you want to live a long life?"

"Yes—but a hundred years! We had a grandmother of eighty-five—well, what a martyr she was! Skin all black, deaf, bent in two, coughing all the while; just a burden to her own self. What sort of life is that, now!"

"So it's better to be a young woman?"

"Why, how else?"

"But in what way is it better? Tell me!"

"What do you mean, in what way? Why, here am I, now, still young, I can do everything—come and go, fetch and carry—and I don't have to ask anybody to do anything for me. What could be better?"

"But to me it's all the same, whether I'm young or old."

"How can you say it's all the same? What you're saying is impossible."

"Well, just you judge for yourself, Theodosia Nicholaievna, of what use is my youth to me? I live all alone, a poor lonely bachelor—"

"That's always up to you."

"That's just it—that it isn't up to me! If only someone were to take pity on me."

Phenechka gave him a sidelong look but did not say anything. "What's that book you have there?" she asked a little later.

"That? That's a learned book, very hard to read."

"But you're still studying? And don't you ever get bored with it? You know everything anyway, I guess."

"It doesn't look that way. Suppose you try to read a little of it, now."

"Why, I won't understand a thing in it. Is it in Russian?" asked Phenechka, taking the stoutly bound book in both hands. "What a thick book!"

"It's in Russian."

"I won't understand a thing just the same."

"Well, I'm not after your understanding it. I want to watch you while you're reading. The tip of your little nose moves ever so charmingly when you read."

Phenechka, who had begun to spell out in a low voice the article "On Creosote" which she had chanced upon, broke into laughter and tossed down the book; it slipped from the bench to the ground.

"I love it when you laugh, too," Bazarov declared.

"There, that'll do!"

"I love it when you talk. It's just like a rill, purling."

Phenechka turned her head away. "What a person you are!" she commented, running her fingers over the flowers. "And why should you be listening to me talk? You've conversed with such clever ladies."

"Eh, Theodosia Nicholaievna! Believe me, all the

202

clever ladies in the world aren't worth the dimple on your little elbow."

"There, what things you won't think of!" Phenechka whispered and put her hands under her.

Bazarov picked up the book from the ground. "This is a medical book—why do you toss it about?"

"A medical book?" Phenechka repeated and turned to him. "But do you know what? Ever since you gave me those drops—you remember?—my, how well Mitya sleeps! My, I can't think how I could thank you; you're such a kind man, truly."

"Well, if you come right down to it, doctors have to be paid," Bazarov observed with a smile. "Doctors, as you yourself know, are a money-grubbing lot."

Phenechka looked up at Bazarov, her eyes seeming still darker because of the whitish reflection falling upon the upper part of her face. She was uncertain as to whether he spoke in jest or in earnest.

"If you like, we'll pay with pleasure. I'll have to ask Nicholai Petrovich—"

"Why, are you thinking it's money I'm after?" Bazarov interrupted her. "No, I don't need any money from you."

"What then?" asked Phenechka.

"What?" Bazarov repeated. "Guess!"

"What good am I at guessing!"

"In that case I'll tell you. What I need is . . . one of those roses."

Phenechka broke into laughter again and even clapped her hands, so amusing did Bazarov's request seem to her. She laughed, and at the same time felt flattered. Bazarov was gazing at her fixedly.

"Surely, surely," she managed to say at last and,

bending over the bench, began picking over the roses. "Which will you have—a red or a white?"

"Red—and not too big a one."

She straightened up. "Here you are," said she, but instantly jerked back her outstretched hand and, biting her lips, glanced toward the entrance into the arbor, then listened intently.

"What is it?" asked Bazarov. "Nicholai Petrovich?"

"No, he drove off to the fields . . . and also, I'm not afraid of him. But when it comes to Pavel Nicholaievich . . . I imagined—"

"You imagined what?"

"I imagined *he* was walking around here. No, there's nobody there. Here you are." Phenechka handed the rose over to Bazarov.

"How come you're afraid of him?"

"He always frightens me. It isn't that he actually says anything, but he does have a way of just looking at one so oddly. But then you, too, have no liking for him. You remember, you always used to argue with him before. I wouldn't know what your argument was about even, but I could see you were twisting him this way and that." She demonstrated with her hands how, in her opinion, Bazarov used to twist Pavel Nicholaievich.

Bazarov smiled. "But if he were getting the upper hand over me," he asked, "would you have stood up for me?"

"Where do I come in to stand up for you? But then, there's no such thing as getting the better of you."

"You think so? Still, I know a hand that could knock me down with just one finger, if it felt like it."

"Whose hand would that be?"

"Come, now, you really don't know? Sniff the rose you gave me—what a glorious fragrance it has!"

Phenechka craned her slender neck and put her face close to the flower. The kerchief rolled off her head down onto her shoulders; a soft mass of black, gleaming, slightly disarrayed hair became visible.

"Wait, I want to sniff it with you," said Bazarov; he leaned over and kissed her hard on her parted lips.

She was startled, thrusting him back with both hands against his chest, but her thrust was weak and he was able to kiss her afresh and prolong his kiss.

A dry cough came from behind the lilac bushes. Phenechka instantly moved away to the other end of the bench. Pavel Petrovich appeared, bowed slightly and, having said "You here?" with a certain malicious despondence, withdrew. Phenechka immediately picked up all the roses and left the arbor. "That was wrong of you, Evgenii Vassil'ich," she whispered as she walked away; one could hear unfeigned regret in that whisper.

Bazarov recalled another recent scene and he became both ashamed and contemptuously vexed. But he at once tossed back his head, ironically congratulated himself upon his "formal induction into the ranks of gay Lotharios," and went off to his room.

As for Pavel Petrovich, he left the garden and, pacing slowly, made his way to the forest. There he remained quite a long while, and when he returned for breakfast Nicholai Petrovich asked him solicitously if he were well: so earthy had his face become.

"You know that I have occasional attacks of jaundice," his brother answered him calmly.

24

Two hours later Pavel Kirsanov was tapping on Bazarov's door.

"I must apologize for interrupting you in your scientific pursuits," he began, settling in a chair by the window and resting both hands on a beautiful cane with a knob of ivory (ordinarily he was without a cane), "but I am under the necessity of asking you to allot me five minutes of your time—no more."

"My time is entirely at your disposal," replied Bazarov, over whose face something odd had flitted as soon as Pavel Petrovich had crossed the threshold.

"Five minutes will suffice me. I've come to put a single question to you."

"A question? What about?"

"Why, here it is. If you'll be kind enough to hear me out, here it is. At the commencement of your stay at my brother's house, when I was not yet denying myself the pleasure of conversing with you, I occasionally heard your judgments on many subjects; but, as far as I recall, the talk, either between us or in my presence, never touched upon single combats, or dueling in general. Will you permit me to learn your opinion on this subject?"

Bazarov, who had stood up to meet his caller, perched on the edge of the table and crossed his arms. "Here is my opinion," he said. "From a theoretical point of view a duel is an absurdity; but from a practical point of view it's another matter."

"That is, you wish to say—if I have grasped your meaning—that no matter what your theoretical view of the duel, in practice you would not allow yourself to be insulted without demanding satisfaction?"

"You have guessed my meaning fully."

"Very good, sir. I am extremely gratified to hear that from you. Your words deliver me from a state of uncertainty—"

"Of hesitancy, you mean to say."

"It's all one, sir. I express myself so as to have you understand me; I am not as learned as a seminary rat. Your words save me from a certain painful necessity. I have decided to fight you."

Bazarov's eyes were goggling. "Fight me?"

"You, without fail."

"But whatever for, if you please?"

"I could explain the reason to you," Pavel Petrovich began, "but I prefer to pass it over in silence. To my taste, you are one too many here; I cannot bear you, I despise you, and if that does not suffice you—"

His eyes took on a sparkle; Bazarov's flared up as well.

"Very good, sir," he spoke up. "There is no need of further explanations. You've struck on the notion of trying out your spirit of chivalry on me. I could deny you this pleasure, but let's have a go at it!"

"I am under a sense of obligation to you," Pavel Kirsanov responded, "and I can now entertain the hope that you will accept my challenge without compelling me to resort to forceful measures."

"That is, speaking without allegories, resorting to that stick?" Bazarov remarked coolly. "Your hope is perfectly justified. It's not in the least necessary for you to insult me. And besides that it might not be an altogether safe procedure. You can remain a gentleman. I, in turn, accept your challenge also in gentlemanly fashion."

"Splendid," Pavel Kirsanov declared, and placed his cane in a corner. "We will very shortly have a few words concerning the conditions of our duel, but first I would like to know whether you deem it necessary to resort to the formality of a slight quarrel, which might serve as a pretext for my challenge?"

"No; it'll be best without formalities."

"I think so myself. I assume it likewise out of place to delve into the real causes of our contention. We cannot stomach each other. What more is needed?"

"What more, indeed?" Bazarov echoed ironically.

"As for the specific conditions of the encounter, since we shall have no seconds—for where are we to get them—"

"Precisely, where are we to get them?"

"—I therefore have the honor of making the following suggestion to you: that we fight tomorrow early, at six, let's say, on the other side of the grove, with pistols, at ten paces—"

"Ten paces? That's right, we do detest each other at that distance."

"We might make it eight," Pavel Petrovich suggested.

"We might—why not?"

"Two shots each, and, to provide against any contingency, each one of us will put a note in his pocket, placing the blame for his own end on himself."

"Now that is something I do not entirely agree to," Bazarov spoke up. "It smacks a bit of the French novel —it isn't plausible, somehow."

"Possibly so. You will agree, however, that it would be unpleasant to incur a suspicion of murder?"

"I agree. But there is a way of avoiding this grievous reproach. We won't have any seconds, but there is the possibility of a witness."

"Who, precisely, if I may inquire?"

"Why, Peter."

"What Peter?"

"Your brother's valet. He's a man who stands on the peak of contemporary culture, and he will play his rôle with all the *comme il faut* required in cases such as this."

"It strikes me that you are jesting, my dear sir."

"Not in the least. After duly weighing my suggestion you will be convinced that it is full of common sense and simplicity. Murder will out; but I will undertake to coach Peter in proper fashion and to bring him to the scene of carnage."

"You are still jesting," Kirsanov declared, getting up from his chair. "But after the courteous readiness you have evinced I have no right to cavil. And so, all the arrangements are made. By the way—you have no pistols?"

"Why should I have pistols, Pavel Petrovich? I'm no warrior."

"In that case I offer you mine. You may rest assured that it is now five years since I fired them last."

"That is very consoling information."

Kirsanov reached for his cane. "And now, my dear sir, it remains for me only to thank you and to let you go back to your pursuits. I have the honor of bidding you goodbye."

"Until the pleasure of our next meeting, my dear sir," Bazarov declared, seeing his visitor to the door.

Kirsanov went out, while Bazarov stood still for a while by the door and suddenly exclaimed: "What the devil! How fine this is—and how foolish! What an act we put on! Just the way trained dogs dance on their hind legs. Yet it was impossible to refuse for, likely as not, he would have struck me, and then"— Bazarov paled at the very thought; all his pride simply rebelled "—in which case I would have had to strangle him like a kitten." He went back to his microscope, but his heart was stirred up, and the calm necessary for making observations had vanished. He happened to see us to-day, he was thinking, but would he really intervene like that just for his brother? And besides, what's so important about a kiss? There's something else involved in this. Bah! Is he in love with her himself, maybe? Of course he's in love; it's as plain as day. What a jam to be in, when you come to think! Things are bad, he decided at last, bad, no matter which way you look at them! First of all, I'll have to offer my forehead as a target for a bullet, and in any case I must leave; and then there's Arcadii—and that blessed little ladybug Nicholai Petrovich. Things are bad—bad!

The day passed in some sort of peculiar quiet and listlessness. Phenechka seemed to have disappeared off the face of the earth; she was entrenched in her little room like a baby mouse in its hole. Nicholai Petrovich seemed to be weighed down by his cares. He had been informed that rust had begun to appear in his wheat, in which he had placed his particular hopes. Pavel Petrovich crushed everybody—even Procophich —with his freezing politeness. Bazarov had begun a letter to his father, but he tore it up and threw the scraps under his desk. If I die, he reflected, they'll get to know about it—I won't die, though. No, I'll be knocking about in this world for a long time yet. He bade Peter come to him on an important matter next morning, as soon as day broke; the valet got an idea that he wanted to take him along to Petersburg.

Bazarov went to bed late and was hagridden by disordered dreams all through the night. Odintsova kept hovering before him—she was, at the same time, his mother; trailing after her was a small cat with tiny black whiskers—and this small cat was Phenechka; then Pavel Kirsanov appeared before him as a great forest, with which he would have to fight, no matter what.

Peter aroused him at four; Bazarov dressed immediately and left the house with the valet.

The morning was glorious, fresh; mottled cloudlets were ranged like woolly lambs against the bleakly clear azure; the dew lay scattered on the leaves and grasses in tiny beads, or gleaming like silver on cobwebs; the dank, dark earth seemed to treasure still the rosy traces of the morning glow; from all the sky the songs of the larks came showering down. Bazarov reached the grove, seated himself in the shade at its edge, and only then revealed to Peter what sort of a favor he expected from him. The cultured flunky became scared to death, but Bazarov calmed him down by assuring him that he wouldn't have to do a thing except stand at a distance and watch, and that he would not be held responsible in any way. "Yet at the same time," he added, "just consider what an important rôle awaits you!" Peter threw up his hands, cast down his eyes and, with his face turning all green, leaned against a birch.

The road from Maryino skirted the woods; the light dust blanketed it, still undisturbed since yesterday either by wheel or foot. Bazarov involuntarily kept glancing along this road; plucking and nibbling blades of grass, he was constantly repeating to himself: What foolishness! The slight morning chill made him shiver once or twice. Peter was looking at him in dejection, but Bazarov merely smiled: he wasn't at all scared.

The stamping of hoofs sounded along the road. A mouzhik came into sight from behind the trees. He was driving two hobbled horses before him and, as he was going past Bazarov, he gave him a look that was somehow odd, without doffing his cap, an omission which evidently disturbed Peter as an ill omen. There, that fellow also got up early, it occurred to Bazarov, but at least it was to do something useful; but what are we up to?

"I think he's coming, sir," Peter whispered suddenly.

Bazarov lifted his head and saw Pavel Petrovich. Clad in a light checked jacket and snow-white trousers, he was striding rapidly along the road; under his arm he was carrying a case wrapped in green baize.

"Pardon me; I believe I've made you wait," he remarked, bowing to Bazarov first and then to Peter, whom at that moment he was treating with respect as being something in the nature of a second. "I did not want to awaken my valet."

"It's nothing, sir," Bazarov replied. "We ourselves arrived here only just now."

"Ah! So much the better!" Kirsanov looked about him. "No one in sight—no one will interfere with us. May we go ahead?"

"Let's."

"You do not, I presume, demand any new explanations?"

"No, I do not."

"Would you care to load?" Pavel Petrovich asked, taking the pistols out of their case.

"No; you attend to the loading and I'll pace off the distance. I have longer legs," Bazarov added with something approaching a grin. "One, two, three—"

"Evgenii Vassil'ich," Peter babbled with difficulty (he was shaking as if he had the ague), "do as you will, but I'm moving off a ways."

"Four, five—move off, brother, move off; you can even stand behind a tree and stop up your ears—only thing is, don't close your eyes; if either one of us keels over, run and lift him up. Six, seven, eight—" He halted. "Will that do?" he inquired, addressing Pavel Petrovich. "Or should I throw in a couple of paces more?"

"Just as you please," the other let drop, ramming down the second bullet.

"Well, we'll throw in two more paces," and he drew a line on the ground with the toe of his boot. "There, that's the barrier. But, while we are at it, how many paces from the barrier is each one of us to take? That, too, is an important question. There was no discussion of this matter-yesterday."

"Ten, I suppose," Kirsanov replied, offering both pistols to Bazarov. "Will you deign to choose?"

"I am deigning. But do admit, Pavel Petrovich, that our encounter is so odd as to border on the mirth-provoking. Do but look at the physiognomy of our second."

"You are still inclined to jest," Pavel Petrovich retorted. "I am not denying the oddity of our encounter, but I consider it my duty to warn you that I intend to fight in all seriousness. *A bon entender, salut*—let him who will, heed!"

"Oh, I haven't a doubt that we're resolved to exterminate each other, but why not have a laugh and blend *utile dulci*—the useful with the agreeable? That's it, then: you let me have it in French, and I'll let you have it in Latin."

"I'm going to fight in all seriousness," his adversary reiterated and walked over to his stance. Bazarov, for his part, counted off ten paces from the barrier and halted.

"Are you ready?" asked Pavel Petrovich.

"Entirely."

"We can approach each other, in that case."

Bazarov moved forward, ever so slowly, while Kirsanov, his left hand thrust in his pocket, advanced against him, gradually raising the muzzle of his pistol.

He's aiming right at my nose, the idea came to Bazarov, and how wholeheartedly he's squinting through the sight, the brigand! It's not an agreeable sensation, though. I'll keep my eye fixed on his watch-chain— Something *pinged* shrilly at Bazarov's very ear and at the same instant a shot rang out. I heard that, so nothing happened, he had time to think in a flash. He took one more stride and, without aiming, pressed the trigger.

Pavel Kirsanov gave a slight shudder and grabbed his thigh. A tricklet of blood coursed down his white trousers.

Bazarov flung aside his pistol and approached his adversary. "Are you wounded?" he asked.

"You had the right to call me up to the barrier," Kirsanov let drop. "As for the wound, it's trifling. By agreement each of us has the right to fire again."

"Well, you'll excuse me—that can wait till another time," answered Bazarov, and he put his arm around

214

the other, who was beginning to lose color. "Now I'm no longer a duellist but a doctor, and I must take a good look at your wound before all else. Peter! Come here! Where did you hide yourself?"

"All this is nonsense—I've no need of anyone's help," Pavel Petrovich managed to say, pausing at each word, "and . . . we must . . . fire again—" He was about to tug at his mustache, but his hand weakened, his eyes rolled up and he lost consciousness.

"This is something new! Fainting! Why should that be?" Bazarov exclaimed involuntarily as he lowered Pavel Petrovich to the grass. "Let's see what all this is about." He took out a handkerchief, wiped off the blood and palpated the region of the wound. "The bone hasn't been touched," he was muttering through his teeth. "The bullet passed through, without any deep penetration; only one muscle, the vastus externus, was grazed. He can be doing a jig in three weeks! Yet he fainted! Oh, but these nervous people annoy me! See how thin-skinned he is!"

"Is he killed, sir?" Peter's voice quavered behind Bazarov, sounding more like rustling leaves than a human voice.

Bazarov looked behind him. "Go get some water quick as you can, brother. As for him, he'll outlive both of us yet."

The perfect servant did not seem to understand him and did not stir from the spot. Pavel Petrovich slowly opened his eyes. "He's passing away!" Peter whispered and fell to crossing himself.

"You're right . . . what an imbecilic physiognomy!" the wounded gentleman managed to say with a forced smile.

"Well, go for the water, you devil!" Bazarov shouted.

"It isn't necessary . . . it was just a momentary *vertige*. Help me to sit up—there, that's it. All this scratch requires is something to bind it and I'll reach home on foot—or else a droshky can be sent for me. The duel, if that is satisfactory to you, won't be renewed. You acted nobly . . . today—today, mind you."

"No need of raking up the past," Bazarov retorted, "and as far as the future is concerned, it doesn't pay to rack one's head about it either, inasmuch as it is my intention to make tracks out of here without losing any time. Here, let me: I'll bandage your leg now; your wound isn't dangerous, but it's always best to stop the bleeding. But first it is necessary to bring this mortal back to his senses."

Bazarov shook Peter by the collar and sent him off for a droshky.

"Watch out—don't frighten my brother," Kirsanov told him. "Don't even think of telling him a thing."

Peter dashed off, and while he was running for a droshky the two adversaries sat on the ground and maintained silence. Pavel Petrovich tried to avoid looking at Bazarov; after all, he did not want any reconciliation with him; he felt ashamed of his arrogance, of his fiasco as a duellist, ashamed of this whole affair which he had contrived, even though he also felt that it could not have wound up in a more favorable manner. At least he won't be sticking around here, he reassured himself, and that's something to be thankful for. The silence, depressing and awkward, became prolonged. Both felt badly; each was aware that the other understood him. Such an awareness is a pleasant thing for those who are friends and a quite unpleasant one for those who are not, especially when it is impossible

216

either to come to an understanding or to go off in different directions.

"Have I bandaged your leg too tightly, perhaps?" Bazarov asked at last.

"No, not at all—it's fine," the other answered and, a little later, added: "One can't fool my brother; we'll have to tell him we had a blowup over politics."

"Very good," Bazarov concurred. "You can say that I was villifying all Anglomaniacs."

"That will do splendidly. What do you suppose that man is thinking about us now?" he continued, indicating the same mouzhik who had driven the hobbled horses past Bazarov a few minutes before the duel and who at this point, coming back along the road, inclined his head in deference and doffed his cap on catching sight of the "masters."

"Who could possibly tell!" Bazarov responded. "Most probably he's not thinking a thing. The Russian tiller of the soil is that same Mysterious Stranger whom Mistress Radcliffe used to mention so often once upon a time. Who will ever understand him? He doesn't understand his own self!"

"Ah, so that's what you think!" Kirsanov began, and then suddenly exclaimed: "Just see what a mess your dolt of a Peter has cooked up! Why, that's my brother himself galloping this way!"

Bazarov turned around and saw the ashen face of Nicholai Petrovich, who was seated in the droshky. He jumped out of it before it stopped and dashed toward his brother.

"What's the meaning of this?" he asked in an agitated voice. "What's all this, Evgenii Vassil'ich, for heaven's sake?"

"It's nothing," his brother answered. "There was no

need for upsetting you. M'sieu' Bazarov and I had a bit of an argument and I had to pay a trifle for it."

"But just what brought the whole thing on, for God's sake?"

"How should I explain it to you? M'sieu' Bazarov voiced certain disrespectful comments concerning Sir Robert Peel. I hasten to add that I am the only one at fault in this matter, while M'sieu' Bazarov behaved most decently. It was I who challenged him."

"But, good heavens, you've got blood all over you!"

"Why, did you suppose I have water in my veins? However, this bloodletting is actually of benefit to me. Isn't that so, Doctor? Help me to get into the droshky and don't yield to melancholy. I'll be all well tomorrow. There, that's fine. Get going, driver."

Nicholai Petrovich started off on foot after the droshky. "I must beg you to attend to my brother," he said to Bazarov, who had attempted to stay behind, "until we bring another doctor from town." Bazarov inclined his head in silence.

An hour later Pavel Kirsanov was already lying in bed, his leg skillfully bandaged. The whole house was thrown into turmoil; Phenechka had been overcome and did not feel well. Nicholai Petrovich kept wringing his hands whenever nobody was looking, but Pavel laughed and joked, particularly with Bazarov; he had put on a shirt of fine cambric, a dandified short morning jacket and a fez, would not allow the blinds to be lowered, and complained whimsically about the necessity of abstaining from food.

Toward night, however, he turned feverish; his head began to ache. The doctor from town showed up. (Nicholai Petrovich had not heeded his brother, and Bazarov himself had desired another medical man to be

218

called in. Bazarov sat the whole day in his room, all jaundiced and surly, and dropped in on the patient for only the briefest of visits; Phenechka he had encountered twice, by chance, but she had sprung away from him in terror.) The new doctor advised cooling drinks; otherwise, however, he confirmed Bazarov's assurances that no danger whatsoever was to be apprehended. Nicholai Petrovich told him that his brother had wounded himself accidentally, to which the doctor responded with a "Hm!" But, on receiving twenty-five roubles in silver, slipped into his hand right then and there, he delivered himself of the opinion: "Do say! Such accidents are of frequent occurrence, and that's a fact."

No one in the house went to bed or even undressed. Nicholai Petrovich kept tiptoeing into his brother's room and tiptoeing out of it; Pavel dozed off from time to time, moaned a little, advised Nicholai: *"Couchez-vous,"* as if his brother could lie down, and asked for drink. Nicholai Petrovich made Phenechka bring a glass of lemonade to the wounded man; Pavel gave her an intense look and drained the glass. Toward morning his fever increased a little; he became slightly delirious. At first Pavel's words were incoherent; then he suddenly opened his eyes and, on seeing his brother by his bedside, bending over him in anxiety, he uttered: "Phenechka does have something about her in common with Nellie, Nicholai—isn't that so?"

"What Nellie, dear Pavel?"

"How can you ask that? Princess R—— . . . Particularly about the upper part of the face. *C'est de la même famille*—there's something akin there."

Nicholai Petrovich made no reply, but wondered to himself about the tenacity of old emotions in man.

Just see when it has come to the surface! he reflected.

"Ah, how I love this insignificant being!" Pavel Petrovich uttered with a moan, clasping his hands behind his head in despondence. "I won't tolerate any insolent fellow touching . . ." He was babbling a few seconds later.

His brother merely sighed; he had not even a suspicion of whom these words referred to.

Bazarov came to him the next day, about eight in the morning. He had already managed to pack his things and to liberate all his frogs, insects, and birds.

"You have come to say goodbye to me?" Nicholai Petrovich asked, rising to greet him.

"Exactly, sir."

"I understand you, and you have my full approval. My poor brother is to blame, of course—that's precisely why he has been chastised. He told me that he placed you in a position where you could not have acted otherwise. I believe that you could not have avoided this encounter which—which is explained to a certain extent by the antagonism of your mutual views." Nicholai Petrovich was becoming entangled in words. "My brother belongs to the old school; he is hot-tempered and stubborn. Thank God this affair has ended just as it has. I have taken all the needed measures to avoid talk—"

"I am leaving you my address, in the event of there being any trouble," Bazarov remarked casually.

"I hope there won't be any, Evgenii Vassil'ich. I regret exceedingly that your stay in my house should have had such—such an ending. This saddens me all the more since Arcadii—"

"I'll probably be seeing him," interrupted Bazarov, in whom every sort of "explanation" and "protestation" always aroused a feeling of impatience. "In case I fail to see him, I beg of you to give him my regards and ask him to accept this assurance of my regret."

"And I in my turn beg of you—" Nicholai Petrovich responded with a bow, but Bazarov did not wait for the conclusion of his sentence and left the room.

On learning of Bazarov's departure Pavel Petrovich expressed a desire to see him and shook hands with him. But even in this instance Bazarov remained as cold as ice, realizing that Pavel Kirsanov wanted to have a fling at magnanimity. As for Phenechka, Bazarov had no luck in trying to tell her goodbye: he merely exchanged glances with her through a window. It struck him that her face looked sad. She'll come to grief, likely as not! said he to himself. Still, she may pull through somehow! Peter, however, was so overcome by emotion that he wept on Bazarov's shoulder, until he cooled him off with the question: "Why the waterworks?" As for Dunyasha, she found it necessary to take to the woods to hide her agitation.

The culprit of all this woe clambered into a cart, lit a cigar and, on reaching a turn in the road after a couple of miles, where the Kirsanov estate with its new manor house spread out before his eyes in a straight line, he merely spat aside and, after muttering "The damned petty squires!" wrapped himself closer in his long overcoat.

Pavel Petrovich improved in a short while; however, he had to be confined to bed for about a week. He endured his *captivity,* as he put it, quite patiently; the only thing was, he fussed too much about his clothes and ordered everything to be deodorized with eau de Cologne. Nicholai Petrovich read periodicals to him;

Phenechka waited on him as before, bringing him bouillon, lemonade, soft-boiled eggs, but a secret horror took possession of her each time she came into his room. Pavel Petrovich's unexpected action had thrown a scare into everybody in the house, but Phenechka had been scared more than all the others; Procophich alone had not been daunted and explained that gentlefolks used to have their set-tos even in his time. "But only the nobly-born gentlemen amongst their own selves; as for any fly-by-nights like them there, however, they'd have ordered them to be flogged in the stable for their impudence."

Phenechka's conscience hardly reproached her, but the thought of the real cause of the contretemps did torment her from time to time; then, too, Pavel Petrovich eyed her so strangely that she felt his eyes upon her even when she had her back turned to him. She had lost weight from her constant inner turmoil and, as it usually happens, had become still more endearing.

One day (it happened in the morning) Pavel Petrovich was feeling fine and had shifted from his bed to the divan, while his brother, having inquired about his health, had left for the threshing barn. Phenechka had brought in a cup of tea and, having set it down on a small table, was about to leave. The invalid detained her.

"Where are you hurrying to, Theodosia Nicholaievna?" he began. "Why, are you busy?"

"No, sir . . . yes, sir . . . I have to pour the morning tea."

"Dunyasha will see to it without you; sit for a short while with the sick. Incidentally, I must have a little talk with you."

Phenechka, without a word, perched on the edge of an armchair.

"Listen," Pavel Petrovich resumed, and tugged at his mustache, "I've been wanting to ask you for a long while—you are afraid of me, it seems?"

"I, sir?"

"Yes, you. Your eyes always avoid me, as if you didn't have a clear conscience."

Phenechka reddened, but she looked at him. He struck her as acting strangely, somehow, and her heart began to throb gently.

"For your conscience is clear, isn't it?" he asked her.

"Why shouldn't it be?" she whispered.

"It could be anything! However, whom could you have wronged? Me? That's improbable. Any other persons in this house? That, too, isn't a thing likely to happen. Unless it's my brother, by chance? But then you love him, don't you?"

"I do."

"With all your soul, with all your heart?"

"I love Nicholai Petrovich with all my heart."

"Honestly? Look at me Phenechka." It was the first time he had called her thus. "It's a great sin to lie, you know!"

"I'm not lying, Pavel Petrovich. If I were to stop loving Nicholai Petrovich, why, I wouldn't want to go on living!"

"And you wouldn't give him up for any other?"

"Why, for whom could I give him up?"

"It could be anybody! Why, it might even be that gentleman who's gone now."

Phenechka stood up. "My Lord God—what are you torturing me for, Pavel Petrovich? What did I ever do to you? How could anybody say such things?"

"Phenechka," Pavel Petrovich uttered in a sorrowful voice, "why, I saw—"

"What did you see, sir?"

"Why, there . . . in the arbor—"

She turned all crimson—to her hair, to the tips of her ears. "But just how was I to blame for that?" she managed to say with difficulty.

Kirsanov sat up a little. "You weren't to blame? No? Not in the least?"

"Nicholai Petrovich is the only one in all the world whom I love, and I'll love him forever!" Phenechka uttered with sudden forcefulness, while sobs were simply straining at her throat. "As for what you saw, why, even on dread judgment day I'll say I'm not to blame and never was, and it would be better for me to die right now if anybody can suspect me of any such thing against my benefactor, Nicholai Petrovich—"

But here her voice failed her, and at the same time she felt Pavel Petrovich seize her hand and squeeze it. She glanced at him and was absolutely petrified. He had become even paler than before; his eyes were glittering and, what was most striking of all, a heavy, solitary tear was rolling down his cheek.

"Phenechka!" said he in a whisper that was somehow odd. "Love my brother—love him! Don't be untrue to him for anyone in the world—don't listen to anyone's speeches! Think—what could be more dreadful than to love and not be loved! Don't ever forsake my poor Nicholai!"

Phenechka's eyes dried and her fright passed, so great was her astonishment. But what were her feelings when Pavel Petrovich—Pavel Petrovich himself!— pressed her hand to his lips and clung to it thus, without kissing it and only sighing convulsively from time to time.

Good Lord! she reflected. Is he having a fit by any chance? Yet at that moment it was all of his perished life which was quivering within him.

The staircase started creaking under rapid footsteps. He thrust her from him and let his head drop back onto the pillow.

The door opened and Nicholai Petrovich appeared, cheerful, fresh and ruddy-cheeked. Mitya, in nothing but his little shift, as fresh and ruddy-cheeked as his father, was bouncing on his chest, his little bare feet catching on the big buttons of his father's rustic over-coat. Phenechka simply flung herself at Nicholai Petrovich and put her head on his shoulder, twining her arms around both him and her son. Nicholai Petrovich was surprised: never had the shy and modest Phene-chka caressed him while a third person was present.

"What's the matter with you?" he asked and, after a glance at his brother, handed Mitya over to her. "You aren't feeling worse?" he asked, approaching Pavel.

The latter buried his face in a cambric handkerchief. "No, not at all . . . everything's the same On the contrary, I feel considerably better."

"You really shouldn't have been in such a hurry about shifting to the divan. Where are you off to?" he added, turning around to Phenechka, but she had already slammed the door behind her. "I had brought my young hero along to show him to you—he's been missing his uncle. Why did she carry him away? However, what's the matter with you? Has anything happened between you, or what?"

"Brother!" Pavel Petrovich uttered with solemnity.

Nicholai Petrovich was startled. He felt uncanny, without himself understanding why.

"Brother," Pavel Petrovich repeated, "give me your word that you will carry out a single request of mine."

"What request? Tell me."

"It is a most important one; the entire happiness of your life, as I understand things, depends upon it. I've been devoting a great deal of thought all this while to what I want to tell you now. Brother, carry out your obligation, the obligation of an honest and noble-hearted man; put an end to the scandal and bad example you are setting—you, the best of men!"

"What are you trying to say, Pavel?"

"Marry Phenechka. She loves you; she is the mother of your son."

Nicholai took a step back and wrung his hands. "Is it you who say that, Pavel? You, whom I've always considered the most implacable foe of such marriages! Is it you who say that? But don't you know it was solely out of deference to you that I didn't carry out what you so justly called my obligation?"

"You were wrong in deferring to me in this instance," Pavel retorted with a despondent smile. "I'm beginning to think that Bazarov was right when he accused me of aristocratism. No, dear brother, it's time we gave up posturing and taking the world into account: we're old folks and resigned; it's time to lay aside all vanities. Let us, just as you say, start carrying out our obligations, and you'll see that we'll yet attain happiness in the bargain."

Nicholai rushed to embrace his brother. "You have opened my eyes fully!" he exclaimed. "I wasn't wrong in always maintaining that you're the kindest and wisest fellow in the world, and now I see that you are just as reasonable as you are magnanimous."

"Easy, easy," Pavel broke in on him. "Don't reopen the wound in the leg of your reasonable brother who, when he was crowding fifty, fought a duel as if he were an ensign. And so, this matter is settled: Phenechka is going to be my *belle-soeur,* my sister-in-law."

"My dear Pavel! But what will Arcadii say?"

"Arcadii? He'll go into raptures, if you please! Marriage goes against his principles, but to make up for that his sentiment of equality will be gratified. And truly, what castes can there be *aux dix-neuvième siècle?* This *is* the nineteenth century."

"Ah, Pavel, Pavel! Let me kiss you once more. Don't be afraid—I'll be careful." The brothers embraced.

"What do you think—shouldn't you let her know your intention right now?" asked Pavel.

"Why rush things?" Nicholai objected. "Why, have you had a talk about this?"

"A talk? *Quelle idée!*"

"Well, that's fine. Go ahead and get well, first of all; this thing won't run away. We've got to think it over thoroughly, take everything into consideration—"

"But you have decided, haven't you?"

"Of course I've decided, and I thank you with all my heart. I'll leave you now—you've got to rest; any excitement is bad for you. But we'll talk about it again. Sleep well, my soul, and God grant you health!"

"What's he thanking me for like that?" Pavel mused when he was left alone. "As if it didn't depend on him! As for me, as soon as he gets married I'll go away, as far as possible, to Dresden or to Florence, and will live there until I peg out like an animal."

Pavel Petrovich moistened his forehead with eau de Cologne and shut his eyes. Lit up by the bright light of day, his beautiful head, now grown gaunt, lay on the white pillow like the head of a dead man.

Yes, for he truly was a dead man.

25

At Nikolskoe, Katya and Arcadii were sitting in the garden on a turf seat in the shade of a towering ash tree; Fifi had disposed herself on the ground near them, her slender body having taken on that graceful curve which hunters call "the lie of the winter hare." Both Arcadii and Katya were silent; he was holding a half-opened book, while she was picking out of a basket the few crumbs of white bread remaining in it and tossing them to a small family of sparrows who, with that poltroonish impudence so characteristically theirs, were hopping and chirruping at her very feet. A faint breeze stirring among the leaves of the ash tree sent splotches of pale gold light wavering to and fro, over both the shady path and Fifi's tawny back; an even shade fell upon Arcadii and Katya, save that at infrequent intervals a vivid streak would flare up in the girl's hair. Both were silent, but it was precisely the way they kept silent, the way they sat side by side, which spoke of a trustful rapprochement: each seemed to be not even thinking of the one sitting so near, yet rejoicing in secret at the other's proximity. Their faces also had changed since we saw them last: Arcadii appeared more calm, Katya more animated, more spirited.

"Don't you find," Arcadii broke the silence, indicating the ash tree, "that the *yassen* is very aptly named in Russian? No other tree creates its traceries against the air so lightly, so radiantly [*yassno*]."

Katya raised her eyes and spoke a "Yes," while Arcadii reflected: There, this one doesn't reproach me for my "pretty talk."

"I have no love for Heine," Katya spoke up, indicating with her eyes the book Arcadii was holding, "either when he laughs or when he weeps; I like him when he's pensive and melancholy."

"But I like him when he laughs," Arcadii remarked.

"That's because of the persistent old traces of the satirical tendencies in you." ("Old traces!" Arcadii reflected. If Bazarov were to hear that!) "You just wait; we'll make you over."

"Who will?"

"My sister; Porphyrii Platonovich, our neighbor, with whom you no longer quarrel; Auntie, whom you escorted to church day before yesterday."

"But it was impossible for me to refuse! And as far as Anna Sergheievna is concerned, she herself, if you remember, agreed with Evgenii in many things."

"My sister was under his influence at that time, just as you were."

"Just as I was! Come, do you notice that I have freed myself of his influence by now?"

Katya let this pass in silence.

"I know," Arcadii continued, "that you never liked him."

"I can't form any judgment about him."

"Do you know what, Katerina Sergheievna? Each

time I hear that answer I disbelieve it. There isn't a person living whom every one of us couldn't form a judgment about! That's simply a lame excuse."

"Well, then, I'll tell you that he . . . it's not that I dislike him, but I feel that he is a stranger to me, just as I am a stranger to him . . . and you, too, are a stranger to him."

"Why is that?"

"How can I tell you? He's feral, while we are tamed."

"And am I tamed too?"

Katya nodded.

Arcadii scratched behind his ear. "Listen, Katerina Sergheievna—why, that really hurts."

"Come, would you wish to be feral?"

"No, not feral—but strong, energetic."

"Those aren't things one could merely wish for. Your friend, now, doesn't even wish for them, yet they're part of him."

"Hm! So it's your supposition that he had great influence on Anna Sergheievna?"

"Yes. But there's nobody can get the upper hand of her for any length of time," Katya added in an undertone.

"Why do you think that?"

"She's very proud—no, that's not what I wished to say: she sets very great store on her independence."

"What person doesn't set great store on independence?" asked Arcadii, yet at the same time the thought flashed through his mind: What's the good of it?—What's the good of it? flashed through Katya's mind as well. The very same thoughts are constantly occurring to young people who forgather frequently and are on friendly terms.

Arcadii smiled and, after edging a little closer to Katya, spoke in a whisper: "Own up—you are a trifle afraid of *her.*"

"Of whom?"

"Of *her,*" Arcadii repeated significantly.

"And what about you?" Katya countered.

"I am, too; mind you, I said: I am, *too.*"

Katya shook her finger at him. "That surprises me," she began. "My sister was never as well disposed toward you as precisely now—far more so than on your first visit."

"Well, now!"

"Come, didn't you notice it? Doesn't that make you happy?"

Arcadii became thoughtful. "In what way could I have merited Anna Sergheievna's good will? Was it possibly because I brought her your mother's letters?"

"Through that, for one, and there are other reasons which I shan't tell you."

"Why not?"

"I shan't tell you."

"Oh, I know that you're very stubborn."

"I am that."

"And observant."

Katya gave him a sidelong look. "Does that irk you, perhaps? What are you thinking of?"

"I am thinking how you could have come by this ability to observe, which you really do possess. You are so timorous, so mistrustful; you shy away from everybody—"

"I have lived a great deal by myself—whether one likes it or not, one becomes reflective. But then, do I really shy away from everybody?"

Arcadii glanced at her fleetingly and gratefully. "All

that is very well," he went on, "but people of your position—in your circumstances, that is—rarely possess this gift; truth has just as hard a time in reaching them as in reaching kings."

"But then, I'm not a rich woman."

He was dumfounded and did not immediately grasp her meaning. Why, true enough, the estate belongs entirely to her sister! it occurred to him; he found the thought not unpleasant. "How well you put that!" he remarked.

"Why, what was it?"

"You put it so well, so simply, without being ashamed and without posturing. By the way, I imagine there must always be something peculiar, a vanity of its own kind, about the way a person feels when he knows he is poor and says so."

"Because of my sister's kindness I haven't experienced anything of that sort; I mentioned my position only because it was apropos."

"Precisely; do confess, however, that you too have a particle of that vanity I was speaking of just now."

"For instance?"

"For instance, you—forgive my question—you wouldn't marry a rich man, would you?"

"If I loved him very much . . . no, I think I wouldn't marry him even then."

"Ah, you see!" Arcadii exclaimed and, after a brief pause, added: "And why wouldn't you marry him?"

"Because even folk songs warn us about unequal matches."

"You want to dominate, perhaps, or else—"

"Oh, no! Whatever for? On the contrary, I'm prepared to submit, except that inequality is hard to bear. As for respecting oneself and submitting, that's some·

thing I understand—it's happiness; but a submissive existence . . . no, there's plenty of that as it is."

"There is," Arcadii echoed her. "Yes, yes," he continued, "it's not in vain that you and your sister are of the same blood—you're every bit as self-reliant as she, but you're more secretive. You, I'm positive, would in no circumstances be the first to voice your feeling, no matter how powerful and holy it might be—"

"Why, how could it be otherwise?" asked Katya.

"Both of you are equally clever; you've just as much character as she, if not more—"

"Don't compare me with my sister, if you please," Katya hastily interrupted him, "that's far too disadvantageous to me. You apparently have forgotten that my sister is both a beauty and a clever woman. And . . . you in particular, Arcadii Nicholaievich, shouldn't be saying things like that, and with such a straight face, too."

"What's the meaning of that 'You in particular,' and what makes you conclude that I am joking?"

"Of course you are."

"Do you think so? But what if I'm convinced of what I say? What if I find that I actually haven't expressed myself in sufficiently strong terms?"

"I don't understand you."

"Really? Well, now I perceive that I surely have overestimated your power of observation."

"How?"

Arcadii made no reply and turned away; as for Katya, she managed to find a few more crumbs in the basket and began tossing them to the sparrows; but she swung her arm too vigorously and they flew off in too much of a hurry to peck at them.

"Katerina Sergheievna!" Arcadii burst forth. "This

233

may not matter to you, probably, yet I'd like you to know that I wouldn't exchange you not only for your sister but for anyone else in the world."

He stood up and hurried away, as if he had been frightened by the words which had escaped him. Katya, for her part, let her hands drop in her lap together with the basket, and for a long while her eyes followed Arcadii. Little by little a crimson tinge emerged ever so faintly on her cheeks, yet her lips were not smiling and the dark eyes bore an expression of perplexity and of some other emotion, as yet without a name.

"Are you alone?" Her sister's voice sounded close to her. "I thought you were with Arcadii when you started out for the garden."

Katya took her time in shifting her gaze to her sister (tastefully, even exquisitely dressed, she stood on the garden path and with the ferrule of her open parasol was making Fifi's ears twitch) and leisurely said, "I am alone."

"So I see," the other replied, laughing. "He's gone to his room, then?"

"Yes."

"Were you reading together?"

"Yes."

Anna took Katya by the chin and tilted up her face. "You haven't had a quarrel, I hope?"

"No," said Katya and quietly put her sister's hand aside.

"How solemnly you answer! I thought I'd find him here and suggest his coming along for a walk. He's always asking me to do so. They've brought you some shoes from town; go and try them on. I noticed just yesterday that your old ones are quite worn out. On

234

the whole, you don't pay enough attention to such things, and yet you have such adorable little feet. Your hands are pretty, too . . . except that they're large, so you must rely on your little feet. However, I know my sister is no coquette."

She resumed her walk along the path, with her beautiful dress slightly swishing; Katya got up from the seat and, taking Heine along, also walked off—but not to try on shoes.

"Adorable little feet!" she was thinking as she slowly and lightly went up the stone steps of the terrace, made almost incandescent by the sun. "Adorable little feet," you say. Well, he'll be lying at them. But she immediately felt ashamed and nimbly ran upstairs.

Arcadii had started going down the corridor to his room when the major-domo overtook him and informed him that Bazarov was waiting for him there.

"Evgenii!" Arcadii muttered, almost with apprehension. "Did he arrive a long time ago?"

"The gentleman came just this minute and insisted on not being announced to Anna Sergheievna, but wanted to be brought directly to you."

Could any misfortune have happened at home? the thought came to Arcadii and, dashing up the staircase, he flung his door open. The sight of Bazarov reassured him, although a more experienced eye would probably have discovered signs of an inner agitation about the shrunken figure of the unexpected caller, despite its appearing as energetic as ever. With a dusty overcoat over his shoulders and wearing a cap, he was sitting on a window sill, nor did he get up even when Arcadii threw himself on his neck with noisy exclamations.

"This is a surprise! What fates bring you here?"

Arcadii kept repeating, bustling about the room like a man who both imagines himself overjoyed and desires to demonstrate that he is. "For everything's in order at home, and everybody's well—isn't that so?"

"Everything's in order in your household, but not everybody is well," Bazarov told him. "Come, stop chattering and instead have some bread-cider brought up for me, then sit yourself down and listen to what I'm going to tell you in a few phrases—few, but I hope they'll be rather vigorous."

Arcadii quieted down and Bazarov told him about his duel with Pavel Kirsanov. Arcadii was exceedingly surprised and even downcast, but did not deem it necessary to show this; he merely asked whether his uncle's wound was really not dangerous and, on getting the reply that it was as interesting as it could be but not in a medical sense, he forced a smile, yet at heart he felt both disturbed and somehow ashamed. Bazarov apparently understood him.

"Yes, brother," he commented, "that's what it means to live with feudal lords for a spell. You turn into a feudal lord yourself and find yourself taking part in knightly tourneys. And so, my dear sir, I upped and set out 'to go to my fathers,'" Bazarov concluded. "And on the way I turned in here . . . I could say it was to inform you of all this, if it weren't that I consider a useless lie plain foolishness. No, I turned in here—well, the devil alone knows why I did. You see, it's a useful thing at times for a man to grab himself by his forelock and pluck himself out, like a radish out of its bed; that's the very thing I did the other day. . . . But I felt like taking one more look at what I had parted from—at the radish bed where I'd been planted."

"I hope these words do not apply to me," Arcadii

responded in agitation. "I hope you aren't thinking of parting from *me*."

Bazarov glanced at him intently, almost piercingly. "Would that really grieve you so much? The way it looks to me, *you* have already parted from *me* You're such a fresh and spic-and-span little fellow. Probably matters between you and Anna Sergheievna are getting along very well."

"What matters between me and Anna Sergheievna?"

"Why, wasn't it on her account you came here from town, my innocent fledgling? Incidentally, how are those Sunday schools doing? Come, aren't you in love with her? Or is it already time for you to play the modest hero?"

"Evgenii, you know that I've always been frank with you; I assure you—I swear to you most solemnly —that you're making a mistake."

"Hm! That has a new sound," Bazarov remarked in an undertone. "However, there's no need for you to get all steamed up for, after all, this doesn't matter to me in the least. A romantic would say, 'I feel that we are coming to a parting of our ways,' but I simply say that we're fed up with each other."

"Evgenii—"

"This, my soul, is no great evil; what won't people get fed up with in this world! And now, I think, shouldn't we say goodbye? From my first moment here I've been feeling ever so abominably, just as though I had crammed myself with Gogol's letters to the good lady of the Governor of Kaluga. By the way, I didn't tell them to unharness the horses."

"Really, this is impossible!"

"But why?"

"I'm not saying anything about myself, but it would

be discourteous to the last degree to Anna Sergheievna, who will inevitably wish to see you."

"Well, that's where you're making a mistake."

"On the contrary, I'm certain that I'm right," Arcadii retorted. "And what are you pretending for? If it comes to that, didn't you yourself come here on her account?"

"That may be true enough, but you're making a mistake just the same."

Arcadii was right, however. Anna Sergheievna did want to see him and sent him word to that effect by the major-domo. Bazarov changed his clothes before going to her: it turned out that he had packed his new suit in such a way that it was easy to get at.

Odintsova received him not in the room where he had so unexpectedly declared his love to her but in the drawing room. She held out the tips of her fingers to him amiably, but her face showed an involuntary tension.

"Anna Sergheievna," Bazarov made haste to say, "I must reassure you, first of all. Standing before you is a mortal who has long since come to his senses all by himself, and who hopes that others as well have forgotten his foolish actions. I'm going away for a long spell, and you will agree that even though I'm not a gentle creature, it would still be no cheerful matter for me to carry away the thought that you recall me with aversion."

She sighed deeply, like one who has just climbed a high mountain, and her face became animated by a smile. She held out her hand a second time to Bazarov and responded to his pressure.

"Let the past bury the past," said she, "all the more so since, speaking in all conscience, I too transgressed on that occasion, if not through coquetry then through something else. In a word, let's be the same friends we were. It was all a dream—isn't that so? And who ever remembers dreams?"

"Who does? Then, too, love—why, it's merely a superficial feeling."

"Is it, really? I'm most delighted to hear it."

Thus spoke Anna Sergheievna, and thus did Bazarov speak; they both thought they were telling the truth. Was the truth, the whole truth, to be found in their words? They themselves did not know this, and the author surely does not know either. But they struck up a conversation which sounded as if they had believed each other perfectly.

She asked him, among other things, what he had been doing at the Kirsanovs'. He was on the verge of telling her about his duel with Arcadii's uncle but restrained himself at the thought that she might think he was trying to make himself interesting and answered that he had been working all the while.

"As for me," Anna told him, "I was out of sorts at first, God knows why; I was actually getting ready to go abroad—imagine that! Then the fit passed; your friend Arcadii Nicholaievich came, and I fell into my rut again, into my real rôle."

"What rôle is that, if I may ask?"

"The rôle of aunt, preceptress, mother—call it whatever you wish. Incidentally, do you know that hitherto I had not understood your close friendship with Arcadii Nicholaievich really well? I considered him quite insignificant. But now I've gotten to know him better and have become convinced that he is clever. But mainly, he's young—young! Not like you and me, Evgenii Vassil'ich."

"Is he still as timid as ever in your presence?" asked Bazarov.

"Why, was he—" she began and, after a little thought, added: "He has become more trustful; he talks to me. Before that he avoided me. However, I didn't seek his society either. He and Katya are great friends."

Bazarov became irked. It's impossible for a woman not to be crafty! he reflected. "He used to avoid you, you say," he uttered with a chill smile. "But, probably, the fact that he was in love with you did not remain a secret to you?"

"What? He too?" escaped from Anna Sergheievna.

"He too," Bazarov repeated, with a resigned bow. "Is it possible that you were unaware of it and that what I have told you is something new?"

Anna Sergheievna lowered her eyes. "You are mistaken, Evgenii Vassil'ich."

"I don't think so. But perhaps I shouldn't have said anything about it." But don't try to be crafty with me in the future! he added to himself.

"Why not? Still, I think that in this instance, too, you are attaching too much significance to a momentary impression. I'm beginning to suspect that you're inclined to exaggeration."

"Let's better not talk about it, Anna Sergheievna."

"But why not?" she objected, yet she herself turned the conversation in a different direction. She was still ill at ease with Bazarov, even though she had told him, and had assured herself, that everything was utterly forgotten. Exchanging the simplest remarks with him, even being facetious with him, she felt a slight constraint of apprehension. Thus ship passengers at sea chat and laugh with never a care, for all the world as if they were on terra firma, but let the slightest hitch occur, let the slightest sign of anything out of the way appear, and at once there will emerge on all the faces an expression of a peculiar alarm, bearing witness to the constant consciousness of constant danger.

Her talk with Bazarov was not kept up long. She began lapsing into pensive spells, into answering absent-mindedly, and at last suggested that they go into the reception hall, where they found the princess and Katya. "But where is Arcadii Nichola'ich?" asked the hostess, and on learning that he had not been seen for more than an hour she sent for him. It took quite a while to find him: he had made his way into the very depths of the garden and, with chin propped up on clasped hands, was sitting there plunged in meditations. They were deep and weighty, those meditations, but not sad. He knew that Anna Sergheievna was closeted with Bazarov, and he experienced no jealousy, as he once had; on the contrary, his face was softly glowing; he seemed, all at the same time, to be wonder-struck by something, and rejoicing, and coming to some resolve.

26

The late Odintsov had had no love for innovations but
tolerated "a certain play of ennobled taste," and consequently had erected in his garden, between the hot-
house and the pond, a structure on the order of a
Greek portico—out of Russian brick. Along the blind
back wall of this portico, or gallery, six niches had
been inset for statues which Odintsov had intended to
order from abroad. These statues were to represent
Solitude, Silence, Meditation, Melancholy, Pudicity and
Sensibility. One of them, the goddess of Silence, holding a finger to her lips, had been delivered and installed, but that very same day some urchins had
knocked off her nose, and although a plasterer in the
neighborhood guaranteed to tack a new nose on her
"twice as good as the one she had before," Odintsov
had ordered her to be removed; and the goddess found
herself in a corner of the threshing barn, where she
stood for many long years, inspiring superstitious terror in the women of the village. The forepart of the
portico had long since become overgrown with dense
shrubbery: the capitals of the columns alone could be
seen over the unbroken greenery. Within the portico itself it was cool even at midday. Odintsova disliked
visiting this place ever since she had seen a grass snake
there, but Katya came there often to sit on the big
stone bench built under one of the niches. Here, amid
the coolness and shade, she would read, work, or yield
to that feeling of utter quietude, probably familiar to
everyone and the charm of which consists of a barely
conscious, mute lying-in-wait for the sweeping wave of

life that rolls ceaselessly both about us and within ourselves.

The day after Bazarov's arrival found Katya sitting on this favorite bench of hers, and Arcadii once more sitting by her side. He had persuaded her to accompany him to the portico.

There was still about an hour left before lunch; the dewy morning was already being supplanted by a sultry day. Arcadii's face bore the same expression as yesterday's; Katya had a preoccupied air. Her sister, immediately after morning tea, had called her into her study and, after a few preliminary caresses (something which always threw a little scare into Katya), had advised her to be more prudent in her conduct toward Arcadii, but especially to shun solitary talks with him, supposedly already noticed by both their aunt and the whole household. Besides that, Anna had been out of sorts ever since the evening before, while Katya herself had felt ill at ease, as if she were conscious of being at fault in some way. When she had yielded to Arcadii's plea she had told herself that this would be for the last time.

"Katerina Sergheievna," Arcadii began with a certain free-and-easy manner engendered by bashfulness, "ever since I've had the happiness of living in the same house with you, we have conversed about many things, and yet there is a certain . . . question which is of the utmost importance to me, but which I haven't yet touched upon. You remarked yesterday that I have been made over here," he added, both intercepting and avoiding the questioning gaze Katya had fixed upon him. "Actually, I have changed in many ways, and you know that better than anybody else—you to whom, properly speaking, I am indebted for this change."

"I? To me?" Katya managed to say.

"I am no longer the overbearing little boy I was when I came here," Arcadii continued. "I'm not over twenty-three in vain; as before, I wish to be useful, I wish to dedicate all my powers to truth; but I no longer seek my ideals where I once did; they present themselves to me . . . considerably closer. Up to now I had no understanding of myself, I set myself problems which were beyond my strength to solve. My eyes have been opened of late, owing to a certain emotion . . . I am not expressing myself quite clearly, but I hope you will understand me—"

Katya made no reply, but she took her gaze off Arcadii.

"I suppose," he began again, by now in a more agitated voice, while a chaffinch high among the leafage of a birch sang his carefree, full-throated song, "I suppose it is the duty of every honest man to be utterly frank with those who . . . with those persons who are . . . in a word, with those who are near to him, and therefore I . . . I intend—"

But at this point Arcadii's eloquence failed him; he went off the track, faltered, and was forced to fall silent for a brief spell. Katya still did not raise her eyes. Apparently she both failed to understand what he was leading up to with all this and was waiting for something.

"I anticipate that I shall surprise you," Arcadii resumed, having pulled himself together anew, "especially since this feeling in a certain way . . . in a certain way, you will notice . . . concerns you. Yesterday, I remember, you reproached me with lacking seriousness," he continued, with the air of a man who has strayed into a quagmire and feels that he is plunging in deeper with every step, but still hurries onward in the hope of getting across as quickly as possible. "That reproach is often aimed at . . . falls upon . . . young men, even when they cease to deserve it, and if I had more self-confidence—" (There, help me—do help me! Arcadii was thinking in despair but, just as before, Katya did not turn her head.) "If I could hope—"

"If I could but feel certain of what you say!" Anna's clear voice broke in on them at that instant.

Arcadii instantly fell silent, while Katya turned pale. A garden path ran right past the bushes that screened the portico. Anna was walking along it in the company of Bazarov. Katya and Arcadii could not see them, but they heard every word, the swish of Anna's dress, their very breathing. They took a few steps and, as if deliberately, halted just in front of the portico.

"There, you see," Anna continued, "you and I have made a mistake; both of us are no longer in our first youth—especially I; we have lived, we are tired; both of us—why be falsely modest—are clever; at first we aroused each other's interest, our curiosity was stirred . . . but afterward—"

"But afterward I became flat," Bazarov quickly interposed.

"You know that that was not the cause of our falling out. But be that as it may, we had no need of each other—that's the main thing; there was too much—how am I to put it—homogeneousness in us. We did not grasp this at once. Arcadii, on the other hand—"

"Have you any use for him?" asked Bazarov.

"There, now, Evgenii Vassil'ich! You say that he is

245

not indifferent to me, and it always seemed to me that he liked me. I know that I'm old enough to be his aunt, but I don't want to conceal from you that I've begun to think of him more often. There is a certain charm about such youthful, fresh emotion—"

"The word *fascination* comes closer to the mark in such cases," Bazarov broke in on her; one could detect seething gall in his calm though stifled voice. "Yesterday Arcadii was secretive with me for some reason and spoke neither of you nor of your sister. A grave symptom, that."

"He's altogether like a brother to Katya," she remarked, "and I like that about him, although, perhaps, I shouldn't have permitted such intimacy between them."

"Is that the . . . sister in you speaking?" Bazarov drawled out.

"Naturally . . . but why have we stopped? Let's walk on. What a peculiar conversation we're having, aren't we? And could I ever have expected that I would be talking to you like this? You know that I'm afraid of you, yet at the same time I trust you because essentially you are very kind."

"In the first place, I'm not at all kind, and in the second, I've lost all significance for you, and you tell me that I am kind. . . . Which is just the same as laying a wreath of flowers on a dead man's head."

"Evgenii Vassil'ich, we have no power over—" she began; but a gust of wind swooped down, swept through the leaves noisily and bore her words away.

"After all, you are free," Bazarov declared a little later.

Nothing more could be made out; their steps receded . . . everything was stilled.

Arcadii turned to Katya. She was sitting in the same position, except that she had bowed her head still lower.

"Katerina Sergheievna," he uttered in a tremulous voice and with his hands clasped hard, "I love you for all time and irrevocably, and I love no one but you. I wanted to tell you this, to learn your opinion of me and to ask for your hand, because, while I am not rich, I feel that I am ready to make all sacrifices. . . . You do not answer? You do not believe me? You think that I am talking frivolously? Recall these last days, then! Is it possible that you haven't long since convinced yourself—do understand me!—that everything else, absolutely everything, has long since vanished without a trace? Look at me, say but one word to me! I love . . . I love you—do believe me!"

She looked at him, and her look was clear and grave, and after long thought, barely smiling, she replied: "Yes."

He leapt up from the bench: "Yes! You said *yes*, Katerina Sergheievna! What does that word mean? That I love you, that you believe me? Or . . . or . . . I dare not finish—"

"Yes," Katya repeated, and this time he understood her. He seized her large, beautiful hands and, gasping with rapture, pressed them to his heart. He could scarcely stand on his feet and merely kept repeating: "Katya, Katya—" while she, somehow guilelessly, burst into tears, while she herself laughed gently at her own tears. He who has never beheld such tears in the eyes of a beloved being has never yet experienced the degree of happiness man can attain on earth, even as he all but swoons from gratitude and shame.

Next day, early in the morning, Anna Sergheievna sent word to Bazarov to come to her study where, with a constrained laugh, she handed him a folded sheet of note paper. It was a letter from Arcadii; in it he asked for her sister's hand.

Bazarov quickly ran through the letter and controlled himself with an effort so as not to betray the feeling of malevolent joy which instantly flared up in his breast.

"So that's it," he declared. "And yet it seems that no further back than yesterday it was your supposition that he loved Katerina Sergheievna with a brother's love. Well, what do you intend to do now?"

"What would *you* advise me?" asked Anna Sergheievna, still laughing.

"Why, I suppose," Bazarov answered, laughing in his turn, although he was not feeling at all gay and did not feel like laughing any more than she did, "I suppose blessings are in order for the young people. It's a good match in all respects; Kirsanov is quite well off, he's his father's only son; then, too, his father is a kind-hearted fellow—he won't stand in his way."

Odintsova took a turn about the room. Her face alternated between flushing and paling. "Do you think so?" she asked. "Well, why not? I can see no obstacles. I'm glad for Katya's sake . . . and for the sake of Arcadii Nichola'ich. Naturally, I'll wait for his father's answer. I'll send him to see his father in person. Still, it turns out that I was right yesterday when I told you that we were both old folks by now. . . . How is it I didn't see a thing? That's what amazes me!" She again broke into laughter, and turned her face away.

"The young people of today have become very foxy," Bazarov remarked, and laughed in his turn.

248

"Goodbye," he spoke again after a brief silence. "You have my wishes for bringing this matter to a most pleasant conclusion; as for me, I'll rejoice from afar."

Odintsova turned to him quickly. "Why, are you going away? Why shouldn't you stay *now?* Do stay . . . talking with you is exhilarating—just as if one were walking along the edge of a precipice. At first it feels scary, but then one picks up courage, without knowing whence it comes. Do stay."

"Thank you for the suggestion, Anna Sergheievna, and for your flattering opinion of my talents as a conversationalist. However, I find that I have been moving too long as it is in a sphere that is not my own. Flying fish can stay in the air for a certain length of time, but they must shortly plop back into the water; allow me, too, to plump back into my element."

Odintsova looked at Bazarov. A bitter smile was making his face twitch. This man loved me! she reflected—and she felt pity for him and held out her hand to him in commiseration.

But he also understood her. "No!" he said, and took a step back. "I'm a poor man, but I've never taken alms up to now. Goodbye, ma'am, and may all be well with you."

"I'm convinced this is not the last time we'll see each other," Anna Sergheievna declared with an involuntary gesture.

"Anything can happen in this world!" answered Bazarov, bowed and walked out.

"So you've gotten a notion of building a nest for yourself?" Bazarov was saying to Arcadii the same day, squatting as he packed his suitcase. "Well, why not? It's a good thing. Only your foxiness was all for nothing. I expected you to go off in an altogether different direction. Or perhaps you yourself were bowled over?"

"Yes, I surely didn't expect this at the time we parted," Arcadii answered. "But why are you being foxy yourself and saying it's a good thing, just as if I didn't know your opinion of marriage?"

"Eh, my dear friend!" Bazarov spoke up. "The way you talk! You see what I'm doing: an empty space turned up in the suitcase, and so I'm filling it with hay. That's just how it is with the suitcase of life: it doesn't matter what you stuff it with, as long as there is no emptiness. Don't take offense, please: you probably remember the opinion I've always held concerning Katerina Sergheievna. Now and then a young lady will be considered clever simply because she sighs cleverly; but yours will stand up for herself, and will do it so well that she'll take you in hand also—but then, that's the way things should be." He slammed down the lid and got up from the floor. "And now I repeat to you in farewell, for there's no use deceiving ourselves: we're saying goodbye for all time, and you feel that yourself. You've acted sensibly; you're not made for our bitter, harsh, lonesome life. There's no daring, no malice in you, but there is a youthful valor and youthful cockiness—and that's no good in our business. Your sort—the gentry, that is—can never get beyond a genteel resignation or a genteel tempest in a teapot, and that's trifling stuff. You, for instance, don't go in for scrapping—yet it's you that imagine yourselves brave lads—whereas we're spoiling for a scrap. But that's not all! Our dust would ruin your eyes, our mire would besmirch you, and besides you're not grown up enough for us; you can't help admiring yourself, you get satisfaction out of upbraiding yourself, whereas we're bored with such stuff—give us men of another stripe! We've got to smash others! You're a fine fellow, but just the same you're a namby-pamby liberal squireling—*et volatoo,* as my progenitor puts it."

"You're saying goodbye to me for all time?" Arcadii uttered plaintively. "And you've nothing else to say to me?"

Bazarov scratched the back of his neck. "I have, Arcadii, I do have other things to say to you, only I'm not going to say them, because that would be romantic stuff—it means turning syrupy. As for you, you just get married, fast as you can, and feather a nest that will be all your own, and make as many babies as possible. They're bound to be clever little things, if only because they'll be born at the right time—which is something you and I failed to do. Aha, I see the horses are ready. Time to be going! I've said goodbye to everybody. . . . Well, what about it—should we embrace, maybe?"

Arcadii flung his arms about the neck of his erstwhile preceptor and friend, and his tears simply spurted.

"That's what it means to be young!" Bazarov declared calmly. "However, I have hopes for Katerina Sergheievna. You'll see how fast she'll console you!"

"Goodbye, brother," he said to Arcadii, after clambering into a cart, and, having pointed to a pair of daws perched side by side on the roof of a stable, added: "There's something for you! Let that be an object lesson to you!"

"What does that mean?" asked Arcadii.

"What? Are you so poor in natural history, or have you forgotten? Why, the daw is the most respectable

251

and family-loving of birds. A model for you! Goodbye, signor!"

The cart began to clatter and rolled off.

Bazarov had spoken the truth. As he talked that evening with Katya, Arcadii forgot all about his preceptor. He was already making a start at submitting to her, and Katya felt this and was not surprised. He would have to go to Maryino the next day to see his father. Anna did not want to embarrass the young couple and only for the sake of propriety would not leave them alone for too long. She magnanimously insulated them against the princess, who had been thrown into a lachrymose frenzy by the news of the impending marriage. In the beginning Odintsova had been afraid that the sight of their happiness might seem a trifle onerous to her, but things turned out altogether differently: the sight not only was not onerous, it engrossed her, in the end it even touched her. She was both gladdened and saddened thereby. Evidently Bazarov was right, it occurred to her. Curiosity, curiosity alone, and love of ease, and egoism—"Children," she said loudly, "what do you think—is love a superficial feeling?"

But neither Katya nor Arcadii even understood her. They fought shy of her; the talk they had involuntarily overheard would not leave their minds. However, Anna soon calmed them down—nor had this been difficult for her: she calmed down herself.

27

The old Bazarov couple was all the more overjoyed by Evgenii's sudden arrival since they had least expected it. Arina Vlassievna became so flustered and kept running all through the house so much that Vassilii Ivanovich likened her to a "hen partridge": the bobtail of her short little blouse really did add something ornithic to her appearance. As for himself, he merely made lowing sounds and kept biting hard on the amber mouthpiece of the long pipe in a corner of his mouth, or, putting his fingers up to his neck, would twist his head, just as if he were testing it to see if it were properly screwed on, and, suddenly opening his wide mouth, would go off into paroxysms of perfectly silent laughter.

"I've come to stay with you for all of six months, old-timer," Bazarov told him. "I want to work, so don't you hinder me, please."

"You'll forget what my physiognomy looks like, that's how little I'll hinder you!" Vassilii Ivanovich told him.

He kept his promise. Having installed his son as before in his study, he all but hid himself from him and restrained his wife from any excessive effusions of tenderness. "You and I, mother of mine," he told her, "pestered our little Gene a trifle on his first visit. We've got to act a bit smarter this time." Arina Vlassievna agreed with her husband, yet she came out but little ahead of the game, since she saw her son only at meals and was now absolutely afraid to address him. "Little Gene," she would occasionally say but, before he had a chance to turn around, there she was, fidgeting with the strings of her reticule and babbling: "Never mind, never mind—it wasn't anything in particular." But later on, having recovered, she would betake herself to Vassilii Ivanovich and, propping up her cheek, say to him: "If I could only find out, darling, what little Gene would like for dinner today—cabbage soup or borshch?" "But why didn't you ask him yourself?" "Why, I'd be pestering him!"

However, Bazarov himself shortly stopped locking himself in: the fever for work *bounced off* him and was replaced by a languishing ennui and dull restlessness. A peculiar fatigue could be noted in all his movements; even his walk, firm and impetuously bold, had undergone a change. He gave up his solitary strolls and began to seek company; he drank tea in the drawing room, wandered about the vegetable garden with his father and, "keeping mum," smoked with him; on one occasion he inquired about Father Alexei.

At first his father rejoiced at this change, but his joy did not last long. "Gene is breaking my heart," he complained in confidence to his wife. "It's not that he's dissatisfied or angry—that wouldn't matter so much; he's been hurt, he's grieving—and that's horrible. He never says anything; it would be better if he scolded us! He's losing weight, the color of his face is so bad."

"Lord, Lord!" the little old woman whispered. "I'd like to put a blessed amulet about his neck, but of course he wouldn't allow it."

The old doctor made several attempts to question his son in the most circumspect manner about his work, about his health, about Arcadii. But Bazarov answered unwillingly and offhandedly, and on one occasion, having perceived that his father was little by little trying to lead up to something in his conversation, he said to him with vexation: "How is it you seem to be tiptoeing around me all the time? That's even worse than the way you carried on before."

"There, there, there—I didn't mean anything!" poor Vassilii Ivanovich hastened to answer.

His political hints remained just as fruitless. During one of their talks he had hopes of arousing his son's sympathy by broaching such subjects as the imminent emancipation of the peasants and progress, but the other responded apathetically: "I was going past a fence yesterday and I heard some of the local peasant boys, but instead of singing some old song they were bawling the latest cheap hit: 'Now the faithful time is coming, the heart feels it is in love.' Well, there's your progress."

At times Bazarov went off to the village and, in his usual bantering tone, would enter into talk with some mouzhik. "There, little brother," he would say to the mouzhik, "expound your views on life to me, for they are saying that all of Russia's strength and future lies in you, that you will launch a new epoch in history, will give us an authentic language as well as laws." The mouzhik would either not answer him at all, or would utter such gems as "Why, we can, lief as not . . . also, on account of, seeing as how . . . depending on whatever our limit has been set at, sort of."

"Suppose you make it clear to me what sort of a thing your *mir* is," Bazarov interrupted him, "and if it's the very same *mir** that rests on three fishes?"

"It's the earth, father of mine, that rests on three

* Bazarov is punning on two of the meanings of this word: *communal council* and *universe*.

fishes," the mouzhik would explain to him soothingly, with a patriarchally good-natured canorousness, "but as against our *mir,* now, as everybody knows, there's the will of the masters, seeing as how you are our fathers. But the stricter the master's demands the more the mouzhik loves it."

After listening to the end of such a speech one day Bazarov shrugged disdainfully and turned away, while the mouzhik ambled onward about his own affairs.

"What was he talking about?" he was questioned by another mouzhik, middle-aged and of glum appearance, who had been following the other's conversation with Bazarov from a distance, standing on the threshold of his hut. "About arrears, or what?"

"It weren't about no arrears, brother of mine!" answered the first mouzhik, and this time there wasn't even a trace of patriarchal canorousness about his voice—on the contrary, one could hear a certain minimizing gruffness in it: "He was just yammering away about something or other; must have felt like chewing the fat awhile. You know how it is; he's a gentleman— would he be likely to understand anything?"

"How could he!" answered the other mouzhik and, tossing back their hats and pushing down their belts, they settled down to discussing their own affairs and needs. Alas! The disdainfully shrugging Bazarov, the Bazarov who knew how to talk with mouzhiks (as he had boasted while disputing with Pavel Kirsanov), this self-assured Bazarov did not as much as suspect that in their eyes he was, after all, something in the nature of a tomfool.

However, he found an occupation for himself at last. Once, while he was present, Vassilii Ivanovich was bandaging a mouzhik's wounded leg, but the old man's hands were trembling and he could not manage the bandages; his son came to his assistance and from then on began to take part in his practice, at the same time without desisting from poking fun both at the remedies which he himself suggested and at his father, who immediately availed himself of them. But Bazarov's jeers did not at all perturb Vassilii Ivanovich —they even consoled him. Keeping his greasy dressing gown together with two fingers against his stomach and puffing away at his pipe, he listened with delight to his son, and the more rancor there was in the latter's outbursts, the more good-naturedly did his happy father laugh, exposing every last one of his black teeth. He even used to repeat these outbursts, which occasionally were dull or pointless, and (to give an instance) for several days in a row kept on saying over and over, without rhyme or reason: "It's no great shakes!" merely because his son, on finding out that he had gone to morning mass, had used that expression.

"Glory be to God! He has stopped moping!" he whispered to his wife. "What a going-over he gave me today—it was marvelous!" At the same time the thought of his having such an assistant threw him into rapture, filled him with pride. "Yes, yes!" he would say to some country wife in a man's thick overcoat and a headdress with points like horns, as he put into her hands a vial of Goulard's Solution or a jar of white ointment. "You ought to be thanking God every minute, dear woman, because my son is staying with me; you're now being treated according to the most scientific and latest method—do you understand that? Napoleon, the emperor of the French—well, even he hasn't a better doctor." But the country wife, who had come to complain that her "innards felt all-overish" (the meaning of which, however, she had been unable to explain herself), merely kept on bowing and reaching into her bosom, where she had four eggs tied up in a corner of a towel, by way of a fee.

Bazarov even had occasion to pull a tooth for a passing dry-goods peddler, and though this tooth was nothing out of the ordinary Vassilii Ivanovich nevertheless saved it as a rare specimen and, as he exhibited it to Father Alexei, kept ceaselessly repeating: "You just take a look at those roots! What strength Evgenii has! The peddler simply rose up in the air. . . . It seems to me that even if it had been an oak it would have popped out!"

"That is praiseworthy!" Father Alexei declared at last, not knowing what answer to make and how to get away from the ecstatic old man.

One day a drab little mouzhik from a neighboring village came in a cart, bringing to Vassilii Ivanovich his brother, who was ill with typhus. Lying face down on a truss of straw, the unfortunate fellow was dying; his body was covered with dark splotches; he had lost consciousness long ago. The old doctor voiced his regret that no one had thought of turning to medical aid earlier and declared that the man could not be saved. And, true enough, the little mouzhik did not get his brother home alive: he died in the cart after all.

Three days later Bazarov came into his father's room and asked him if he had any lunar caustic.

"Yes; what do you want it for?"

"To cauterize a cut."

"For whom?"

"For myself."

"What do you mean, yourself! What's all this about? What kind of a cut is it? Where is it?"

"Right here, on my finger. I rode over to the village today—you know, the one they brought that mouzhik with typhus from. For some reason or other they were getting ready to do an autopsy on him, and it's been a long time since I've had any practice of that sort."

"Well?"

"Well, so I made a request to the district doctor. Well, then, I happened to cut myself."

Vassilii Ivanovich suddenly turned all white and, without saying a word, dashed to his study, from which he returned at once with a bit of lunar caustic in his hand. Bazarov was about to take it and leave.

"For God's own sake," said the father, "let me attend to this myself."

Bazarov smiled a little. "How eager you are for practice!"

"Don't joke about it, please. Let me see your finger. The cut isn't so extensive. Does that hurt?"

"Press harder; don't be afraid."

Vassilii Ivanovich desisted. "What's your opinion, Evgenii—wouldn't it be better if we cauterized it with a hot iron?"

"That should have been done earlier; but now, if you come right down to it, even the lunar caustic is useless. If I've been infected it's too late now."

"What do you mean . . . too late—" the father could barely articulate.

"I should say so! It's four hours and more since it happened."

Vassilii Ivanovich cauterized the cut a little more. "Why, didn't the district doctor have any lunar caustic?"

"He didn't."

"My God, how could that be? A doctor—and he doesn't have such an indispensable thing?"

"You ought to take a look at his lancets," Bazarov remarked and walked out.

Until the very evening and all through the following day the father grasped at all possible excuses to drop in on his son, and though he not only avoided any mention of the cut and even tried to talk on the most irrelevant subjects, he nevertheless peered so insistently into his eyes and observed him with such trepidation that Bazarov lost patience and threatened to leave. Vassilii Ivanovich gave him his word that he would not worry, all the more readily since Arina Vlassievna (from whom, naturally, he had kept all this a secret) was beginning to pester her husband as to why he couldn't sleep, and what had come over him. For all of two days he restrained himself, even though he didn't like the looks of his son, whom he kept eyeing by stealth. On the third day, however, while they were at dinner, he could stand it no longer. Bazarov was sitting with his eyes cast down and would not touch a single dish.

"Why don't you eat, Evgenii?" asked the father, putting on a most carefree expression. "The food seems to be tastily prepared."

"I don't feel like it, and so I'm not eating."

"Have you no appetite? And what about your head?" he added in a hesitant voice. "Does it ache?"

"It does. And why shouldn't it?"

The mother straightened up and became all ears.

"Please don't get angry, Evgenii," Vassilii Ivanovich went on, "but won't you let me feel your pulse?"

Bazarov half rose. "Even without feeling my pulse I can tell you I'm running a high temperature."

"And did you have chills?"

"Yes, I've had chills too. I'll go and lie down, and you can send me some linden tea. I must have caught a cold."

"No wonder I heard you coughing last night," Arina Vlassievna remarked.

"I've caught a cold," Bazarov repeated and withdrew.

The mother busied herself with preparing the linden-flower tea, while the father went into an adjoining room and clutched his hair in silence.

Bazarov did not get up again that day and passed the whole night in heavy, semiconscious dozing. About one in the morning, having opened his eyes with an effort, he saw by the light of the image-lamp his father's pale face bent over him, and he told him to leave; the latter submitted but immediately returned on tiptoe and, half-screened by the door of a closet, watched his son without taking his eyes off him. The mother did not go to bed either and, opening the study door just the tiniest crack, kept constantly coming up to it to listen how "little Gene was breathing," and to have a look at Vassilii Ivanovich. All she could see was his motion-less, bowed back, but even that afforded her a certain relief.

In the morning Bazarov made an attempt to get out of bed; his head became dizzy, his nose bled; he lay down again. Vassilii Ivanovich tended him in silence; Arina Vlassievna came into his room and asked him how he felt. "Better," he answered—and turned to the wall. Vassilii Ivanovich shooed his wife away with both hands; she bit her lips so as not to cry and went out.

Everything in the house suddenly seemed to darken; all faces became drawn; a strange hush prevailed; some loud-throated rooster was taken out of the yard and carried off to the village, long unable to grasp why they were doing this to him. Bazarov was still lying with his face close to the wall. Vassilii Ivanovich tried to put various questions to him, but they tired Bazarov and the old man huddled motionlessly in his armchair, merely cracking his knuckles at rare intervals. He would go out for a few moments into the garden, stand there like a graven image, as if overwhelmed by ineffable bewilderment (the expression of bewilderment never left his face throughout), and then go back again to his son, trying to evade his wife's questionings. She caught him by the arm at last and convulsively, almost threateningly, spoke to him: "Come, what's wrong with him?" Thereupon he came to and forced himself to smile in reply to her, but to his own horror, instead of a smile laughter welled up from somewhere within him.

He had sent for a doctor at daybreak. He had deemed it necessary to warn his son of this, to avoid any chance of angering him.

Bazarov suddenly turned on the divan, looked dully at his father and asked for a drink. Vassilii Ivanovich gave him some water and took advantage of the opportunity to feel his son's forehead. It was simply on fire.

"Old-timer," Bazarov began in a hoarse, slow voice, "my goose is cooked; I've been infected and in a few days you'll be burying me."

Vassilii Ivanovich rocked on his heels, as if someone had struck at his legs. "Evgenii!" he babbled. "What are you saying! God be with you! You've caught a cold—"

"That'll do!" Bazarov broke in on him, speaking slowly. "It's not permissible for a doctor to talk like that. All the symptoms of infection are present—you know that yourself."

"Where are those symptoms of . . . infection, Evgenii? Do be reasonable!"

"And what do you call this?" Bazarov asked and. pulling up the sleeve of his nightshirt, he showed his father the ominous red splotches that had erupted on his skin.

A shudder ran through the old man and he turned chill with terror. "Let's suppose," he spoke at last, "let's suppose . . . that if . . . that even if there is something in the nature of . . . an infection—"

"Of pyemia," his son prompted him.

"Well, yes—something in the nature of . . . epidemic—"

"Pyemia," Bazarov repeated sternly and distinctly. "Or have you forgotten your notebooks?"

"Well, yes, yes—have it your own way. But just the same we'll cure you!"

"Cure me, fiddlesticks! But that's not the point. I didn't expect I'd die so soon. This, to tell you the truth, is a most unpleasant happenstance. Both you and mother ought to avail yourselves now of your strong religious belief; here's your chance to put it to the test." He took another sip of water. "Well, there is one thing I want to ask of you—while my head is still under my control. Tomorrow, or the day after, my brain, as you know, will hand in its resignation. Even now I'm not altogether certain whether I'm expressing myself lucidly. As I was lying here it seemed to me all the time that there were red dogs running around me, while you made them point at me, as if I were a woodcock. Just as if I were drunk. Do you understand me clearly?"

"Please, Evgenii, you're talking absolutely properly."

"So much the better. You told me you sent for a doctor. You did that to cheer yourself up. Cheer me up, too: send as fast a messenger as you can find—"

"To Arcadii Nicholaievich—" the old man put in eagerly.

"Who's Arcadii Nicholaievich?" Bazarov uttered, as if in reflection. "Ah, yes, that fledgling! No, don't trouble him: he's gotten in amongst the daws now. No need of you wondering; this isn't delirium yet. You just send a messenger, fast, to Odintsova, Anna Serghei-evna; there's a lady by that name, with an estate in this vicinity. . . . You know about her?" Vassilii Ivanovich nodded. "Say Evgenii—Bazarov, that is—bade to send his greetings, and bade to say that he is dying. Will you carry that out?"

"I will. But is such a thing possible—that you should die—you, Evgenii . . . Judge for yourself! Where is justice, after that?"

"That's something I know nothing about; you just send that messenger, now."

"I'll send him this very minute, and I'll write a note myself."

"No, what for? Say that I bade to send my greetings; you don't need anything more. And now I'll go back to my dogs. A strange thing! I want to fix my thoughts on death, and nothing comes of it. I see some sort of a red blotch—and nothing more."

He turned ponderously to the wall again; as for his father, he walked out of the study and, having somehow

264

made his way to his wife's bedroom, simply slumped to his knees before the holy images.

"Pray, Arina—pray!" he moaned. "Our son is dying."

The doctor, that same district doctor who had not been able to find a piece of lunar caustic in his office, arrived and, after examining the patient, advised sticking to watchful waiting and, while he was at it, said a few words about the possibility of recovery.

"Have you ever chanced to see people in my condition *failing* to set out for the Elysian fields?" Bazarov asked him and, suddenly grabbing the leg of a heavy table standing near his divan, shook it and budged it from its place. "The strength, now—the strength is still all there," he muttered, "yet one must die! Take an old man: he at least has had time to break the habit of living, but I . . . Yes, go and try to renounce death. Death will renounce you—and that's that! Who's that weeping there?" he added, after a brief pause. "Mother? The poor thing! Whom is she going to feed now with her amazing borshch? And you, Vassilii Ivanych, are also turning on the waterworks, it looks like? Why, if Christianity is of no help to you, be a philosopher, a stoic or something! For you did boast you're a philosopher?"

"A fine philosopher I am!" Vassilii Ivanovich wailed, and the tears fairly dripped down his cheeks.

Bazarov worsened with every hour; the progress of the disease became rapid—something which usually occurs in surgical infections. He had not lost consciousness and understood what was being said to him; he was still putting up a fight.

"I don't want to rave," he whispered, clenching his fists. "What nonsense all this is!" And immediately he would say: "Well, take ten from eight—what's the remainder?"

Old Bazarov walked about like one demented, suggesting first one remedy, then another, and did nothing but keep covering his son's feet. "Try a cold pack . . . an emetic . . . mustard plasters on the stomach . . . bloodletting . . ." he kept saying with an effort. The doctor, whom he had entreated into remaining, yessed him, drenched the sick man with lemonade, and as for himself, requested now a pipeful of tobacco, now a "fortifying and warming tonic"—meaning vodka. Arina Vlassievna sat on a footstool near the door and only from time to time would she leave to pray. A few days before a small looking glass had slipped out of her hands and shattered, and this was something which she had always held to be an ill portent; Anphissushka herself could say nothing to comfort her. Timotheich set out for Odintsova's place.

It was a bad night for Bazarov. He was tortured by a cruelly high temperature. Toward morning he felt easier. He asked his mother to comb his hair, kissed her hand, and took a couple of swallows of tea. Vassilii Ivanovich revived a little.

"Glory be to God!" he kept repeating. "The crisis came . . . the crisis is past."

"Think of that, will you!" Bazarov declared. "See what a word means! He found it, said 'crisis'—and is comforted. An amazing thing, the way man still believes in words. If people tell him he's a fool he'll get blue, even if they don't give him a beating; if they call him a clever fellow he'll feel gratified, even if they don't give him any money."

266

This little speech of Bazarov's, recalling his previous "outbursts," stirred his father's emotions. "Bravo! Excellently put—excellently!" he exclaimed, pretending to clap his hands.

Bazarov smiled sadly. "Well, just which is it, according to you?" he asked. "Is the crisis over, or has it come?"

"You're better—that's what I see, that's what makes me rejoice," the father answered him.

"Well, that's splendid; rejoicing is always not a bad idea. But what about sending someone to her—do you remember? Did you send anybody?"

"That I did—how else?"

The change for the better did not last long. The disease renewed its attacks. Vassilii Ivanovich was sitting near his son. Some particular anguish was apparently torturing the old man. Several times he was getting ready to speak—and could not.

"Evgenii," he uttered at last, "my son, my dear one, my beloved son!"

This unusual appeal had an effect on Bazarov. He turned his head a little and, visibly trying to struggle out from under the crushing weight of a coma, he asked: "What is it, my father?"

"Evgenii," Vassilii Ivanovich went on, and he sank to his knees before Bazarov, although the latter did not open his eyes and could not see him, "Evgenii, you're better now; God willing, you'll get well; but avail yourself of this time, comfort your mother and me—fulfill the duty of a Christian! Think how I must feel to be telling you this—it is dreadful; but it's still more dreadful . . . why, it's for all eternity, Evgenii . . . you just think what it's like—"

The old man's voice broke off, while something strange crept over his son's face, even though he still lay with his eyes closed.

"I am not refusing, if it can be of any comfort to you," he uttered at last, "but it seems to me there's no need for haste yet. You yourself say that I am better."

"You are better, Evgenii, you are, but who can tell —why, it's all as God wills, whereas, having fulfilled your duty—"

"No, I'll wait awhile," Bazarov broke in on him. "I agree with you that the crisis has come. But if you and I have guessed wrong—well, what of it! Why, they give the viaticum even to those who are unconscious."

"Evgenii, for mercy's sake—"

"I'll wait a while. But now I want to sleep. Don't disturb me." And he put his head back in its previous position.

The old man raised himself, sat down in the armchair and, holding his chin, fell to biting his fingers.

The noise of a carriage on springs, that noise which is so peculiarly noticeable amid a rustic quiet, suddenly struck upon his hearing. Nearer and nearer the light wheels came rolling; by now even the snorting of the horses could be heard. Vassilii Ivanovich sprang up and dashed over to the small window. A two-seated carriage, drawn by four horses harnessed abreast, was entering the courtyard of his small house. Without any pause for reflection, under the impulse of some senseless joy, he ran out on the front steps. A footman in livery was opening the doors of the carriage; a lady veiled in black, in a black mantilla, was stepping out of the carriage.

"I am Odintsova," she announced. "Is Evgenii Vassil'ich still living? You are his father? I have brought a doctor with me."

"My benefactress!" Vassilii Ivanovich cried out and, seizing her hand, convulsively pressed it to his lips, while the doctor whom Anna had brought, a manikin in spectacles, with a German physiognomy, was leisurely emerging from the carriage. "He's still living, my Evgenii is still living, and now he'll be saved! Wife, wife! An angel from heaven has come to us—"

"Lord, what's all this!" babbled the little old woman, running out of the parlor, and, unable to understand anything, she fell at the feet of Anna Sergheivna right there, in the entry, and began kissing her dress like a madwoman.

"What are you doing! What are you doing!" Anna kept saying, but the older woman would not heed her, while all that Vassilii Ivanovich could do was to repeat "Angel! Angel!"

"*Wo ist der Kranke?* And where iss it the patient iss?" the doctor spoke up at last, not without a certain degree of exasperation.

Vassilii Ivanovich remembered his manners. "Right this way, right this way, my most estimable colleague —please follow me, *werthester Herr Kollege,*" he added, dredging up whatever he could recall of his rusty knowledge of German.

"*Ach!*" the German exclaimed, baring his teeth in a sour grin.

Vassilii Ivanovich ushered him into the study. "The doctor from Anna Sergheievna Odintsova has arrived," said he, bending down to his son's very ear, "and she herself is here."

Bazarov suddenly opened his eyes. "What did you say?"

"I'm telling you that Anna Sergheievna Odintsova is here and has brought this medical gentleman to see you."

The sick man's eyes took in the scene about him. "She's here. . . . I want to see her."

"You shall see her, Evgenii; but first it is necessary to discuss things briefly with the doctor. I'll tell him the entire history of your illness, because Sidor Sidorich"— this was the name of the district doctor—"has left, and we'll hold a short consultation."

Bazarov glanced at the German. "Well, do your discussing quickly, only not in Latin; after all, I understand that *iam moritur* means . . . he's on his way out—"

"Der Herr scheint des Deutschen mächtig zu sein," began the newly-arrived foster-child of Aesculapius, turning to Vassilii Ivanovich.

"Ich habe . . . We'd better drop German," said the old man, who could hardly be said to have mastery of that language as attributed to him by the doctor.

"Ach, ach! Shoost so! Shoost as you blease—"

And the consultation began.

Half an hour later Anna, accompanied by Vassilii Ivanovich, came into the study. The German doctor had managed to inform her in a whisper that it was useless even to think of the patient's recovery.

She glanced at Bazarov—and halted near the door: to such an extent had she been struck by that enflamed and at the same time deathly face, with its turbid eyes directed upon her. She was starkly frightened with a certain chill and agonizing fright; the thought that she would have felt otherwise if she truly loved him flashed in an instant through her head.

"Thanks," he began to speak with an effort. "I did not expect this. This is a good deed. There, we have chanced to see each other again after all, just as you predicted."

"Anna Sergheievna has been kind enough—" old Bazarov began.

"Leave us, father. You will permit that, Anna Sergheievna? It would seem that now—" He indicated with his head his prostrate body, bereft of all its strength.

Vassilii Ivanovich left.

"Well, thanks," Bazarov repeated. "This is a queenly action. Queens too, they say, visit the dying."

"Evgenii Vassil'ich, I hope—"

"Eh, Anna Sergheievna, let's speak the truth. I'm done for. I'm caught under a wheel. And now it turns out that there was no use in thinking of the future. Death is an old trick, yet it strikes everyone as something new. Up to now I have no craven fear of it . . . and later on there will be a coma and—up the chimney you go!" He made a feeble nugatory gesture. "Well, what am I to say to you . . . I loved you! That had no sense whatsoever even before, and surely it hasn't any more now. Love is a form, and my own form is already decomposing. I'd do better by saying how fine you are! And even now you're standing there, so beautiful—"

Anna gave an involuntary shudder.

"Never mind; don't upset yourself . . . sit over there. Don't come close to me—after all, my illness is contagious."

She swiftly crossed the room and sat down in an armchair near the divan on which Bazarov was lying.

"Magnanimous one!" he whispered. "Oh, how near,

271

and how young, fresh, pure . . . in this loathsome room! And now, farewell! Live long, that's the best thing of all, and make the most of it while there is time. Just look—what a hideous spectacle: a worm half-crushed, but writhing still. And yet I, too, was thinking: I'd bend so many things to my ends; I wouldn't die— that's not for me! If there's a hard nut to crack—why, that's what I'm a giant for! But now the only hard nut the giant has to crack is how to die decently—although that really doesn't concern anybody. . . . Just the same, I'm not going to wag my tail."

Bazarov fell silent and began groping for his glass. Anna gave him a drink of water, without taking off her gloves and breathing apprehensively.

"You will forget me," he resumed. "The dead man is no fit companion for one living. My father will be telling you: see, now, what a man Russia is losing. That's poppycock, but don't disillusion the old man. What does it matter what toy soothes a child as long as it won't cry—you know the saying. And be kind to mother. Why, such people as they aren't to be found in your grand world if one were to seek them in broad daylight with a lit candle. Russia needs me—no, it looks as if she doesn't. And besides, whom does she need? She needs the cobbler, she needs the tailor, she needs the butcher . . . he sells meat . . . the butcher does . . . hold on, I'm getting mixed up. . . . There's a forest here—" Bazarov placed his hand on his forehead.

Anna leaned toward him. "Evgenii Vassil'ich, I'm here—"

He at once took his hand away and raised himself a little.

"Farewell," he said with sudden energy, and his eyes gleamed with a last gleam. "Farewell . . . Listen . . . Why, I didn't kiss you that time . . . Breathe on a dying image-lamp, and let it go out—"

Anna put her lips to his forehead.

"And that is enough!" he uttered, and sank back on the pillow. "Now . . . darkness—"

Anna quietly left the room.

"Well?" Bazarov's father asked her in a whisper.

"He fell asleep," she answered in a barely audible voice.

Bazarov was not fated to awaken. Toward evening he sank into total unconsciousness, and the following day he died.

Father Alexei performed the last religious rites over him. When extreme unction was being administered to him, when the consecrated chrism came in contact with his breast, one eye opened and it seemed as if at the sight of the priest in his vestments, of the smoking thurible, of the tapers before an icon, something that resembled a shudder of horror was for an instant reflected upon the death-stricken face.

And when, finally, he breathed his last and all in the house lamented as one, a sudden frenzy came upon Vassilii Ivanovich. "I said I would rebel," he screamed hoarsely, his face flaming and distorted, shaking his fist as if he were threatening someone, "and I will rebel, I will!" But Arina Vlassievna, all in tears, hung upon his neck and both fell prostrate. "Side by side," Anphissushka told the story later in the servants' quarters, "that's how they fell; and they let their poor heads droop, like little lambs at noonday—"

But the sultriness of noonday passes, and evening

comes, and night, and then, too, the return to a calm haven, where sleep is sweet for the tortured and the weary. . . .

28

Six months went by. White winter reigned, with the cruel quiet of cloudless frosts, packed crunching snow, trees covered with rose-tinged rime, a sky of pale emerald, caps of smoke over chimneys, billows of steam from doors opened for an instant, faces full of freshness and looking as if they had been nipped at, and the fussy trotting of little nags that have been chilled through and through.

The January day was already drawing to its close; the cold of evening was clamping the still air more tightly than ever in its vise, and a blood-red sunset was rapidly expiring. Lights were springing up in the windows of the manor house at Maryino; Procophich, in black frock coat and white gloves, was with particular pompousness setting the table for seven. A week ago, in the small parish church, two weddings had taken place, quietly and practically without witnesses: that of Arcadii and Katya, and of Nicholai Petrovich and Phenechka, while on this very day Nicholai Petrovich was giving a farewell dinner to his brother, who was setting out for Moscow on business. Anna Serghei-evna had also gone there immediately after the weading ceremonies, having made very generous presents to the newlyweds.

Precisely at three all gathered around the table. Mitya had his place right there; he had already acquired a nanny with an elaborate Russian headdress of glazed brocade. Pavel Petrovich was enthroned between Katya and Phenechka; the "husbands" had ensconced themselves close to their wives. Our friends had changed of late; they seemed to have grown better looking and more mature; Pavel Petrovich alone had become thinner—which, however, added even more elegance and a still greater air of the grand seigneur to his expressive features. And Phenechka, too, had become a different woman. In a new gown of silk, with a wide ornament of velvet on her hair, wearing a thin gold chain on her neck, she sat with an immobility that denoted respect—respect for herself, respect for everything surrounding her—and was smiling as though she would say: "You must excuse me; I'm not to blame." Nor was she the only one smiling—all the others were, and they, too, seemed to be apologizing; they were all feeling a trifle awkward, a trifle sad and, in reality, very well. They all helped one another with amusing solicitude, as if they had agreed to play out some sort of artless comedy. Katya was the most composed of all; she kept glancing about her trustingly, and one could notice that Nicholai Petrovich had already managed to grow dotingly fond of her. Just before the end of the dinner he stood up and, glass in hand turned to his brother:

"You are forsaking us . . . you are forsaking us, dear brother," he commenced, "not for long, of course, but still I cannot help but express to you that I . . .

that we . . . how much I . . . how much we. . . .
There, that's just the trouble—I don't know how to
make speeches! Go ahead, Arcadii—you say something."

"No, Dad, I'm not prepared."

"Well, I certainly prepared myself thoroughly! Well,
brother, let me simply give you a hug and wish you all
good luck—and come back to us as soon as you can!"

Pavel Petrovich exchanged kisses with everybody,
without excluding Mitya, of course; when it came to
Phenechka he also kissed her hand, which she did not
know how to offer properly yet, and drinking off his
glass, which had been refilled, he uttered with a deep
sigh: "May you be happy, my friends! *Farewell*." This
English flourish went unnoticed, but just the same they
were all touched.

"To the memory of Bazarov," Katya whispered in
her husband's ear and clinked glasses with him. Arcadii pressed her hand hard in response, but could not
find the resolve to propose this toast for all to hear.

We have reached the end, haven't we? But perhaps
some reader or other may wish to learn what each one
of the characters we have introduced is doing at present—the actual present. We are ready to satisfy his
curiosity.

Anna Sergheievna has recently married—not for
love but for convincing reasons—one of the up-and-
coming Russian men of action, a very clever man, a
jurist, possessed of a strong sense of the practical, a
firm will, and the gift of remarkable eloquence; a man
still young, good-natured, and as cold as ice. They live
in great harmony with each other and, perhaps, will

live long enough to attain happiness . . . perhaps love. The Princess Kh—— died, forgotten on the very day of her death. The Kirsanovs, father and son, have settled down at Maryino. Their affairs are on the mend. Arcadii has turned into a fervent husbandman, and the *farm* is already bringing in rather considerable revenue. Nicholai Petrovich has become one of the mediators appointed to carry out the emancipation reforms and works at it with all his might and main; he is forever traveling all over the district, delivering long speeches (he holds to the opinion that the lowly little mouzhiks ought to be "reasoned with"—that is, to be reduced to exhaustion through the frequent repetition of never varied phrases); and yet, truth to tell, he does not satisfy fully either the cultured gentry who talk either with *chic* or with melancholy about the 'man-cipation (Frenchifying the word by sounding the *an* syllable through the nose), or the uncultured gentry, who unceremoniously curse "this here 'mun*cipation." And to both the one camp and the other he is far too much of a softy.

Katerina Sergheievna has given birth to a son, Nicky, while Mitya runs about like a fine young lad and chatters as if he were speechifying. Phenechka—now Theodosia Nicholaievna—deifies no one so much (next to her husband and son) as her daughter-in-law, and when the latter sits down at the grand piano she would not mind spending the whole day at her side.

Incidentally, we may mention Peter. He has become altogether hidebound with stupidity and pompousness and has evolved a very fancy enunciation, giving all his *e*'s the sound of *u;* but he, too, has married and gotten a considerable dowry with his bride (the daughter of a truck-gardener in town), who had turned down two worthy suitors because neither had a watch, whereas Peter had not only a watch but a pair of patent-leather half-boots.

In Dresden, on Brühl Terrace, between two and four in the afternoon (the most fashionable time for sauntering), you are likely to come upon a man of fifty or thereabouts, by now entirely gray and apparently afflicted with podagra, but still handsome, exquisitely dressed and with that special impress which a man acquires only by living for many years in the higher strata of society. This man is Pavel Petrovich. From Moscow he had gone abroad to better his health and has settled down in Dresden, where he consorts for the most part with Englishmen and transient Russians. With the Englishmen his conduct is simple, almost modest, but not without dignity; they find him a bit of a bore, but respect him for being, as they put it, "a perfect gentleman." With Russians he is more free and easy, gives vent to his spleen, pokes fun at himself and at them, but in his case all this comes off very charmingly, and nonchalantly, and decorously. He adheres to Slavophile views: this attitude, as everybody knows, is regarded in the highest society as *très distingué*. He reads nothing Russian, but you will find on his desk a silver ash tray shaped like a mouzhik's sandal of plaited bast. He is very much run after by our tourists. Matvei Ilyich Kolyazin, finding himself among the "temporary opposition" (or political outs), paid him a majestic visit on his way to take the waters in Bohemia. As for the natives (with whom, however, he has very little to do), they all but worship him. No one can obtain a ticket for the court chapel, for a theater, and so on, as readily and quickly as *der Herr Baron von*

Kirsanoff. He is constantly doing good, insofar as it lies in his power; he is still creating a modest stir in the world—it is not in vain that he was a lion on a time. Life is a burden to him, however, more of a burden than he himself suspects. . . . To be convinced of this one has but to catch a glimpse of him in the Russian church, when, leaning against a wall off to one side, he falls into deep thought and stays thus for a long time, never stirring, his lips compressed in bitterness, and then, suddenly coming to with a start, and almost imperceptibly, crossing himself.

Kukshina, too, found her way abroad. She is now staying at Heidelberg, and it is no longer the natural sciences she is studying but architecture, in which, according to her, she has discovered new laws. Just as before, she is hail-fellow-well-met with students, particularly with young Russians who are going in for physics and chemistry, who swarm in Heidelberg and who, astounding the naïve German professors by their sober views on things, subsequently astound those same professors by their utter inactivity and absolute laziness. With two or three chemists just like himself, who cannot tell oxygen from nitrogen, but who are brimming over with negation and self-esteem, and also with the great Elisevich, Sitnikov, who in his turn is readying himself for greatness, is knocking about in Petersburg and, according to his own assertions, is carrying on the "work" of Bazarov. There is talk of someone having beaten him up not so long ago, but Sitnikov paid this fellow back with interest: in an obscure little article, published in an obscure little journalette, he hinted that the man who had beaten him up is a coward. This he calls irony. His father rides rough-shod over him, as before, while his wife considers him a little ninny—and a littérateur.

There is a small village graveyard in one of the remote nooks of Russia. Like almost all our graveyards it looks woebegone; the ditches surrounding it have long been choked with rank growths; the weather-beaten crosses of wood are leaning over and rotting under their gableboards, which had at one time been painted; the gravestones are all dislodged, as though someone were nudging them upward from below; two or three puny trees with tattered foliage begrudgingly cast a scanty shade; sheep browse over the graves, with no one to tell them nay. . . . But among these graves there is one untouched by man, untrodden by any beast; the birds alone perch thereon and sing at morning glow. An iron fence surrounds it; there are two young firs there, one planted at the head of the grave, the other at its foot: it is Evgenii Bazarov who is buried in this grave.

Often, from a little village not far off, two little old people, man and wife, decrepit by now, come to visit this grave. Supporting each other, they move with heavy steps; they draw near the grave and fall to their knees, with their faces close to the railing, and weep, long and bitterly, and long and intently gaze at the mute stone under which their son is lying; they exchange some brief phrase, brush the dust from the stone and set straight a branch on one of the firs, and pray anew, and cannot leave this place, where it seems to them that they are nearer to their son, to their remembrances of him. . . .

Can it be that their prayers, their tears are fruitless? Can it be that love, holy devoted love is not omnipotent? Oh, nay! No matter how passionate, how sinful and riotous the heart that has hid itself in the grave, the flowers growing thereon gaze untroubled at us with their innocent eyes; it is not solely of eternal peace that they speak to us, of that great peace of "indifferent" nature; they speak, also, of eternal reconcilement and of life everlasting.

MODERN LIBRARY COLLEGE EDITIONS